# BEAT
## OF THE
# JUNGLE

## A DEADLY FORCES NOVEL

# ERIN MOIRA O'HARA

# Also by
# Erin Moira O'Hara

The Knight of Castle Kildare

Conspiracy in Emilia Romagna

Beat of the Jungle

## Steel Ops Series

The Kalista Diamond

Precious Gems

Jewel of the Kimberley

The Amethyst Code

## Bindarra Creek

Tempting Fate

Date with Destiny

A Twist of Fate

*To my great friend and cohort, S E Gilchrist.*
*As usual, it's been a pleasure working alongside you.*
*No matter whether it is research, brainstorming,*
*or just catching up, we always have fun.*

*To my family and friends,*
*who have grown accustomed to me vanishing*
*into a world of research, writing and deadlines.*
*Thank you for your perseverance, I love you all.*

~ 1 ~

Noxious fumes billowed from the rusted funnel above the fishing trawler's cabin. A decent gale could easily snap it in two. Jack Callaghan stared into the murky water, watching fish dart away from the churning froth. He'd lay odds there'd be a piranha or two among them.

A skeleton wharf came into view, reeds and grasses growing up through the missing timbers. For the first time in days, his mind calmed. The payoff for this job would finance his disappearance, as long as his involvement stayed a secret.

He paced to the stern, searching for any sign of pursuit. Other than the wake roiling away in an arrow of white foam, the river remained empty. The Rio Solimões ran deep and with the end of his contract in sight, it made the perfect place to ditch his weapons.

With a twinge of regret, he reached for his duffle bag, upending the contents into the murky depths. Ammo, handgun, rifle and knife sank to the riverbed.

"*Señor*, we are arrived."

Jack nodded to the white-whiskered captain. The man had been well paid for his services and silence, barely raising an eyebrow when advised of their destination three days ago. Seldom without a cigarette between his weathered lips, the captain had held to his part of the bargain, and now smoothly maneuvered his vessel alongside the wharf.

Habit had Jack scanning the area. He spent precious seconds examining the sedan he'd parked under what remained of a leaning tin shed. Faded paintwork, dents and bald tires made it forgettable. He wished he could say the same for himself, but people tended to notice big guys.

He exhaled slowly. No pissed-off police or mercenaries waiting to ambush him. Rustling grass caught his attention, holding him inert, until a mangy black and tan dog emerged on the bank, craning forward to lap from the river. All appeared as it should, yet he never took anything for granted.

Picking up his pack, he stepped onto the only plank stable and strong enough to take his weight. "Let's go."

Without argument, the other two passengers clambered over the side of the boat. They followed him along the narrow pier, passing over wide gaps and rotted timber to solid ground.

Jack unlocked the sedan's trunk and held it open. Neither companion spoke as they scrambled in and curled up together. A jagged hole in the rear seat ensured enough air reached the trunk. If anyone noticed him passing, it would be as a solo occupant of an unmemorable vehicle.

Closing the trunk, he strode to the driver's door, pausing to watch the trawler pull away from the wharf. Now nothing tied him to this place. The humidity had been steadily rising all morning. Sweat soaked his chest, back and armpits, leaving him grimacing at the odor. He'd need to wash and change at the airport. Glancing up at the heavy bluish-gray clouds, he figured they'd dump their contents any minute. An earlier storm had dished out lightning and thunder, but barely any rain.

He checked his watch. Twelve hundred hours. If he wanted to shave off his stubble before the flight to Manaus, he needed to move his ass. It would have been nice to get reacquainted with the Brazilian city, but that wasn't on the cards this visit. Get in, do the job, get out.

The drive to Sào Paulo de Olivença airport took twenty minutes and at this time of day, he foresaw no holdups, unless things went drastically wrong.

A snuffle instantly drew his attention. The mangy dog trotted past to lift his hind leg on the front tire. With a wide yawn, he disappeared back into the undergrowth.

Jack unlocked his door and slid in behind the wheel, grateful the tin roof had kept the vehicle relatively cool. His passengers had water bottles, so they'd be fine for the time being.

Backing blindly through tall grass wasn't ideal, but other than small tussocks nothing impeded his passage to the dirt track. Once facing the right direction, he concentrated on avoiding large ruts until he reached the road into Sào Paulo de Olivença. Smooth sailing.

Almost.

Two minutes from the airport, the vehicle in front slowed to a crawl, veering off to the side of the road. He silently cursed. Ahead, a roadblock had been set up, manned by one rifle-toting soldier.

The soldier waved Jack forward, gesturing for him to park behind the other car. If he meant to search each vehicle, Jack would have a major problem.

Easing down on the accelerator, he calculated his best strategy. The soldier could be dealt with easily, but the single occupant of that car might prove problematic.

Staying in his lane, several yards behind the other vehicle, Jack cut the engine and lowered his window. He was motioned to the side of the road again. When he didn't move, the soldier trudged forward, his gut wobbling like blubber. He wore no name or army insignia. This wasn't a regular soldier, which meant he could be a mercenary, and on the lookout for at least one of Jack's passengers.

The man reached the car, a hefty scowl twisting his features as he pointed to the other vehicles. "*Parque al lado de la carretera, señor.*"

Jack tapped his watch. "Late for flight. What's the problem?"

The man bent, his gaze searching the interior. "*No hay problema, señor. Eres Americano?*"

Jack wasn't American, but disguising his true nationality was paramount. "*Sí*, and late for my flight." He tapped his watch again and pointed to the airport.

The man stared at him. "Open trunk. I check if you have a woman, maybe two, inside?"

*Fuck.* Jack forced a laugh. "I wish. Two women might make up for missing my flight."

The man snickered. "You pay me twenty American dollar and I no make you wait."

He could have asked for two thousand. It was nothing compared to what Jack would receive for the trunk's cargo. Pulling out his wallet, he handed over a twenty. "Am I good to go?"

"No, *señor.* I still look in your trunk, but I not make you wait behind other car."

*Damn.* Jack released the seatbelt and opened his door. He needed to get rid of this guy. He paced to the back of the sedan, out of sight to the parked car's driver. Fumbling, he dropped the keys, and as he'd anticipated, the mercenary bent to retrieve them.

Jack moved in with a knife-blow to the back of the neck, dropping the man at his feet. He dragged him to the left side of the car then lugged him onto the back seat. The rifle, he hurled into a mud ditch beside the road.

*Now for the witness.* He strode to the other vehicle and tapped on the window. An oriental man looked up from his phone, not the least agitated.

Jack waved him on.

With a quick nod of thanks, the man pocketed his phone, released his handbrake and shot forward, just as droplets of rain began to fall.

Jack returned to the sedan. Opening his pack, he pulled out masking tape and para cord then gagged and bound the mercenary. The looming storm would conceal any ruckus from the trunk, where he intended to stow the mercenary, once he unloaded its present cargo.

On reaching the airport, Jack parked well away from other vehicles. He opened the trunk. "Go. Our flight leaves in forty minutes. I expect to see the money in my account in three days." Without waiting for a reply, he strode to the back door, dragged the bound man out and deposited him in the trunk. The rain would keep the car cool, so the guy didn't cook, but once it stopped raining, any noise he made would draw immediate attention and rescue.

After wiping down the steering wheel, handbrake, door handle and trunk, Jack grabbed his pack and ran.

Entering the building, he headed for the departures counter, relieved to see no queue. The woman behind the counter beckoned. "*Hola, señor.*"

"How ya doing? I know I'm cutting it fine, but can you get me on my flight?" He handed over his ticket and faux ID.

She glanced at them. "Do you have check-in luggage, *señor*?"

"No, ma'am."

"Lucky for you." She handed him his boarding pass. "Enjoy your flight, *señor.*"

"Thanks." He walked toward the men's restroom, his mind racing. He'd taken every opportunity to cover his tracks and disguise his companions, but any delay could have grievous consequences for all of them.

Freshly shaven, washed and wearing clean gear, Jack dumped his filthy clothes in the trash can. He had five minutes to kill before boarding commenced. A quick check of his reflection revealed a casually dressed, relaxed looking guy. Few if any would imagine he'd trekked through inhospitable jungle, armed to the hilt, to retrieve something worth so much to so many.

Sweeping up a discarded Spanish newspaper, he let the restroom door swing shut behind him. Pulling his baseball cap lower, he slung his pack over one shoulder and made for the departure area, dropping the car keys in another trash can. Now nothing tied him to the vehicle.

He found a wall to lean on then eased to the floor between two leafy pot plants, spreading the newspaper wide, as he examined those around him.

His gaze drifted over two white-haired women deep in conversation. He picked up Canadian accents. To his right a Brazilian family squabbled over who would sit beside who on the plane. His attention shifted to an attractive young woman dressed in drab colors. Interestingly, her gaze didn't shift from her lap. Maybe the yuppie couple behind her, having a heated argument, had captured her attention.

Moving on, Jack studied an elderly man, mollycoddling a boy much too old to be babied in such a way. Next to them, a middle-aged African-American couple held hands. Numerous people sat about reading books or newspapers. Most passengers existed in their own insular cocoon, oblivious to all others as they concentrated on electronic devices. Nobody gave him cause for alarm.

A pair of toned, slim legs stepped in front of him. His gaze rose to the short, brightly colored dress obstructing his vision. The woman lifted her left foot, hopping as she adjusted the loose strap of a red sandal.

His gaze fixed on her nicely rounded ass, just as she dropped a wisp of green material. She scooped it up without turning, so he didn't see her face, but he caught her fragrance—gardenias. A wave of nostalgia hit, as he pictured the soft scented shrubs in front of his parents' porch. A memory he'd never experience again.

On this woman, the fragrance reminded him of sultry summer sunsets and the innocence of youth. Her reddish-gold hair had to be long as the high ponytail came half way down her back. She twisted left and right, as if searching for someone. It had to be a guy. A woman like her would hardly be without a male escort.

Oblivious to his scrutiny, she lowered a rucksack to her feet and proceeded to smooth down the stretchy material over her hips. He almost offered to help. She had a body he wouldn't mind enjoying for an hour or two. She flexed her fingers several times. No rings.

A clap of thunder frightened her back a step. Another one would land her in his lap, drawing unwanted attention. He raised the paper and nudged her sandal with the toe of his boot.

She murmured an apology and shifted beyond the pot plant to his right.

Heavy rain sheeted against the window, effectively drowning out nearby conversations. An announcement declared boarding could commence for the flight to Manaus. The elderly and those with children were invited to come forward.

Jack didn't move a muscle as a group of passengers ignored the polite request, converging *en mass* to form a scraggly line. A gray-haired man complained loudly before joining the line. The Brazilian family continued arguing as they gathered their bags.

A male flight attendant stood by the exit door. He held his hand out for the old man and child's boarding pass.

The young woman beside Jack joined the line, her attention fixed on the entry doors. Whoever she waited on hadn't made it. A guy with dreadlocks bumped into her and she jerked as if stung. Her face remained a mystery, but Jack would lay odds she'd be pretty.

He focused on the other passengers as the queue moved forward. An athletic-looking guy met his gaze before strolling toward the end of the line. His companion was a much older, white-haired lady. Their relaxed attitude deemed them non-threatening.

Jack's attention swung to a new arrival. The middle-aged, olive-skinned man stood alone. Like most businessman, he wore a pressed, long-sleeved shirt and pants. Yet he lacked a briefcase or computer bag, and his cold gaze drilled into the waiting horde.

Jack stiffened as the newcomer began prowling the room, his gaze skimming each person. The queue dwindled, which meant Jack would get his money, if he stayed alive long enough to withdraw it.

He wiped a bead of sweat from his brow, well and truly over Brazil's heat and humidity. The Caribbean beckoned. He folded the newspaper and stood, briefly drawing the man's focus, before it fixed on two fair women huddled by the window. Several other people lounged about the room, probably waiting on the next flight out.

Jack strolled across to the flight attendant and handed over his boarding pass.

"*Gracias, señor.*" After scanning it, the guy handed it back.

"Thanks." Jack stepped through the exit door and onto the wet tarmac. Holding the paper over his head, he jogged to the plane. With a grin, he mounted the empty stairway. Never again would he shoot to kill. Never again would he stake out a target. From now on, he would turn his back on the past and everyone who ever knew him. From now on, he'd please only himself.

Men like this didn't inhabit her orbit—ever.

Steady rain and the dirge of propeller engines might lull most passengers into a snoozing state of immobility, but Kitarna Ashford remained alert and wired, thanks entirely to the man beside her. He'd been the last to board, leisurely scanning each face, halting beside the last row of seats, at the rear of the plane.

Up close he could be an advertisement for '*come join the marines*', warping her tongue into a twisted knot, inhibiting her from stringing two sensible words together. After a brief hesitation where his amber eyes had held her captive, he'd stuffed a bulky pack into the overhead locker.

She'd probably commandeered his seat and he was too polite to object. It certainly wasn't where she should be sitting, but thinking all passengers were on board, she'd claimed the window seat, with the intention of getting Bernie to join her once they were airborne.

Riveted, Kitarna had immersed her senses, soaking up his mouth-watering physique as he folded his big frame into the seat beside her. He'd bent forward to re-tie a shoelace, and his black T-shirt had stretched across the wide expanse of male perfection.

It came as a welcome relief when he eased back in the seat and closed his eyes, giving her seized lungs the air they craved, and vanquishing the need for her to utter a single word of breathless drivel.

Hollywood-handsome did not apply to this ruggedly captivating man. The epitome of a fallen angel with a lock of deep-chestnut hair curled against his wide forehead, his all-knowing, king-of-the-jungle eyes a perfect match to the patriarchal nose. He exuded arrogance and a will of steel. Not a man to be messed with, yet his physical presence—clean-shaven jaw, and sexy lower lip—had Kitarna fantasizing. Her mind slipped into a mutiny of erotic images.

For goodness sake, at twenty-five with a degree in botany and a good sense of self-preservation, what was wrong with her? She'd never lost the plot over a man like this, but she had to admit, she'd never had such a fine specimen to analyze. He'd taken her mind off the disappointing cancellation of her trek into the Amazon's interior.

Now at cruising height, they'd entered the eye of the storm, turbulence jolting the plane like a bus with no suspension. Her gaze lingered on his huge chest, annoyingly veiled by the T-shirt. His hands rested palms-down on solid thighs.

You could tell a lot by a man's hands. His were large. Well accustomed to manual labor if the calluses were anything to go by. His fingernails were clean and evenly clipped, a point in his favor.

Her gaze slid down long legs encased in navy khaki, to a pair of hiking boots crammed under the seat in front. She blinked twice at his whopper-sized boots compared to her size seven sandals. Bernie maintained the size of a man's feet was relative to the size of his...

With a gasp, her gaze shot to his lap, covered by a waterproof black jacket. Her cheeks heating rapidly, she glanced up to find his lion-like eyes observing her from under golden-brown eyebrows.

"Oh." Mortification filled her as his lips curved in a knowing smile.

He leaned close, his breath tickling her ear. "How badly do you want to know?"

His voice, barely more than a low rumble, sauntered across her senses in a warm Australian accent, reminding her of the two holidays she'd spent there. He raised a hand and caught one ringlet of her unruly mane. Why it wouldn't stay confined in a hair clip was a conundrum she lived with every day. Salvation could only be found in a braid or very high ponytail.

She replayed his words, her breath hitching as she grasped the implied invitation. Seeking enlightenment had always been her Achilles heel, and backing down wasn't in her nature. Even so, she hesitated.

His eyes danced with wicked promise. Yes, definitely a fallen angel who, after throwing down a gauntlet laced in devilment, now waited to see how she'd respond.

Licking her lips, she drew in a much-needed breath. "You could just tell me, although without seeing the evidence with my own eyes, I only have your word. Such a pity we're not somewhere private."

He laughed, apparently tickled by her audacity. He tweaked her hair, drawing her so close she caught a whiff of peppermint on his breath. "You're welcome to judge for yourself."

Unable to form words, her mouth gaped like a fish starved of water.

His deep chuckle drove home one point. He would rise to any challenge she set.

"No, thank you." She eased away and with feigned calmness, returned to her book on medicinal and edible plants of the Amazon. She leafed through to *Matricaria matricarioids*, otherwise known as pineapple weed. Her own remedy for repelling insects was extremely effective, but she could always improve on it.

Unfortunately, her anticipated jaunt into the world's largest rainforest wasn't to be this trip. Fury and disbelief were high on the list of emotions she'd dealt with over the last hours, yet ignoring the threat could mean death.

The page blurred as her mind returned to the weird call from her father. Crackling static had obscured everything but one disjointed sentence. Still, the urgency and distress in his voice had filled her with trepidation as she'd handed the phone to Bernie.

*Get out, get out...Jaguar after you...Go to Embassy.*

What did it mean? Kitarna shivered. If not for that call, she and Bernie wouldn't be fleeing on this plane.

They'd be on a small boat, heading into the hidden depths of the Amazon, to face...what?

There were jaguars in Amazonas, but that made even less sense. They preferred to stay well away from humans, not hunt them.

Maybe a gang that went by the name 'Jaguar' required a westerner for ransom, but why Bernie? Why not both of them?

She glanced at the man beside her. He certainly radiated the strength of a large cat, yet the wicked glint in his eyes and lingering smile filled her with excitement, not fear.

He'd closed his eyes again, so she looked her fill. His bearing screamed military, and from his steady scrutiny of each passenger, he reminded her of the bodyguards who protected her father. Eyes were the windows to a person's soul and she hadn't detected an ounce of malicious intent, only steadfast interest and wicked promise.

She and Bernie were safe. For now. Hopefully that would remain so once they landed in Manaus.

The flight attendant wandered along the aisle, her eyes skimming passengers, occasionally stopping to speak before strolling on again.

Kitarna glanced across the aisle to a young boy snuggled against an elderly man. The boy's haircut seemed a touch severe, and by the death grip he maintained on the man's arm, the little guy didn't like flying in storms. Who could blame him? She didn't much like it either, but a little turbulence beat a slit throat.

The old man's thoughts appeared to be elsewhere, as he stared blank-faced at the seat in front, rubbing the boy's skinny shoulder.

As the flight attendant reached their row, her gaze roamed over the man next to Kitarna for an annoyingly long time. Eventually her gaze shifted. "*Señorita*, can you shut your blind, please? Once we're free of the storm you can open it again."

"Sure."

The flight attendant's gaze swept back to the lion, who now had his eyes open. "Is there anything you need, sir?"

Kitarna blinked at the husky overtures in the woman's voice.

"What's on offer?" drawled the opportunistic devil.

"I'm certain I can cater to your needs."

*What a pair of outrageous flirts.* Kitarna stiffened as annoyance and maybe a little jealousy spiked. *Ridiculous.* She didn't even know him. Still, now that she'd finished her degree, why not study the human courting ritual in more depth? This presented an opportunity to gain insight and much-needed pointers.

The lion glanced at her. "I'm famished. What about you? Care to indulge?"

"Erm...yes." She tore her gaze from his amused eyes and looked at the flight attendant. "I would like some bottled water please, and...nuts."

Something between a snort and choke brought her attention back to him. He cleared his throat. "I'll have a couple of bottles of water, thanks. And nuts for me too."

"Certainly." The flight attendant's smile centered on him. "I won't be a minute." She sashayed away, the hip-swaying so overdone she'd probably keep a hula-hoop spinning for hours.

Kitarna met his lazy gaze. "You do realize she's coming on to you, don't you?"

He smiled. "Uh-ha. You really want nuts, or is this payback?"

"Yes, I want nuts." She frowned, mindful of his stillness. "Why would you think me wanting nuts is payback?"

He shook his head, "Nothing, forget it. So, what are doing in South America?"

"I'm a b..." A sixth sense made her pause. Until they reached Manaus, she couldn't risk revealing her profession or identity to anyone. "Butterfly enthusiast. Did you know there are over seven thousand species in the Neotropical region, and some of the most beautiful and toxic are found here in the Amazon."

"Really? I didn't know butterflies could be toxic."

"Oh, yes. The *Heliconius erato* and *Heliconius melpomene* are extremely poisonous. During their caterpillar stage, they ingest the leaves of poisonous flora, and that makes them deadly to avian predators."

His lips twitched. "Beautiful, but deadly. They should come with a warning."

"They do—bright wing markings are a warning of their toxicity." She really hoped he didn't ask questions. Her knowledge on butterflies was flimsy at best. "So, what are *you* doing in South America?"

"Traveling."

"Would I be right in assuming you're a soldier on leave?"

If she'd considered him still before, now he morphed into a wall of granite, his fists clenched so tight the knuckles stood out white against his deeply tanned skin. His jaw looked in danger of cracking and his eyes haunted.

She searched for a lighter subject to fill the tense silence. "You're Australian, right? I've been there twice. The first time I spent a couple of weeks on an island in the Great Barrier Reef. The second visit I stayed in Cairns and did an eco-tour through the Daintree rainforest." God, now she couldn't stop babbling.

He flexed his fingers. "My family run eco tours into the Daintree, but I'm headed to the Caribbean." He paused, shooting her a flirty smile. "Wanna come?"

She couldn't help but grin. "The Caribbean. Hmm, I'll think about it."

The flight attendant returned and passed across a bottle of water, two packets of nuts, and a napkin. She turned a very private smile on the Australian as she handed him water and packaged nuts.

Kitarna watched bemused as the woman held a napkin with writing on it between her finger and thumb, waving it suggestively. The napkin fell, sweeping the Australian's left knee before floating to the floor between Kitarna's feet. She released her belt and bent forward.

He did too.

Their fingers brushed, tangled. Tiny tremors shot up her arm, her breath caught as his heated gaze touched hers, swirling them into their own private time lock.

"Please, can someone help my wife," a man called out from the front of the plane, bringing them back to earth with a jolt.

They reversed positions, as the flight attendant rushed away.

Tugging the napkin from his fingers, Kitarna read the message. *Meet me at the door to the rear luggage compartment in five minutes.*

She raised an eyebrow. "For what?"

His lips twitched. "I'm guessing she wants to make out."

Eyes wide, she could only stare at him. "Why that's...that's so brazen."

He stuffed his water and nuts in the seat pocket. "I'd prefer to make out with you." His sexy smile promised sensual delight. A promise she wanted to exploit, but...

"I don't even know your name."

"Jack Callaghan. Be a devil, come join me in the luggage compartment?"

"What's wrong with doing it here?"

"I like a little more privacy when I'm...indulging." He shot a quick glance across the aisle as if to point out they had spectators.

She looked at the elderly man and boy. Both had their eyes closed, so she leaned closer to Jack and whispered, "Passengers aren't allowed in the luggage compartment. What if we get caught?"

"Risk is half the fun."

So tempting, except he was a stranger. Could there be a worse time to put her trust in a man she didn't know? She almost gave him the standard I'm-really-not-interested line. But what single woman in her right mind would pass up the chance of a lighthearted dalliance with a man like him?

"Your kissing ability better be worth this."

His lips curled into a carnal smile. "I guarantee joining the Mile-High Club will be an experience neither of us will forget."

Mesmerized, she stared into eyes shining with the promise of a damn good time. Whatever the Mile-High Club embodied, he made it sound wickedly exciting.

A sharp cry had him leaning out into the aisle. "It looks like some sort of commotion up front. I'd say this is an opportunity we should use to our advantage." He took her water and nuts and shoved them in her seat pocket.

"What are you doing?"

He stepped into the aisle and offered his hand. "Fulfilling my promise. Come."

Kitarna gave him her hand. Excitement welled, pushing away the last remnants of doubt. No kiss to date had ranked high on her scale of memorable experiences. No kiss had stirred her enough to lose her head.

Hopefully Jack would prove the exception. Make her forget her father's warning and the danger that stalked her and Bernie. A glance over her shoulder proved him right. With everyone focused on the drama up front, no-one paid attention to the two of them.

He towed her to the small alcove at the rear of the plane, where he reached for the luggage compartment's door handle.

As a pocket of turbulence hit, he lifted her inside and locked the door.

Squashed between the wall and his chest, she exclaimed, "Are you mad? We can't be in here."

"I would have preferred a bed, but it isn't an option." He sat on a bulky crate and pulled her across his thighs, hiking her short dress obscenely high.

"Jack, I'm not letting you kiss me in a cramped luggage comp—"

He captured her lips in a kiss that knocked every coherent thought into orbit. They could have been making out in the cockpit for all she cared. Deep—sensual—worshipful. She kissed him back, clinging to his huge shoulders, urging him on, tasting *Jack*, oblivious to everything except his worshipful lips and provocative tongue.

Permission granted, he plunged them both into an inferno of sensation. Never had she been kissed like this. The heat from his hands seared her back, molding her against his chest. With only two thin layers of cotton between them, her nipples throbbed, sensitive to each shift of his body.

He plundered her mouth, his hands gliding down her spine to caress her backside, squeezing once, before sliding lower. He cupped the undersides of her bare thighs, and lifted her against his erection.

"Oh God!" She clung, her wits scattering as warmth blazed through her body, melting her bones, blowing her mind.

He refused to release her mouth.

She'd hoped for an interlude to remember, to appreciate true desire. She hadn't expected to be devoured, ravaged. He stole her breath then gave it back again as their mouths melded and tongues dueled. Her fingers sunk deep into his thick mane, her breasts crushed against his chest. Shocked and embarrassed by her response, she pulled back, attempting to regain her breath and some space.

He allowed it, reluctantly. Her lips prickled like pins and needles as the blood flowed back into them.

They both breathed raggedly. Her mind blanked by the unconcealed lust in his eyes. She barely had time to blink before he bent his head again, his lips searing a blaze down her throat, tantalizing the skin over her collarbone.

She should call a halt before they were discovered.

His breath heated her skin, sending every hormone into rebellion, warring against her sanity, which hung by a thread.

She moaned. Captive, caged between his hard chest and muscle-bound arms, spellbound by clever lips and so much raw virility. She craved more. Skin to skin, pressed against the place she needed relief.

"I want you."

His deep, gruff words blew across her skin, sending her blood racing. Wisdom fled. Her airways filled with the spicy essence of his cologne. Intoxicating.

Awareness spiked as he settled his hand on her waist, his fingers dipping into the hollow of her lower back. The other hand traced a path up her left arm. He pushed the thin strap off her shoulder then set his lips to cruise and electrify. A shudder racked her body.

He smiled. "Ready for more?" He tugged at the neckline of her spandex dress.

"Wait."

Too late, his fingers caressed her naked breast, knowingly, sensually. He played to her fantasies, his tongue and lips tickling her throat. She couldn't quell the moan or shivers.

"So sensitive." His thumb flicked her nipple, boldly cupped her breast and kneaded. "So responsive."

"More," a whispered plea she couldn't hold in.

"Yes, ma'am." He transferred his fingers to her left breast.

She squirmed, grinding her hips against him, as a yearning she'd never faced begged for relief. This was madness—he needed no encouragement.

He shifted, worked her dress down to below her waist, exposing her tummy. His gaze lifted to hers. "Breathtaking. I need to taste you." He descended, closing his hot, wet mouth over her right nipple.

She gasped, tensed, gasped again. Waves of pure pleasure crashed through her, shocking her, awakening greedy, starved senses as he slowly, deliberately laved, nipped, suckled, then moved to her left breast. His hands on her back stroked soothingly.

This was nothing like the fumbling she'd encountered with Jeff, an interlude she'd quickly put behind her.

Jack's coiled tension seeped into her awareness. He couldn't back off now. She pulled her hands free of the dress and clutched his head, holding him to her, unable to let go. Through lowered eyelashes, she watched him feast on her swollen breasts, giddy at his intimate reverence. There appeared to be so much more to making out than she'd ever imagined, but then Jack knew exactly how to please a woman.

Rationality crashed through her passion-hazed brain. She knew nothing about Jack Callaghan. He could be married. With kids. And a dog.

Squirming, Kitarna pulled away, her gaze meeting his lust-filled eyes. She opened her mouth, not even sure what she wanted to say. Stop. More. He cut off the words, seizing her lips in another drugging kiss that flung caution to the wind. He could be the maestro, playing her, a violin in the sweetest symphony. Their music floating sensually out across the waves.

He slid his hand between her thighs.

"Jack!" With her legs spread wide and her arms locked around his neck, she froze, paralyzed as he pushed her bikini pants aside and set his fingers to intimately explore, stroke, tease.

"Oh, God." She dropped her head to her arm, boneless on his shoulder. Her adventure had gone in a direction she hadn't planned. This was an experience not to be missed.

He nudged her back, lowered his head and captured a nipple again, then pushed a finger inside her, hesitated, his breathing suspended. "You're so damned tight." It came out as a growling murmur against her aching breast.

Was tight good or bad? Her mind snagged on his whopping shoes. "Women have been accommodating men since the beginning of time. I'm sure... I'll cope." Had she really said that out loud? She felt breathless, intensely aware of his thrusting finger and the blaze igniting at his touch.

He chuckled, the sound vibrating though her chest. "I promised you satisfaction and that's what you'll get." His thumb stroked that one incredibly sensitive spot.

She cried out. Wet, hot and frantic. A desperate longing surged through her veins. "Please, Jack."

His lips closed over her nipple, sucking hard as one finger circled that spot and another thrust deep.

She shattered, arching as wave after wave of euphoria crashed through her. He withdrew his hand and she collapsed in a daze of blissful stupor, panting against his hard chest. Dragging in air, she eventually lifted her head and looked him in the eyes. "I had no idea making out could be so mind-blowing. I can't believe I've been missing out on this." She waved a hand between them.

"Missing?"

She felt him stiffen and looked down to see his pants open and a huge bulge straining against black briefs.

His hands suddenly clamped on her thighs. "What do you mean by *missing*?" His voice rumbled with foreboding.

Lifting her gaze, she met his intense stare. "I've never experienced anything like that—this." She licked her lips.

He tracked the movement with wary eyes. "An explosive orgasm or making out in a plane?"

A giggled escaped. "Both. An explosive orgasm and making out in a plane. You're the first guy to give me an orgasm anywhere, and you bypassed the whole dating ritual."

"Dating ritual?"

"You know, flowers, chocolate, movies, romantic dinners, getting to know each other. If all goes well, moving on to the physical side of things. Not that I'm complaining. You certainly know what you're doing."

"Christ almighty, you're a virgin. Why the hell didn't you say something?"

"Keep your voice down. I'm not a virgin. It's just that my previous dates left me uninspired."

His eyes narrowed. "How many men have you slept with?"

"I've been busy studying, so I haven't had a lot of time for...for that stuff."

"How many?" He almost growled the words.

She swallowed. "One."

"And how many times did you have sex with this uninspiring sap?"

"I don't see what that..."

"How many?" his clipped tone would slice through steel.

"Once. He barely touched me, except for removing my panties and...you know. The act itself didn't motivate me to repeat the experience. Happy?"

Jack drew in a deep breath, his chest expanding, drawing her gaze. She slid her hands from his broad shoulders, spreading her fingers as she explored. "You remind me of a very agitated lion." Grinning, she slid her fingers under his shirt. "This is what you meant by the Mile-High Club, isn't it?"

He groaned and pulled her against his chest, trapping her hands. "Don't move an inch. How old are you?"

"Twenty-five, old enough to know what I want."

"I know you're old enough. I'm just wondering if all the men you hang out with are blind or halfwits."

"They're too old, too boring, too immature or married. And they aren't like you." She leaned forward and kissed his neck. "I want you to show me all I've been missing. Do you have protection?"

He groaned, holding her back. "This isn't going to work."

"Of course it will. I'm willing, and you said you never break a promise."

"You're new to this, and I'm... I'm..." He sighed. "Darlin', you're the sort of girl who should be wined and dined. You need to be made love to leisurely, in a bed, not fucked in a cramped compartment, a mile above the earth."

This might not have been what she'd planned originally, but his words only heightened her aroused state, making her fidget with his watchband. "I don't want to stop. You can wine and dine me in Manaus, and afterwards we can go to a hotel and do it leisurely."

He studied her face for a moment. "Darlin', it's Manaus or nothing."

"But you've done this before."

"No, not in a plane. It would have been a first for me too." He ran a hand through his hair. "Look, we can do the wine and dine thing in Manaus, but then I'm gone. You're free to change your mind, no hard feelings."

He wasn't going to budge. "Not fair." With time to consider this so-unlike-her wantonness and the fact she needed to get out of South America ASAP, there would be little chance they'd ever meet again. And in all honesty, she dreamed of being wooed like her stepfather had wooed her mother. But what if this intense attraction was a once in a lifetime chance, a prelude to their merging of souls?

*For heaven's sake.*

He wasn't the wooing type—he must be the fast and furious type, promising an exciting gallop before disappearing into the Caribbean sunset.

He lifted her off his lap. "You go first." His gaze lingered on her naked breasts. "I need a few minutes alone." He glanced down.

Her gaze dropped to the substantial bulge and understanding dawned, instantly infusing her overly hot body with more heat. Quickly she righted her dress. Avoiding his eyes, she opened the door. "I'll see you back out there."

Amazingly no one spared her a glance as she slid into her seat, hot and flustered. She reached for her rucksack, needing some moist wipes to cool her face. Nothing like this had ever happened to her. No man had ever touched her like Jack Callaghan.

To be on the same plane and to share such a powerful attraction—what were the odds? He'd almost missed the flight. She froze.

Could her lion be the Jaguar? The person she and Bernie were running from?

~ 4 ~

*Almost a virgin, for fuck's sake.* Exiting the luggage compartment, Jack cursed silently. The signs had been there, in her expressive green eyes, breathless gasps and tentative touch.

*Holy shit, she really hadn't known what the 'mile high' club meant.* Her blushes should have been a dead giveaway, and irrational though it was, he still wanted her. If only for one night, where he'd seduce her as she deserved.

If he wanted to keep his body under control he'd need to avoid looking at her long legs or ripe breasts, a perfect fit for his hands. Being the man to introduce her to a world of exquisite pleasure stirred him like nothing had in a very long time, but he doubted she would go through with it. He didn't even know her name.

He never used to be such a cad. Once he'd been a guy full of ambition, at the top of his field, surrounded by family and friends. And he'd know a girl's name within minutes of striking up a conversation. He'd sunk to an all-time low.

He shouldered the opposite door as the plane banked left. His gaze fell to the slanted aisle. Why were they descending?

Taking three paces, he dropped into his own seat. No, not his seat. *She* occupied that.

Looking ahead, he observed the flight attendants. Their attention on a passenger in the front row, and by their faces, they were concerned.

This was supposed to be a direct flight to Manaus. Maybe the pilot intended off-loading the passenger in Tefè. That would explain their descent to the port side.

He glanced across the aisle to where Ross Dalton dozed. He might be seventy, but due to years of hiking and mountaineering, the man retained remarkable fitness. It was one reason Jack had accepted his involvement. The other being eighty-grand for a job no man in his right mind would consider. Not that Jack was insane, but with his specialized skills and one woman's desperate plea, he'd taken the job. The buzz and planning of this operation also kept his mind from dwelling in the past.

Strategy and patience were second nature to him. Everything had gone smoothly.

Roscoe opened his eyes. "Any idea why we're turning off course?"

"Could be something to do with what's happening up front."

"From what I can make out, a passenger had a seizure."

"That sucks." Jack fastened his belt then glanced at the lovely creature beside him. She'd slipped on the deep-green wisp of material that had fallen at his feet in the departure lounge. A bolero. It tied under her breasts and matched the green swirls on her sexy little dress. It also hid her erect nipples, which had been an instant turn on when he'd found her in his seat. A delectable peach that had his taste buds humming.

Her eyes were closed, but he doubted she slept. The temptation became too much to resist. He leaned across and brushed his lips over hers as he lifted the blind.

She gasped. "What are you doing?"

He stared out into thick cloud. They were still banking left, but other than driving rain, he couldn't see a thing. "We're descending and I'm wondering why." He closed the blind. "Oh, you mean the kiss—I couldn't help myself."

Her eyes turned solemn. "Maybe the pilots are trying to avoid turbulence."

"Possibly, although I would have expected them fly above the storm, not under it." He picked up her delicate hand and ran his thumb over her soft palm, pleased when she trembled. "I know we got off to an unusual start, but...don't you think I should know your name?"

She considered him for several heartbeats, almost as if she might refuse his request. "It's Kit." Her fingernails dug into his hand. "You don't think we're turning back to Sào Paulo de Olivença, do you?"

"No, but we might be diverting to one of the larger towns along the Solimões River." He wondered if Kit was short for some other name. Along with her sharp little claws, her striking green eyes reminded him of a frightened kitten.

Although very slight, the plane continued to bank left. At this rate they'd be heading west, over nothing but dense jungle, which surprised him.

The flight attendant arrived with a beverage cart and sent him a black scowl. Maybe she'd noticed him dragging Kit into the luggage compartment, or was annoyed he hadn't taken up her offer.

All cool efficiency, she looked straight past him. "Sorry about the delay, madam, we've had a medical emergency. Would you like tea, coffee, or an orange juice?"

Kit smiled. "A white tea, please. Is the passenger all right?"

"We are monitoring her." The flight attendant handed the cup and a packet of biscuits across Jack.

Stifling a grin, he glanced at Kit, easily reading her amusement that the flight attendant would ignore him on purpose. He looked to the woman and waited.

Her attention remained on Kit. "Am I right in assuming you're my missing passenger from 9D?"

"Yes. The man in the aisle seat wore strong cologne. I couldn't stay there?"

"Passengers are supposed to stay in their allocated seats." She hesitated. "Where are you from? Your accent is confusing me."

To Jack's surprise, the shutters came down over Kit's eyes. "All over—I spend a lot of time travelling. It's had an impact."

"Hmm." The flight attendant glanced toward the front of the plane.

Contrition rode Jack. He'd noticed Kit's soft accent when they'd first spoken, but over the last few years he'd lost interest in idle chitchat. Getting his rocks off had taken precedence to learning anything about her. He was a jerk and sick of the flight attendant ignoring him.

"I'll have a black coffee, no sugar, and two packets of biscuits, thanks." His cool words succeeded in catching the woman's attention.

"Certainly, sir." Her bored tone reinstated his amusement. After handing him the coffee and biscuits, she attended to Roscoe and the kid. Then the bloody woman clipped his elbow as she dragged the cart back down the aisle.

His gaze flitted over the heads he could see, checking their positions against his memory. He'd waited to board until the last minute in case he needed to make a run for it. Old habits died hard. Everyone appeared to be where he or she should be.

All but the beauty beside him.

The plane could seat sixty-eight passengers, although he'd counted eight empty seats scattered about the plane. One other passenger had drawn his interest, a white-haired woman who returned his incisive scrutiny. In her eyes he encountered a perceptiveness he hadn't expected.

Draining his lukewarm coffee, he grabbed his jacket off the floor. From the inside pocket, he withdrew a creased photo and passed it to Kit. "I'm going to renovate that shack into a beachside bar."

She smiled. "Let me guess, it's in the Caribbean, right?"

"Yep. It's taken me months to convince the owner to sell. We finally settled on a price and I have five days to seal the deal."

She passed the photo back. "How old are you?"

"Thirty."

"Are you married?"

He stiffened. "I wouldn't have propositioned you, if I was married."

"Good." She grinned. "So, no dog either?"

Unable to help it, he laughed. "No dog. I might get one when the shack's finished."

"Followed by a wife and kids?"

"Not in this life. Any ideas what I should call my bar?"

She studied his face for a moment. "How about Jack's Shack?"

"I like it." He slid the photo back inside his jacket then draped it over one knee. His mind turned to this latest job, a risky exercise that had taken weeks of planning. The execution had gone without a hitch. Much better than he'd anticipated. Next week he'd be living the dream, a new beginning.

He glanced across as she raised the blind. The gray cloud had broken up, giving him a clear view of dense vegetation. "What the fuck?"

She clutched his arm. "Jack, why are we so low?"

"I don't know. The captain should have made an announcement."

"Maybe he did, while we were…busy." She looked at him, her eyes large pools of shimmering emeralds.

His gut tightened. If they crashed through the rainforest canopy, being concealed from rescuers would be the least of their problems. Besides impenetrable jungle, deadly snakes, spiders and predators, they'd encounter drenching rain and killer humidity. The plane had to be flying too low for regular radar to detect them, but in a worst-case scenario, the plane's transponder would give their position, impregnable though the rainforest might be.

And if they did go down, he'd rather it wasn't anywhere near Luis Rodriguez, a man with resources to retrieve what had been stolen from him. The punishment for the thief would be a slow, painful death.

Jack had enough on his plate without worrying about a beautiful young woman, or for that matter, any of the women on the plane. From his research, kidnapping, torture and murder had all been attributed to Rodriguez and his mercenaries.

"Go to sleep, kitten. If there's a problem, we would have been informed."

She laid her head against his shoulder. "I like you, Jack Callaghan."

His smile lasted all of two minutes until the plane banked left again. He checked the compass on his watch and stiffened. No, that couldn't be right.

She lifted her head. "What is it?"

"We've turned back."

"What?" She bolted upright. "Why?"

"I have no idea." A bad feeling coiled in his gut, like a snake about to strike.

The flight attendant bustled along the aisle. When she came abreast of their seats, Jack held up a hand. "Why are we flying so low?"

"There is a minor mechanical problem. Don't worry, the co-pilot has advised me everything is under control."

He looked at his watch. "If there's a problem, shouldn't we be landing in Tefè?

"Due to the weather, we are making for an airstrip where we can land safely."

"What airstrip?" A delay in reaching Manaus was bad enough, but turning back could have grave consequences. He glanced across the aisle.

The kid started crying. "I want Mommy."

A guy with dreadlocks stood up. "Hey, we've got connecting flights in Manaus. What happens if we don't make this other airstrip? I heard the Amazon jungle has cannibals. Go tell the captain we want to land in Tefè, where we can catch another plane to Manaus."

Several passengers called out their agreement.

Above, the seat belt warning flicked on.

"The pilots know what they're doing," the flight attendant cleared her throat. "Please remain seated with your belts fastened."

Jack watched her pull a seat down on the back wall, sit and fumble as she buckled up. Her eyes darted away from him to the floor. She knew more than she let on. Maybe the problem wasn't mechanical, but why head west when Tefè was so close?

Tears welled in Kit's eyes. "Jack, I can't go back."

He agreed whole-heartedly, not because of cannibals, that was utter rubbish. The small tribal groups remaining isolated preferred to hide from outsiders. His aversion to landing anywhere near Columbia lay in the fact it bordered an area controlled by Luis Rodriguez.

Leaning across the armrest, he brushed a fleeting kiss over her pillow-soft lips, then entwined his fingers in her silken locks. She had the prettiest hair he'd ever seen. Not red, not brown. More mahogany with highlights of burnished-gold and her deep-emerald eyes could only be described as soul stealing.

Her stalling measures worried him. The hesitation with her name, and again when he'd asked what she was doing in South America. Damn it all, maybe he'd lost his edge.

The turbulence turned volatile and the plane bore a battering by gusty winds and driving rain. With every shudder and plunge, passengers wailed and shrieked. The nauseating stench of vomit invading the cabin had Jack wanting to puke. It didn't help that Roscoe kept throwing him rattled glances.

The further west they flew, the edgier he became. This did not make sense. If the plane had a mechanical fault, they should have landed in Tefè.

A grating drone sounded under them. "What's that?" whispered Kit.

He prized her fingers off his arm and took hold of her hand. "Landing gear." Leaning across her, he grimaced at the thick canopy. Were they about to crash? Best be prepared.

Unzipping the rucksack at her feet, he shoved in the bottled water, nuts and book she had on her lap. "Brace over your rucksack, and stay down."

"Bernie!"

Any other time, he would have asked about

Bernie, but he had more urgent matters on his mind. Ignoring the flight attendant yelling at him, Jack stood, opened the overhead locker and dragged down his and Roscoe's packs. They contained essential items that could mean the difference between life and death.

If the passengers survived the initial impact, they'd likely be incinerated within minutes. He wouldn't have time to waste, and didn't fancy burning alive.

Slamming the locker, he tossed Roscoe's pack at him. "Jam that under your feet and don't leave without it."

Above the sobs and screams, he could hear a male voice over the intercom, calling for passengers to brace in the crash position.

Dropping into his seat, Jack wedged the pack between his legs. He stuffed the water and nuts in the side pockets then buckled up. Leaning against the seat in front, he met Kit's gaze. "I haven't fulfilled the rest of my promise yet, darlin'."

"I'll hold you to that, Jack Callaghan." She squeezed her eyes shut.

The wheels hit solid ground and bounced. A roar sounded in his ears as the reverse thrusters engaged. The plane slid sideways, righted itself, then swung the other way.

Her eyes remained clenched. She didn't utter a sound. No doubt, terror kept her silent as tears leaked down her cheeks. He wanted to reassure her, but it would be a hollow declaration.

Cursing, he wrapped his arm around her. The plane had been flying west long enough to be near the Columbian border, which put the passengers in great danger. They could be held captive for ransom or worse. He needed a weapon.

The plane slowed, but continued to slide every which way, so he figured it had to be a dirt surface. That didn't bode well for them either. Dirt in this region would imply little use, an ominous sign. Kit moved to lift her head and shoulders. He held her down. The plane suddenly plummeted, along with his stomach.

Screeching, tearing and grinding erupted around and under the plane. Ripping metal competed with terrified screams. They were traversing downward, off the side of a mountain, but into what?

The sudden explosive impact threw him back in the seat. The plane swiveled to the right. A horrendous tearing surrounded them. Jack flinched, praying he was wrong, but only a giant tree made such a spine-chilling noise before it crashed to the ground. And God only knew where it would fall.

The crash sounded like a cannon firing, but after spending eight months working for a logging company, he knew better. A savage blow hammered the plane. The sound of tearing metal screamed throughout the plane. Debris flew around him. The acrid smell of rain, rotting forest and hot metal filled his nostrils.

Powerful vibrations shuddered under his feet. The stench of vomit assaulted his airways, filling his lungs until the acid taste of bile rose in his throat. An oxygen mask caught the edge of his eye with a sting worthy of a wasp. Hysterical screaming dragged him back into the past, to the carnage he could have prevented with one extra bullet.

Shearing metal competed with torrential rain and the roar of jet engines, which didn't make sense. This plane was a propeller job.

He lurched sideways, confirming his worst fears. A deluge of water poured through jagged cracks, thanks to an enormous tree trunk, which had crushed the middle section of the plane like an aluminum can. There would be no survivors.

All that remained of the rear section was row twelve to seventeen, but he could definitely hear what sounded like jet engines.

"Bernie," Kit screamed the name, barely distinguishable under all the noise.

*Who the hell is Bernie?* He blinked as passengers raised their blinds, flooding the cabin with murky light, crying out as they noticed the destruction.

"Come on, kitten, we have to get off the plane." He pried her arms from around her thighs then released their belts. "Follow me." It would be an uphill climb for the other passengers, but if they followed his instructions, it needn't be a battle.

Jack untangled his large frame. Gripping the back of the seat, he threw his jacket and pack around the wall. Hauling himself up, he clambered into the rear passage of the plane. As long as they weren't on fire, staying put would be wise, but they were in a humid jungle, and it wouldn't take long for dead bodies to attract dangerous scavengers and insects.

His gut instinct urged him to find another way to Manaus before Luis Rodriguez discovered them. But if the weather forecast held true, the monsoonal rain would hamper rescuers for a day or two. He had no intention of hanging around here that long.

They would need to find a river and a boat. It would be longer, but local airports were out of the question. Rodriguez owned too many people in this region.

The burden of responsibility sat heavily on his shoulders. This was a completely different scenario to the bazaar in Afghanistan, full of innocent civilians.

*I'm not responsible for these people.*

The flight attendant cursed in Spanish as she tried to undo her belt without sliding off her seat and tumbling down the aisle.

He turned his attention to unarming the exit door and releasing the emergency chute. Lifting the plastic cover, he gripped the release handle and raised it.

Drawing a deep breath, he pushed the door out of its frame. Instantly, lashing rain battered him, along with the engine-like roar, which turned out to be a mob of teeth-baring, branch-shaking howler monkeys. He'd seen a couple once at Western Plain's Zoo back in Australia, but they hadn't displayed this degree of ferocity.

He pushed the door back against the outside of the plane and the chute instantly began to inflate out over the mangled vines and foliage.

The flight attendant finally managed to get across the gap and Jack helped her onto the wall then assisted a gray-haired couple up.

They thanked him before holding hands and jumping onto the chute.

The flight attendant opened a wall locker above, bringing the contents tumbling down. She picked up a medical kit and several thermal emergency blankets. Opening a second locker, she pulled out a folder and small bag. Once she had everything stowed in the case, she stepped to the exit. "If you can help the other passengers out, I'll gather everyone together and check off their names." She jumped without waiting for his answer.

He turned back as a sniveling woman with bits of vomit clinging to her hair climbed onto the wall. The guy with dreadlocks shouldered Jack aside then shoved the woman out the door.

She hit the chute and yelped as she bounced over the side.

"You bloody idiot." Jack glared at him. "Get down there and check she's okay."

"Keep ya hair on, mate. It's not exactly a concrete jungle out there." He laughed at his pathetic joke as he jumped.

Shaking his head, Jack turned to help Roscoe and the kid onto the wall. "Take your time, and when you're on the forest floor, climb to the top of the hill. See if they've got any fast transport out of here."

Roscoe hitched his pack onto his shoulders. "Will do. See you at the top." He picked up the kid and carefully edged onto the chute.

Two white-haired women followed, both shaking badly.

"Easy does it, ladies. Once you're at the bottom, make your way up the hill."

Thanking him, they slid down without a backward glance.

What could be taking Kit so long? He threw his pack down the chute then dropped to his knees and leaned round the wall. He heard a mixture of English and Spanish voices debating whether to stay. Others were yelling at people to get out of their way. He couldn't see her.

Wiping the water out of his eyes, he looked further down the dimly lit aisle where several people were working their way up.

Kit balanced below them, swiping at her cheeks. He could only surmise she'd gone to see if there were any survivors under the wreckage. She had her rucksack hanging off one shoulder and looked overwhelmed.

"Kit, come on."

She nodded and climbed to a bottleneck held up by a blonde with a low neckline, spray on jeans, and black heels. Amazingly the woman tried to hoist a small suitcase up with her.

Jack rolled his eyes. "Ditch the bag, you're holding everyone up."

"Let me take that, babe." A fair-haired guy took the case and tossed it into the row above then bent to take the woman's hand. Several passengers aired their irritation as they clambered past.

Jack assisted two teenage boys and an older couple he assumed to be their parents. Next came two young men. After they jumped, Jack looked to where Kit balanced, staring at two leather shoes protruding from a row of seats.

"Shit." He swung down past the yuppie couple.

Her tear-filled eyes met his. "I think that man is dead."

"I'll check. Take my jacket and get out of the plane." He braced his feet either side, on the back of two seats to pull her up. "Climb the hill. I'll catch up."

She twisted back. "No, I need to check on…on the passengers in front."

"Just climb the damn hill."

He watched her clamber from seat to seat, unable to drag his eyes away. Once she disappeared from view, he leaned over the man to find a pair of lifeless brown eyes staring vacantly. On closer examination, he discovered the man's head at an odd angle. He hadn't been wearing his seat belt.

Jack froze as a fearsome tearing rendered through the forest, overshadowing the monkeys. "Fuck."

He bolted up the seats, hoping Kit, Roscoe and the kid had found cover. A resonating explosion vibrated through him as another prehistoric tree crashed to the ground.

He jumped onto the chute, slid down and rolled onto wet, mushy foliage at the base of a gigantic root ball. The howler monkeys hadn't let up their horrific noise, but at least they seemed to be moving away. He ripped away a clinging vine from his trousers and clambered to his feet, almost falling over his own pack. *Where's Kit?*

"Jack!"

Looking up, his gut clenched. "Jesus Christ." She dangled from a gigantic upended tree root. Leaping forward, he braced to catch her. "Let go, I've got you."

He caught her against him, keeping her close as he lowered her to the ground.

"Thank you." She wore his saturated jacket, shivering like a bedraggled pup. "The tree is blocking my path, Jack. You have to help me get over there."

"Why? Is Bernie on the other side?"

"Who?" She blinked rapidly, clinging to his T-shirt. "When I heard that second crack, I thought you would be crushed, and when the tree hit the ground, it shook me like a rag doll. That's why I lost my grip."

Her evasive tactics were impressive, but he didn't have time to interrogate her. "Why are you still here?"

"I'm looking for survivors."

"*Hola!*" The call came from the male flight attendant who had scanned Jack's boarding pass. He stepped carefully along the enormous trunk, leading a group of saturated passengers. Two men supported a dazed woman between them.

Kit wiped water out of her eyes. "Is everyone out?"

"Almost. My name is Juan, do you have any injuries or fatalities?"

Jack nodded. "One male is deceased, and I'm quite sure all the passengers in row eleven were killed by the tree."

"*Mierda.*" Juan jumped down in front of them and addressed the female flight attendant, who had materialized beside Kitarna. "Solana, do you have the passenger manifest?"

"Yes, Juan, and the medical kit?"

"Good. That tree wiped out rows eight to eleven. We need to do a passenger check."

Noticing Kit had no intention of leaving, Jack stood beside her and waited as nine passengers climbed down from the tree, some to mill around with others in stunned shock. The rest began climbing the mangled slope.

Kit pulled out of his arms and touched Juan's shoulder. "What's keeping the rest of the passengers?"

He grimaced. "A few went to check on the pilots. This should be the last of them now. Something is very wrong. We should not be here."

~ 6 ~

Looking up, Kitarna spotted five more drenched people climbing down through the tree roots, her sister among them. "Thank God." She went to rush forward, but stopped when Bernie shook her head sharply.

Accepting Bernie's reasoning for wanting their connection to remain secret, she visually checked her sister for injuries. But other than a bandage across her forehead Bernie seemed fine. They were so different in looks and character that few would pick them as sisters. For now they were safe.

Kitarna sank against Jack's chest, savoring his heat when he wrapped his arms around her. Along with bits of fern, rotting leaves and dirt, her hair and clothes were plastered to her skin. Knowing Bernie had survived, her spirits lifted and her mind turned to the man holding her. What she'd give for that hotel room, a deep bath, and Jack, so they could explore this connection between them. Her heart beat faster at the notion.

"Let's go." He released her then swung his pack onto his back. "We need to get up that hill and assess our options."

She swiveled to face the climb. "With luck we can get a hot cup of coffee while we wait for transport to the nearest town."

"I fear you're in for a big disappointment, kitten. From what I could see as we came down, this is a remote mountaintop, there won't be much in the way of transport or sustenance. Just mosquitoes once it stops raining."

"I expected the mosquitoes, but thanks for making me feel *so much* better."

He chuckled. "After such an ordeal, you're taking this very well, Kit."

"Believe me, it's all an act." She glanced back to where Bernie assisted a young woman. *I'm only calm because I know my sister is safe.*

Kitarna's sandals slid from under her, and Jack helped her up. "May I ask why my jacket's pockets are bulging?"

"*Bixa orellana*." She pulled a bright-red, spiny fruit out to show him.

"What the hell is that?"

"It's commonly known as lipstick plant. The Amazonian tribes use the seeds for red dye and add it to fish oil to make insect repellant. After I slid down the chute, I stumbled into it. The seeds will come in handy if we're stuck here for any length of time."

Squaring her shoulders, she started up the hillside, stumbling and crawling over the trail of ravaged vegetation, thankful for Jack's help.

She emerged at the top to see the runway, a

quagmire grooved with deep gouges where the plane's tires had fought for grip. The airstrip had been cut out of the top of the mountain, surrounded on both sides by dense forest.

Stinging rain cut through her inadequate clothing, and her teeth chattered. Her mouth fell open at the sight of a rusted metal roof, supported by four uneven saplings. A group of the passengers had congregated under it, their faces pale with shock.

A man sobbed uncontrollably, and she wondered if he'd lost a loved one. By the number of missing passengers, she surmised they were either dead or still climbing.

"Jack, where on earth are we?"

"I dread to think."

"Come see!" Juan, the flight attendant waved them over to the far edge of the runway, where it looked like a mudslide had taken a chunk of rainforest away. "The army is here."

Kitarna ran to the edge and stared down through the curtain of rain to a road several hundred feet below. Two tarpaulin-covered trucks were parked before the washed-out road, their headlights beaming through the downpour. A section of hillside had collapsed, taking mud and foliage sweeping past the front of the first truck. It wouldn't be coming up any time soon.

How many hours would it take before rescue choppers arrived? She glanced at her watch. Three-forty. It looked like they were in for a long, cold wait.

Men carrying rifles and wearing waterproof ponchos stood in front of the vehicles watching as others shoveled the mud aside. She frowned. "They're wasting their time, and it's dangerous. We're better off climbing down to them."

Juan passed her a satchel with a red cross on it. "With the storm, those soldiers might not know we're here. I'll go alert them before they give up and leave." He pulled two palm fronds from a tree then leaped onto the thick mud, shooting down the slope in an impressive piece of showmanship.

"That doesn't look good." Jack spoke quietly beside her. "We should get out of here before they see us."

"What are you talking about? Those soldiers can help us."

"I don't think they're soldiers, at least not the good kind. And believe me, you don't want them anywhere near you."

She kept her eyes on the men below. "What do you mean by 'not the good kind'?"

"Mercenaries." Jack urged her back. "Spread the word for everyone to head back to the plane. We'll have to hide in the jungle. Up here we're open targets."

"But Juan has gone down there."

"Fuck."

They watched as Juan zoomed downhill, waving wildly. She couldn't hear him, but the soldiers' attention suddenly shifted. A man climbed out of the cabin of the second truck.

He stepped forward as Juan clambered off his makeshift toboggan. They exchanged words. The soldiers looked up the hill to where several passengers waved at them.

Suddenly Juan turned and ran. A gunshot rang out.

Kitarna watched in horror as the flight attendant slammed face first into the sludge oozing down the mountain.

A woman screeched, making Kitarna jump. Around her, chaos broke loose. Passengers began yelling and running about with no real direction, panic taking hold. She stood stunned, her brain attempting to process what her eyes had just seen.

"Who will help us?"

"We help ourselves. Come on." Jack grabbed her hand and sprinted to the aluminum shelter where quite a few passengers still stood, unaware of the imminent danger.

A clap of thunder boomed above, and the downpour swelled.

He had to shout to be heard. "Folks, there are mercenaries on the road below. With the mudslide and heavy rain, it will take them time to get up here. Head for the plane then veer off to the southeast. Once you hit a river, go east. Eventually you will find a town. Avoid villages as they could be under the control of the mercenaries."

"We can't tell which way is east in this weather," someone called.

"When you get to the plane turn left and, in the morning, look for the brightest bit of sky, that's your east. Let's go" He picked up the young boy under one arm and sprinted through the downpour, Kitarna hot on his heels. Mud oozed between her toes as she fought to stay on her feet.

"Jack, wait. I can't go without..."

"Kit!" The anguished, distant cry came from her right.

She turned and ran through the blinding rain toward her sister's voice. "Bernie!"

Barely able to see through the rainstorm, she almost crashed into her sister.

"Kit?" Bernie hugged her fiercely. "How were you not squashed by that tree?"

"I moved seats before takeoff."

"You're going to send my hair white, Kit Kat."

Kitarna clung to her older sister. "Mercenaries just shot the flight attendant."

"Yeah, I know." Bernie tugged her into motion again. "Listen, you've got the knowledge to survive the jungle, but just in case we get separated or run into this Jaguar, I recommend we hide our identities and pretend we're traveling alone."

"Okay."

They broke into a jog, side by side, running toward the shelter.

"Have you got your rucksack?" Bernie shot an anxious look over her shoulder.

"Yes, under this jacket."

"Good." Bernie flicked the edge of Jack's jacket as they ran. "Who gave you this?"

She lengthened her stride to match Bernie's. "Jack Callaghan, he's Australian, and I think he might be a soldier." She repeated the instructions Jack had given the group.

"Have you got your compass, Kit?"

"Yes."

Bernie gave a low whistle as they came across Jack at the end of the runway, gesturing to other passengers to hurry. His stern frown softened slightly when he saw Kitarna.

"You took your sweet time, kitten. Let's move it." He charged down the flattened foliage.

Bernie gripped her hand. "Be careful, Kit Kat. Don't trust anyone. We'll meet up along the road. Now go, and no matter what happens, keep moving forward."

"Okay." She plunged down the bank after Jack, only just able to make out his shape through the dense rain. After catching her feet twice in tangled roots, she gave her full attention to the downward drop, with no choice but to trust Bernie would follow.

Reaching the plane, she discovered luggage sprawled over the ravaged earth and a man with his back to her rummaging through a suitcase.

Jack had stopped too and strode over. "What the hell are you doing?"

The guy almost jumped out of his skin. "Looking for anything useful; lighters, repellant, water. Who knows what we might need?"

"No time," called Jack. "There are mercenaries chasing us. Get down the mountain."

"Yeah, no worries."

Kitarna spotted her huge pack near the one of the twisted wheels. "Wait." Switching her rucksack to her chest, she scrambled over bags and flattened shrubs to the pack.

"Forget it," yelled Jack. "Don't bring anything that will slow you down."

"My hiking boots and supplies are inside. We're going to need them."

"Shit." Passing her his pack, he hauled hers onto his shoulders. "Keep up with me and don't stop for any reason. Let's go."

"I'm right behind you, Jack." She pulled on his pack. It was weighty, but definitely lighter than hers. With the heavy rain, she couldn't tell if Bernie had caught up and passed or taken another path. Picking up the first aid satchel, she trudged after a string of passengers and Jack, into wet, slippery, tightly packed, clinging jungle. A perfect haven for leeches. She cringed.

The monkeys had moved on, but the racket still echoed through the forest. Their aggressive barking and shaking of branches had made her hair stand on end, as did the automatic rifles she now heard discharging on top of the mountain.

She could only be thankful they had enough light filtering through the canopy to allow them to see where they were going. A quick glance at her watch showed five-thirty. Almost twilight. How had so much time passed?

She glanced over her shoulder again, looking for Bernie. That might be her, eight or nine people back, behind the flight attendant. The deep shadows made it difficult to tell.

Either from fear or agreement, none of the passengers spoke above a whisper as they held palms aside for each other or lent a helping hand over fallen trees.

The guy with dreadlocks barged past, knocking her sideways into a *Theobroma grandiflorum*. Sending him a dagger stare, she clambered to her feet then picked as many of the chocolate-flavored fruit as she could squeeze into her rucksack. High in antioxidants and nutrients, they'd be good to have on hand.

The fair man and blonde woman who had held everyone up on the plane jogged past her. Surprisingly, the woman now wore a sleeveless sweatshirt, active-wear tights and runners. She'd discarded the small suitcase.

So, not a dumb blonde. Kitarna instantly felt ashamed. As her father would say, never make assumptions. For all she knew the blonde could be a brain surgeon and Jack could be part of some private army. He certainly looked the part.

Jack disappeared ahead of the scraggly line of sodden men, women and several teenagers. Breathing hard, Kitarna continued placing one foot in front of the other, treading over clumps of ferns, pushing aside vines, and ducking low branches.

She stepped onto a mud track with two ruts running parallel to each other. Zigzag impressions cut into the mud where the ruts weren't waterlogged. She glanced right, fully expecting to see the trucks and mercenaries bearing down on them. Instead she found a continuous barrage of rain and an empty track, meandering uphill and around a bend.

A round of gunfire, somewhere on the mountain above, had her praying they weren't shooting at Bernie. She helped two white-haired ladies down the bank. On the plane, they'd been in the row ahead. "Just follow the crowd." She pointed down the road.

"Thank you, dear." One lady squeezed her fingers before hurrying after her friend.

An older couple jumped out of the rainforest further down.

Realizing her sister wasn't one of the stragglers, Kitarna turned to follow the ladies around the curving track. Quite possibly Bernie had taken a longer route and would emerge further down the road. The sky grew darker and she wondered if they should make some sort of camp.

The low rumble of an engine and grinding gears sounded behind her. "Quick, everyone, get off the road." She caught up with the ladies. "Hurry, hide yourselves."

The older couple and several men turned around. She gestured toward the lower side of the jungle. "Hide into the rainforest, quick."

Around the next bend, the road straightened for several hundred feet. A group of people stood before the next bend. The rain must be obscuring the engine noise. "A truck is coming. Move!"

Everyone scattered.

She scrabbled to get up the right-hand bank, but it veered too high. "Not good."

She ran across the track, crashing into a wall of strangler vines. No way through. No choice but to run to the next bend. She sprinted past walls of impregnable jungle. Everyone had disappeared, and the trucks were nearing. A strangled sob escaped her.

Jack stepped out from behind an enormous mahogany tree and she almost peed her pants, screeching in fright. He clamped a hand over her mouth and lifted her off the ground, around the tree's impressive roots.

"Shush, I've got you, kitten." He backed through a screen of thick maidenhair fern, before lowering her feet to the ground. "Follow me."

Breathing raggedly, she jumped over tree roots and ploughed through undergrowth behind him, praying Bernie had found a safe hiding spot.

Jack pushed vines and ferns aside until they came to a tree so ancient it stole her breath. Moss-covered roots rose from the squelchy earth to well above her head, supporting an enormous trunk that disappeared into the canopy. She followed him around its thick girth to a gap large enough for two people to crawl through. He stood back. "Stay here, I'm going to check on the others."

"Wait." She didn't relish the idea of him leaving. What if the mercenaries found her, or a prowling, hungry animal? Noises always sounded spookier at night, but there were others out there alone. "How long will you be?"

"If I'm not back by morning, keep going downhill. Find a river and follow it east." He dropped her big pack and retrieved his from her back. "I might need this."

She watched the jungle swallow him. "Oh, God, please bring him back before it gets dark." Rolling thunder crashed overhead, absorbing her whispered plea. She could only be thankful the monkeys had ceased their horrendous noise.

The canopy took the brunt of the rain. Something she could be grateful for. *I'm going to need light.* She shifted her big pack into the hollow tree then pulled out her headlamp. A quick wave around the interior revealed an empty area big enough to garage a small car. Raising her flashlight, she encountered a hairy, bird-eating tarantula.

"Shit." She lurched backward, tripping over the pack and landing on her butt. Her heart raced. Where had it gone? Scooting back, she considered her options. No way would she sleep in there with that thing. Her gaze dropped to her pack. It contained the latest lightweight tent and sleeping bag. She could erect the tent inside the tree.

She froze as the rumble of a truck drew closer. Her heart remained in her mouth until it passed along the road. She heard male voices calling to each other in Spanish. Mercenaries on foot, and one voice seemed to be ordering them into positions.

It had been a long time since she'd conversed with her father's Spanish kitchen and ground staff. But some things stayed with you forever.

"*El* Jaguar *estará muy enojado si no encuentro a el arqueólogo.*"

*The Jaguar will be very angry if we don't find the archeologist.* Trembling, she snatched her rucksack and backed around the tree. The mercenaries knew the Jaguar, and the Jaguar hunted Bernie, but how could he know she'd been on that plane?

He couldn't. Kitarna pushed aside wet ferns. Not unless the mercenaries had found the manifest. Maybe another archeologist had taken their flight? Perhaps she'd misheard. Anthropologist, or *antropólogo* sounded similar. She might as well be clutching at straws.

Her brain and body were too tired to figure it out, but she needed to find her sister. The temperature had dropped. She couldn't stop shivering as she stumbled uphill, through the thick foliage. She had to move parallel to the road and work her way back to where she'd last seen Bernie. *Where is the damn road? It has to be close.*

A *maracuya* vine blocked her path. Food was the last thing on her mind, but she picked a handful of the passion fruits. They would need sustenance to keep up their energy. "Oh, oh." Unable to hold it, she sneezed loudly.

A snapping twig followed by a Spanish curse jolted her. Sweat beaded on her upper lip as she slowly turned. She stared at the thick foliage surrounding her. No place to hide, nowhere to run. She held her breath as palm fronds separated and she stared into the inky black eyes of the mercenary who had shot Juan.

A slow smile curved his thin lips. "*Este debe ser mi dia de suerte.*" She automatically translated in her head. *This must be my lucky day.*

As if her day couldn't possibly go any further downhill. The nightmare loomed before her. She'd be dragged kicking and screaming to his camp, used until she resembled a dirty rag, then she'd be tossed aside like stale bread. Her shaking knees wouldn't hold her up much longer.

If he thought her easy prey, he was in for a shock. She wouldn't go willingly. He looked to be around forty, and almost handsome, but for his cold eyes. He held a flashlight in one hand and a machete in the other. A menacing rifle hung across his chest.

If she screamed, would Jack come to her rescue? No, how could he without any kind of weapon? Her screams would just bring more mercenaries to defile her body. And, if Bernie heard the scream she'd come tearing through the forest like a crazed matriarchal elephant. They'd both be captured.

"*Hablas español, señorita?*" He demanded, waving the machete at her.

It might be more of an advantage if he thought she didn't understand Spanish. His clean-shaven arrogance and cultured accent gave her pause. This man was no mere foot soldier. Could he be the Jaguar?

She needed to play ignorant, stall for time, get him to let down his guard then knock him over the head. *Great idea, Kitarna, what are you going to hit him with, a rotting stick?* Bernie would kick his ass.

"I'm sorry, I don't understand what you're saying."

His eyes narrowed. "What is your name, *señorita*?"

"K...imberley. I was on a plane and we crash-landed on the top of the mountain. Who are you? What do you want?"

"My men call me *Capitán* Pérez. As you belong to me, *señorita*, you may call me Andrés."

"Like hell she will," came Jack's menacing voice.

The mercenary twisted, grabbing for his rifle. Jack slogged him with a jagged sapling, knocking him off his feet, into the gnarled root of a massive tree. Dazed the man rolled over. Kitarna gasped at the blood pouring from his torn chin.

Jack strode forward, seized the rifle and leveled it on the captain's chest. "None of the passengers want trouble. We're only interested in getting out of here as quickly as possible."

The mercenary's black gaze never left Jack. He raised a hand, touched his jaw then regarded his bloodstained fingers. Using the tree for support, he stood. "I am going to kill you. Not fast or simple. You will be staked to the ground, your intestines hanging out as enticement for scavenging animals to gorge on."

"Not happening." Jack slung the leather strap around his neck so the rifle fell across his chest. "Search parties will descend on this area in the next few hours. Your best option would be to collect your buddies and leave before the army arrives."

"No army will come. You will die in agony knowing I, Andrés Pérez, took your woman for a camp whore." He unsheathed a long-bladed knife and threw it.

Kitarna screamed, but somehow Jack blocked the knife with the rifle and came at the mercenary, smashing him across the skull with the butt. The mercenary crumpled.

The terror she'd been keeping at bay erupted into choking sobs. "Is...he...dead?"

"Not yet." Jack pulled her into his arms. "Speak in whispers. We now have a machete and automatic assault rifle. Way to go, kitten."

"I can't stop shaking."

"That's understandable. Why didn't you stay where I left you?"

"I heard mercenaries."

"Yeah, the trucks are dropping them off every eighty feet so they can work their way back up the mountain by foot. My guess is they intend to surround us, herding everyone into a group. What they won't realize until morning is most of us are already outside their net."

She stared at the unconscious man. "What about him?"

"I saw this guy at Sào Paulo de Olivença Airport. He must have taken a chopper to get here so fast." Jack reached for his knife. "Turn your back."

The horror of what he proposed choked her. "No. I can't have his death on my conscience. Let's tie him up."

For a moment he looked like he might argue. "Hold this." He passed her the rifle then took off his pack.

Intrigued, she picked up the flashlight and held it close to the ground, while he pulled out a ball of cord. "Is that strong enough?"

"It's para cord, very strong."

"Why do you carry para cord?"

"It's good in an emergency." He drew the cord taut and ran it against the machete blade. "We should take his poncho too." He removed the waterproof cape and a belt holding a knife sheath. "We don't want him alerting his friends." He tied Andrés Pérez's hands and feet then tore a strip of material from the mercenary's shirt and gagged him.

"That gash needs stitching. What if a wild animal comes along?"

"Darlin', this piece of scum murdered Juan in cold-blood and would have done appalling things to you."

"Yes, I know."

"Indeed." Jack stood, attaching the knife sheath to his own belt. "Let's get out of here, *Kimberley*."

"My name isn't Kimberley. I just told *him* that."

He picked up the machete. "I'd bet my entire savings it's not Kit either."

"Please don't. I'd hate to be responsible for you living on the streets." She pursed her lips. "I don't know how to thank you, Jack."

"I'll show you when we get to Manaus." He chuckled softly as he led the way.

They trekked much faster with him in front, shoving foliage aside for her. He moved with the stealth of a large cat. When they reached the hollow tree, she discovered the man and boy from across the aisle huddled inside with a young dark guy.

She pointed the flashlight up. "There's a bird-eating tarantula up there."

The boy shot out. "I hate spiders. The kids in the village used to catch tarantulas to cook and eat."

"Alex, keep your voice down." The older man stepped out of the hollow and laid his arm around the boy's shoulders. "Spiders won't bother us if we don't bother them."

Kitarna wanted to disagree, but her brain had fixated on the village kids. To her knowledge, eating tarantulas was a tribal delicacy. "Have you been staying with a tribe?"

"No." The man answered. "Alex has a vivid imagination."

Shrugging out of Jack's jacket, she glanced at the scowling young boy.

He brightened. "Did you know the Amazon basin is as large as the entire United States?"

"Yes." She smiled and held out her hand. "I'm Kit."

"I'm Lexi...I mean Alex, and this is Roscoe, my grandpa."

Roscoe frowned at the little boy before turning to Jack. "We need to keep moving."

"Too dark and we can't risk using the road." Jack took the rifle from Kitarna and propped it inside the tree. "I'll get rid of the spider then I'm going to cut some camouflage to hide the entrance." He glanced at her. "Get what you need from your big pack, because it's not coming with us."

"But I need everything."

"You can bring the rucksack, so choose wisely. That little number you're wearing stays behind." He ducked inside the tree.

She seethed at his broad back. He had no right to tell her what she could bring. He wasn't an authority on plant diversity, ecology and evolution. He hadn't gained an encyclopedic knowledge of rainforest plants. This holiday should have been an opportunity to study and collect undiscovered specimens, her chance to be taken seriously by her peers.

*As for this little number*...She caught the knot of her green bolero. No way would she toss away her birthday presents. This French ensemble had cost her mother a small fortune, and the *kansashi* hairpin Bernie had given her lay in the bottom of her pack. If need be, it would pierce a mercenary's throat or vital organs.

What Jack Callaghan didn't know wouldn't hurt him.

~ 8 ~

After years of stalking his prey or lying patiently in wait, it came as second nature for Jack to place each boot prudently, before shifting his weight forward. The rustle of leaves or snap of a twig could spell instant death. Painstakingly, he worked his way toward the roughly hewn track, mindful of the overhanging branches.

Although jaguars avoided humans, they did hunt at night, and could just as easily drop from a limb as leap from the dense undergrowth. He'd left the rifle behind on purpose for Roscoe. The hunting knife and machete were all he needed, and a little more time before complete darkness fell.

After fifteen minutes of cutting giant, palm fronds and shearing quietly through bamboo, he heard a whimper, then a louder, male voice.

"For Christ sake, stop being such a baby, Marley."

A female answered. "You're an asshole, Brett. I hurt my stomach when you threw me out of the plane. What if I've ruptured something?"

"Fuck, that's all we need. I should have dumped you in Rio and gone with Alison."

"I wish you had. Now we're going to die, because you're a cheat and a liar."

Jack lifted a large palm leaf aside and looked down on the guy with dreadlocks and the skinny girl who had tumbled off the emergency chute. Two pairs of terrified eyes stared up at him.

*These two are going to be trouble. I just know it.* "Stay completely silent and follow me. Utter one word and I'll leave you for the mercenaries." He led them in a roundabout way back to the tree, uneasy at the crunching of their feet amongst the forest waste.

"Get in there and stay quiet." Holding onto his temper, Jack placed his bundle of bamboo and palm fronds beside the tree. "Roscoe, throw these palms down, they'll be more comfortable to sleep on than soggy mulch."

"Sure, Jack. Want me to make up a door with that bamboo?"

"Yeah, use this to tie the lengths together." He passed the para-cord over. "Don't cut it, as we'll take it with us tomorrow. If you need a flashlight inside, stick some palm fronds across the gap to hide any light. I'll cut branches to conceal the opening." He took two steps and froze as the sound of someone moving toward him reached his ears. Sliding behind a moss-covered tree, he waited, concentrating on the placement of feet. There were three of them moving quietly but steadily through the forest toward him. Lifting the machete to his shoulder, he braced for a hard swing.

"I know it's here somewhere."

*Kit. Jesus, I'm going to strangle that girl.* He lowered the machete and crept forward. Her voice although low, sounded too calm to be bringing mercenaries back for him to deal with. It had to be more passengers. A gray-haired man and woman emerged from the forest. They stood aside for Kit to take the lead. She almost walked into Jack before she saw him.

He put a finger against her lips and whispered, "Do you ever do what you're told?"

"I needed to pee. This is Piers and Juliette," she whispered back. "They're doctors."

He nodded at the couple. "I'm Jack. Our accommodation is three steps behind me. Can you check on a passenger? She hurt her stomach falling from the plane."

"Of course." Piers took his wife's elbow and guided her past.

Jack looked into Kit's pleased face. His annoyance wilted under her wide smile. "Darlin', you can't run off on your own. It's too risky."

"So we pee in pairs?"

A chuckle escaped. "Yeah. We do everything in pairs from now on."

"I like the sound of that." She kissed his cheek. "Shall we join the others?"

"You go, I'll be along soon." Ducking under a thick fern, he waited several minutes, but could detect nothing bar the occasional roll of thunder, crickets, night birds and the constant patter dripping through the canopy.

By the time Jack approached the tree with a second load of bamboo and palm fronds, complete darkness had descended under the canopy. He was relieved to hear no voices as he felt his way round the tree. With luck the mercenaries had returned to their camp for the night. If the rescue teams didn't land first thing in the morning, stray passengers could spend days wondering in circles as the mercenaries tightened the net.

A dim glow revealed Roscoe and Piers crouched on the ground, fixing the bamboo together. Kit stood over them holding a flashlight and wearing the assault rifle across her chest. Hell, she had to be the sexiest woman he'd ever met. He wished he had her somewhere safe and naked. She hadn't heard him. It would really top his day off if she panicked and shot him.

He lowered his bundle then eased over a high root, taking a minute to study his mark. The drenching rain had plastered the skimpy dress to every luscious curve.

*Focus! This is not the time to get a hard-on.*

She raised her arm, wiping the drizzling rain out of her eyes with her sleeve. He sprang, covering her mouth with one hand and caging her and the rifle within his arm.

"Oomph." Pain slammed across his forehead. The blasted female had hit him with the damn flashlight.

She pushed back, sending them both crashing through the makeshift fronds of the palm door. Her teeth sunk into his fingers.

"Hell, woman, it's me."

"Jack! For goodness sake, why did you sneak up on me?"

He released her and rubbed his forehead. "I didn't want that rifle going off."

She scrambled to her knees. "I had the safety catch on and was listening for you."

"You won't hear me." He came up on his haunches, taking in the surprised faces. "Sorry, folks. I didn't expect Kit to hit me."

She huffed. "I'm not going to let a mercenary grab me without reacting."

"Good to know." Although they'd kept their voices low, he feared exposure. "Where did those other flashlights come from?"

Kit propped the rifle next to her large pack. "They're mine. I gave Juliette the headlamp and I carry a spare flashlight just in case."

*A headlamp? She gets more interesting by the minute.* "Turn them off until we have the doorway covered properly." Jack ducked back outside to drag in another pile of bamboo and palms. "I've cut a couple of thick branches to add a bit of camouflage."

A piercing scream echoed through the night, setting off multiple squawks and fluttering in the canopy above.

Kit grasped his arm. "Was that a woman or an animal?"

"I'm not sure."

A second scream had her pushing him aside. He caught her waist in both hands and lifted her back inside. "Stay here, I'll go." Releasing her, he unzipped an outer pocket of his pack and grabbed the night vision goggles.

"Wait, take this." Her hand shook as she held out the rifle.

"No, you keep it."

Fitting the goggles, he crept into the jungle.

Everything took on an eerie green glow through the night vision lenses. Warily he eased aside foliage and ducked under limbs, placing each foot carefully. Guttural male laughter and Spanish curses almost drowned out a woman's frantic, English pleas.

*Christ.*

They were twenty or thirty feet away. Campfire smoke assailed his nostrils. Hard to tell how many, at least two. The woman swore vengeance if they didn't back off.

Easing round a high tree-root, he found his quarry. By the edge of the road, a tarp had been tied between trees, sheltering the fire's struggling flames from rain. To his left a lantern swayed from its perch on a low branch.

Underneath two mercenaries, hampered by ponchos, attempted to get tight leggings off a struggling blonde. She kicked and scratched for all her worth, adding to their battle.

Dealing with the men wouldn't be a problem, but her screeching would bring reinforcements. Whipping off his goggles, Jack slid the blade from its sheath. He crept up on the mercenary, who now had the blonde's arms anchored, under his knees, beside her head.

His sleazy snicker became a choked gasp as Jack yanked him off the woman, hammer-punched him twice in the kidney, then shoved him head-first into bracken fern.

The other mercenary, who'd been intent on getting his trousers down, reared back, scrabbling to swing his rifle from under his arm and get on his feet.

Jack kicked him in the shoulder with his steel-capped boot, knocking him flat on his back.

Grunting, the mercenary raised his rifle.

Jack dived, bashing the weapon aside with his forearm. He landed heavily on the man's chest, cracking the soldier's ribs. Before the man uttered a sound, Jack head-butted him. He clenched his fists and swung, a one-two motion smashing him in the jaw. The man stayed down for the count.

Detecting movement from behind, Jack lunged side-ways, avoiding the first mercenary's knife by a whisker. Springing to his feet, he kicked out, striking the man's wrist and dislodging the knife.

The mercenary went for his rifle, leaving Jack no option but to throw the long-bladed knife he'd taken from Pérez. It wedged deep in the man's chest, the shock on his face lasting three seconds before death claimed him.

Jack dragged the body under a mass of giant palms then crouched, listening for approaching feet, while the blonde fixed her clothes, sobbing softly.

Once certain they weren't about to be ambushed, he withdrew the knife and wiped it through a clump of wet grass. The mercenaries were out of sight, but blood would bring scavengers.

Of more concern, had the blonde's screams alerted other mercenaries? He could only hope they would assume she'd been captured and taken to their camp.

Sheathing the knife, he held out a hand. "Let me help you."

She reared up, and flew at him, sending him staggering back a step when she jumped him, wrapping her arms and legs around his body.

He had to forcibly peel her off and set her on the ground. "We can't hang around. Are you good to go?"

She nodded. "Yes. No. Wait." She snatched up a black drawstring bag, pushed a clump of ferns aside and began walloping a curled-up shape. "You bastard, you would have cowered there and let them rape me."

Jack leaped forward and pulled her away, clamping his hand over her mouth. "For Christ sake, be quiet."

She slumped against him.

A man crawled from under the fern. "I'm sorry, babe, I was paralyzed with fear."

She ripped away from Jack. "You fucking liar. You were saving your own skin and couldn't give a…"

Jack clamped her mouth again and whispered, "Shut up, or you'll get us shot."

She nodded.

He released her and picked up the rifles, his goggles and the flashlight. "Follow me and stay close."

She gripped his belt, staying so close he found it awkward to push through the thick foliage. His goggles exposed the forest clearly in two circles of green, yet even using his compass; Jack couldn't locate their hideout.

A short, sharp shrill caught his attention. "This way."

The intermittent sound led him to the tree where Kit balanced on a low branch, her lips pursed to emit the sharp birdlike tweets.

She scampered down like a monkey. "Sorry, I know you said to stay inside, but I thought you might get lost."

Unclamping the blonde's fingers from his belt, Jack stepped forward and eyed her lush lips. "Clever thinking." He leaned the rifles against the tree and pulled off his goggles. "I appreciate the help, but you put yourself and the others at risk. Don't do it again."

"I can mimic forest birds. Did you make it in time?"

"Yeah."

Adrenalin still pumped through his body. He noted the stubborn tilt of her chin and felt the strongest urge to kiss her. Instead he looked over his shoulder at the blonde and her companion, who were glaring at each other stony-faced. He turned back to temptation personified, almost groaning at the sight of her erect nipples, under a dress he wanted to rip off her. Touching her became more important than life itself.

The branches he'd cut earlier had been speared deep into the ground completely hiding any sign of what lay behind. "Let's get these two inside."

"It's quite cozy in there now." Kit pulled the branches back then edged the bamboo gate aside.

Jack directed the blonde and her partner inside and took the gate from Kit. He leaned it across the opening. "We have something important to discuss."

"We do?"

"Yeah." He lifted her off her feet and kissed her, harder than he'd intended, but hell, it barely scratched his itch. Other than her gasp of surprise, she didn't object, running her hands through his hair as their tongues dueled.

Her soft moan was like a kick in the head. He risked endangering everyone. Returning her feet to the ground and stepping away took immense willpower.

"I'm glad we understand each other." He collected the rifles, bent and entered the snug space, her sexy chuckle ringing in his ears. He should have put up with the bloody itch, now he had to hide a blazing erection.

He laid the weapons on the ground. Once she squeezed past, he fitted the gate between the tree and two bamboo stakes. Palm fronds had been added on both sides, effectively blocking any light from escaping.

"Good job." He kept his voice low, even though the rolling thunder and continuous pattering of rain should cover their voices. When he turned, ten people were watching him. They were seated in a semi-circle, on a large piece of green plastic. "What's this?"

"It's mine," whispered Kit, extinguishing a headlamp. "It hangs over my hammock, so I don't get wet."

*She has a hammock?* He scanned the items arranged about her and recognized a compact hammock and sleeping bag much like his own. "Your big pack stays here, and we're going to need the rucksack to carry essentials."

The defiance in her eyes and stubborn tilt of her chin amused him. She was a puzzle he enjoyed more and more. "At least you've got dry clothes. You should change before you shiver to death."

"It is wrong for her to bare her body in front of any man other than her husband."

Jack glanced at the young, dark-skinned guy who had spoken. "Would you rather she freezes when there's dry clothes in her pack?"

"You should not allow your woman to dress this way. What she is wearing—" he waved a hand in Kit's direction, "—is inappropriate."

*My woman. I like that.* Jack stared at the young guy. "The way any person dresses is their business, and never a reason to be judged."

"The natives wear nothing," said the kid. "Well, nothing but a tiny fringe to hide their privates."

The young guy scowled. "They are pagans. It is different for them, living here in the jungle."

Jack wasn't going to get into an argument with a guy who probably considered women should be covered from head to foot. He looked at the two doctors. "Did you examine the girl?"

The woman answered. "*Ja*, Marley's stomach is bruised and bloated. She assured us she isn't pregnant, so we are concerned she has internal bleeding. The sooner we're rescued the better." She spoke with a melodic accent.

Jack nodded. "Army choppers should be here by morning." These people weren't his concern and he'd gladly hand them all into the care of rescuers. In Manaus, he'd collect his eighty-grand and disappear. His gaze rested on Kit's downturned head as she rummaged in her pack. He'd have gone to great lengths to keep *her*, if not for his past.

~ 9 ~

Dropping to his haunches, Jack examined Kit's belongings. She was an extremely efficient packer. Everything had been rolled tightly or secured in net pockets. He pulled out army-green cargo pants and a paler green long-sleeved shirt, then a pair of thick socks and hiking boots. "These are the only clothes you'll need."

"But..."

"Your big pack will get caught on branches, and drown you if we need to swim across a river."

The blonde gasped. "There are alligators and piranhas here."

"Keep your voice down. Piranhas will only attack if you're bleeding." He pulled out the compact sleeping bag and hammock then lowered his voice to a whisper so only Kit could hear. "I would expect a butterfly enthusiast to stay in hotels, not camp out in the jungle."

She shrugged her slim shoulders. "The butterflies I'm interested in don't inhabit cities. I've got a tent too, in case there's no trees close enough for my hammock."

"Now that *will* come in handy." He pulled out the tent and looked around the faces watching. "Who wants to carry this?"

Piers held out his hand. "I can, if we attach some loops for my shoulders."

Jack nodded. "In that case you and...Juliette get to use it."

"Hey." Kit scowled at him. "You can't give away my things."

"There are eleven of us, and you won't need your hammock or sleeping bag."

"What?"

He threw the hammock at the blonde. "Empty your bag and put that in. Without a tent, it will be safer to sleep above the ground."

"What about us?" The guy with dreadlocks pointed a finger at his own chest.

"Find a tree." Jack glanced at each of the women then rummaged through Kit's clothes. "You ladies need something to protect your arms against insects."

She shouldered him aside. "You have no right to give away my gear. I'll do it." She handed each of the ladies a long-sleeved shirt, and after a tiny hesitation gave the lady doctor a pair of fawn cargo pants. "These will protect your legs."

With genuine surprise, Jack sat back and watched as she passed the ladies socks, T-shirts and plastic vials of brown stuff. "This will keep flies and mosquitoes away."

"What is it?" asked the skinny girl, her lips thinning in disgust.

"I don't actually have a name for it." Kit dragged out her sleeping bag and offered it to Piers. "You may as well have this too. I won't need it, as I'll be sharing Jack's hammock and sleeping bag."

He resisted grinning when she tilted her chin, daring him to refuse. As that had been his plan all along, he merely raised an eyebrow. "Of course."

She glared at him before unzipping her rucksack. She placed a small camera beside her then pulled out two packets of nuts, a handful of what looked like lemons and several brown things the size of grapefruit.

"Where did you get those?"

She leaned over, unsheathed his knife and sliced one of the brown things into several pieces. "These are a relation to cacao. It tastes like a mixture of chocolate and pineapple. The yellow things are a cousin to passion fruit and full of pro-vitamins A, vitamin C and iron."

He picked up a piece and sniffed. "Did you buy them at the market?"

"No, I picked them in the rainforest, but I assure you they are safe to eat."

"We can't risk it, kitten. A lot of fruit and berries are poisonous."

"No, she's right." The kid took a quarter. "We ate this in the village."

Roscoe glowered. "If anything happens to Alex, I'll..."

"It's okay, Roscoe," said the kid, taking another piece and happily biting in to it. "The natives wouldn't dare give me anything poisonous."

Jack jumped in before Alex gave away too much.

"All right, but as a general rule, don't eat any berries or fruit."

"Or, ask me first." Kit smiled sweetly at Alex. "I've been in the Amazon a few times, and know a bit about what is and isn't safe to eat."

*More and more interesting.* Jack bit into the pulp and immediately his taste buds took flight, soaring with the rich flavor. "This is delicious."

"Told you." She set about cutting up the rest of the fruit. He noticed she put all the husks into a zip-lock plastic bag, of which she had a roll. They would come in handy to protect passports. He'd also noticed specimen jars. Maybe she hadn't lied about being a butterfly enthusiast. *I wish my life could be that simple.*

Jack handed over his collection of nuts and water to Kit. Between them they had four twelve-ounce bottles of water. He and Roscoe had hydration bladders inserted in their packs that would need filling once they found drinkable water. He noticed Kit had one in her rucksack.

He glanced around the group again. "I suggest we introduce ourselves. It's the best way to break the ice." Jack focused on the guy with dreadlocks, sitting on his left. "You wanna go first?"

"Sure. I'm Brett Ogle, and this is Marley Simpson, we're from New Zealand and we're backpacking."

Jack noticed neither had taken any fruit or nuts.

The blonde went next. "I'm Victoria Hayes, I'm from California and I'm a Human Resource Manager." She glanced at the fair man beside her. "Your go."

"Robert Northcote, I'm also from California, and a Director of the building company Victoria and I work for. We've been negotiating an upcoming project."

Jack noticed the wedding band Robert wore and wondered if his wife knew about the blonde.

The older couple introduced themselves as Piers and Juliette Willems, newly retired doctors from Belgium, who had been volunteering at a mission for the past month. They had been on their way to Argentina for a holiday.

Roscoe went next. "Ross Dalton, from Florida. Me and Alex have been on a boat trip, and now we're going home."

The dark guy met Jack's gaze. "My name is Ahmed, I'm Iranian and a fourth-year medical intern. I have been working at the same mission as the Willems."

Jack looked at Kit, kneeling on his right. "Your turn, darlin'."

Her gaze dropped to her interlocked fingers. "I'm here to photograph butterflies, and after we're rescued I plan to spend time with my mother in Paris." She looked up and smiled at him. "I might even head to the Caribbean for a cocktail on the beach. I hear there's a great bar opening there."

He liked the thought, but wondered at her hesitation.

"So, you're part French," asked Robert, his lingering gaze a little too personal for Jack's liking.

"I'm a bit of everything." She raised a fine eyebrow at Jack. "Your turn, honey."

*She's accepted the challenge.* More interestingly, she hadn't supplied her last name, occupation or nationality, nor made any mentioned of Bernie. Jack determined to learn more about his newly acquired partner, even though their liaison would only last until their rescue. He had enough on his plate without subjecting her to his torment and guilt.

She nudged him. "Jack?"

"Sorry, I'm Jack, Australian, and for the last twelve months I've been working for a logging company in Florida."

Kit jerked, her eyes widening. He'd swear her lips trembled before she looked down. Something had spooked her—logging or Florida?

Watching her closely, he continued. "Before that I spent ten years in the army." No point hiding it, she'd already guessed. And if they were to survive, these people needed to follow his lead. "Once we're rescued, I'm heading to the Caribbean."

He caught Kit's frown as she glanced between him and Roscoe. They'd called each other by name several times over the last few hours, had she picked up on that, or had the kid let something slip? *Damn, bring a child into a dangerous situation and everything goes to shit.*

Kit turned her back. "I need to change."

"Good idea." His gaze stayed on her as she lifted the dress, exposing smooth, golden skin and a pair of black bikini pants. *Damn she's hot.* Watching her would give him a hard-on, so he dragged his eyes to the task of what she could keep. Why she had a large collection of empty, plastic jars he didn't know, but they could stay behind. There were several scarves the other ladies could use to carry things or protect their heads.

He glanced across the hollow to see Victoria, Marley and Juliette pulling on shirts. Ahmed kept his eyes down. Brett and Robert stared blatantly at Kit as she struggled to do up the ties of a bikini top, which were getting caught in her hair.

"Here, let me." Jack shifted closer, blocking their view. She held up her hair while he tied the strings.

"Thanks." She shrugged into a blue tank top, the shirt and pants he'd chosen. Once she had the socks on, Jack shifted back to the edge of the tree and pulled out his sleeping bag and a dry T-shirt then peeled off his wet one.

"Oh. My. God."

Jack looked up to see Victoria ogling him.

"You must be really good at swinging an axe."

Robert snorted. "Bloody showoff."

"If you've got it, flaunt it." Victoria grinned at Jack. "And he's got it."

The skinny girl, Marley, stared so hard she risked popping her eye sockets. "His breasts are bigger than mine."

Victoria scoffed. "They're called pectorals, sweetie, and I bet the rest of his anatomy is just as impressive."

Robert hissed. "Victoria, I'm sitting right beside you. Use a little decorum."

"Go to hell, Robert. Jack saved me from being raped, while you cowered under a fern. I'd be happy to do a lot more than just look at his body."

"You realize he killed those men," whispered Robert, loud enough for all to hear.

"What's your point?" asked Victoria. "We're alive and those two bastards will never hurt another woman."

*Shit.* Jack shot a glance at Kit. She had both hands clasped over her mouth, her wide eyes staring at him, as if seeing him in a totally different light. He'd hoped Victoria and Robert had been too traumatized to notice his actions. He pulled on the T-shirt. "Climb inside my sleeping bag, kitten. You're shivering."

"Wait." She opened her rucksack and passed a space blanket to Marley.

Jack wondered at the items around her. A small camp stove and billycan stuffed with firelighters and waterproof matches, things he would take on a stakeout. No wonder her pack had been so heavy.

He glanced at Roscoe, holding the flashlight upward, casting a soft glow as he watched over his grandchild wrapped in a sleeping bag beside him. Piers and Juliette were cuddled up under the sleeping bag. Marley moved closer to Victoria to share the space blanket. Brett, Ahmed and Robert leaned against the tree, their arms crossed, and wearing sulky, irritated, and in Robert's case, anxious expressions.

Jack didn't give a fuck. He held his sleeping bag open then covered Kit as she slid inside. "I didn't have a choice." He kept his voice to a whisper. "Those mercenaries would have killed me and captured you. That doesn't bear thinking about."

Roscoe turned off the flashlight, leaving them in a cocoon of pitch black.

"You did what you had to. I'm grateful." She spread the bag over him.

"So, why were you looking at me like I shocked your socks off?"

"When did you last look in a mirror? Don't worry, I'll protect you from the ladies and their jealous boyfriends."

He chuckled. "That works both ways. Sleep well, *Katherine.*"

"Not even close. Goodnight, Jack."

*Intriguing—Why would she hide her identity?* He had plenty of time to ponder, as a full night's sleep was a luxury he hadn't enjoyed in a long time.

~ 10 ~

Shocked—to her very core. Jack. A *killer.*

The storm covered Jack's groans during the night, but his agitation and distress were evident each time he thrashed beside her. Deep sleep had only claimed him when she'd held him close, caressed his face and whispered soothingly against his ear.

She couldn't abandon him. Jack had become her best hope of finding Bernie and leading all the passengers to safety. Leaving him to deal with the messy stuff wasn't fair, yet the people she knew didn't go about killing others, even if they were mercenaries. Not that she'd ever met any of those either, until last night.

Yes, he'd saved Victoria, but the horror in Robert's eyes couldn't be faked. Is that what disturbed Jack's dreams or, as a soldier, had killing become second nature? Images of him knocking Andrés Pérez unconscious troubled her. Would he have killed that mercenary too, if she hadn't been there? Had he stabbed the other two mercenaries with that knife?

She'd used it to cut up fruit.

There appeared to be different sides to Jack Callaghan, and all of them were beyond her experience, beyond her comprehension. Yet irrespective of what he'd done, some basic instinct assured her she was safe with him. He'd woken her senses. She wanted to know him, and trust him.

He stirred, tensed momentarily before drawing her close. "I can't recall sleeping so well. I don't think I woke once."

"Maybe the storm lulled you." She touched a fingertip to his lips. "The rain has stopped, I can hear birds."

He captured her fingers, holding them gently against the steady beat of his heart as they lay in the dark, listening to a sonata of whistling and squawking, twittering and chirping. Their feathered orchestra occasionally joined by a throaty trill, or a sharp bark.

"We need to get moving." He kissed the inside of her wrist then released her hand. A soft glow illuminated his jaw as he checked his watch. "It's almost five-thirty. Bring only what you need." He threw the cover off. After a minute of rustling, a flashlight beam lit up their small haven. "Time to get up, folks."

Drawing up her knees, Kitarna shook her boots then dragged them on. She was of two minds. Get away from here fast, or stay and search for her sister. The fact Bernie hadn't come to Victoria's aid suggested she wasn't within hearing distance, or she'd been captured. So, should they look for the mercenaries' camp?

No, that would put everyone's lives in danger, and Bernie would never forgive her. She had to trust that Bernie could take care of herself, while she put her trust in a killer. A stark reminder for her to be wary, but at least now she knew Jack wasn't the Jaguar.

Victoria groaned. "That has got to be the worst night's sleep I've ever had."

"Yeah, me too," muttered Robert. "Our rescuers better hurry up, or I'll be very angry. I'm lodging a complaint to that airline, insisting the pilot be dismissed."

"Won't do any good. He died in the crash." Jack pulled their makeshift door aside and began untangling the para cord. "We can't wait to be rescued. Those mercenaries will scour this area."

Robert sneered. "And they'll be after revenge, thanks to you. We haven't killed anyone, but will they care? No."

"You ungrateful jerk." Kitarna came up on her knees, snatching her rucksack. "What do you think would have happened once those mercenaries raped Victoria? They'd shoot you and drag her back to their camp. If we'd stayed with the plane, the men would all be dead and us women wishing we were."

She rolled her space blanket and jammed it in with her other essentials. "Stay here by all means, we will move faster without—"

A low reverberating rumble drowned her hoarse whisper. An answering growl rolled across her skin, raising the fine hairs on her arms.

Jaguars.

The birds' chatter grew to a crescendo, as if to warn all the small creatures on the forest floor to run and hide. *To be an ant right now would be just dandy.*

Jack shoved the door back in place, leaned on it and whispered. "Kill the light. They're tracking the scent of blood."

*Shit, all cats have an incredible sense of smell. We're sitting ducks. Unless…*

Cursing the darkness, Kitarna blindly dug through her rucksack. Fumbling, she pressed a jar of insect repellant into Jack's hand. Stretching up, she touched her lips to his ear. "Use the gel to cover our scent."

"Hell, this smells vile." Jack muffled a cough.

They smeared the door's frame in the gel, its pungent stink up there with onions, bringing tears to her eyes. This stuff might be excellent for keeping insects away, but she'd never find a market to sell it. Closing the lid, she wiped some gel on her hands, neck and face then pushed the jar back into her rucksack.

No one spoke. No one moved.

The jaguars were so close their rumbles vibrated through her entire body, like a mild earthquake deep below the earth's crust. Her concentration became so intense that the rustling leaves and soft pad of the predators' paws competed with her thudding heart.

"Darlin', give me a touch of light," whispered Jack, his breath tickling her ear.

She switched on her headlamp, keeping it low to the ground, and watched as Jack donned the night vision goggles. Why he carried such an item was another thing to contemplate. He parted some palm leaves and leaned close to the door. After a minute he slowly drew back, lifted the goggles and placed them on her head. Taking the headlamp, he motioned for her to look outside.

At first, she only saw the surrounding trees and plants in a weird haze of green and black. The branches they'd stuck in front of the entrance had fallen over.

Movement caught her attention and she gulped. What she'd supposed to be a stump several feet to her right was a huge black jaguar looking directly at the tree. He turned his head away and sniffed then made a low throbbing sound, like a motorbike left idling with the choke too high. She couldn't take her eyes off the magnificent cat. He snarled, and she jumped.

So did Jack. Several people gasped.

Kitarna remained mesmerized by the magnificent animal, so close she could make out darker markings under his fur. Suddenly he leaped onto a fallen log and slunk low, his belly touching the bark.

A low, rumbling yowl drew her attention further to the right where a smaller jaguar prowled toward her mate. Black paw-like prints covered her lighter coat, which thanks to the goggles had a green-gray hue instead of the traditional yellowish-brown.

The black jaguar snarled again before bounding out of sight. His mate soared over the fallen tree and vanished after him in the darkness.

"They've gone." Sitting back on her heels, she grinned at Jack. "If I live to be ninety, that is something I'll never forget." She handed him the goggles. "I've never seen a black jaguar and the female was gorgeous."

"Damn, I missed her." Jack shifted the door again and began disassembling it. "Jaguars tend to avoid humans, so I think we're safe to go." Turning up the headlamp, he gestured for her to roll up his sleeping bag and the ground sheet. Once he had the para cord in a ball, he passed everyone a length of bamboo, cutting one down to size for Alex. The rifles he passed to Roscoe and Piers, keeping the scoped one for himself. He grabbed his jacket and pack then ducked outside.

Her heart in her mouth, Kitarna followed. She could still hear the jaguars in the distance, and by their snarky calls, they'd found what they were tracking. It didn't sit well on her conscience, but survival in the depths of the Amazon meant kill or be killed. Did she have it in her to take another person's life? She truly hoped she never faced such a dilemma.

With no more than an arm's length between each person, Jack led them downhill, hacking his way through the dimly lit rainforest, over moss-covered, rotting trees and around sharp cycads. Under the constant strains of bird chatter and whistles, they traipsed through groves of wet bracken ferns and tall trees.

Surprisingly, as the morning passed, the rainforest's interior opened, becoming easier to navigate the sparse undergrowth and thin layer of tree litter. A large group of red-faced *uaraki* monkeys put on a stage-show-worthy performance, mock fighting, swinging crazily through the trees. One showed off, juggling a mango. The orange-furred, short-tailed, bizarre-looking monkey deserved an Oscar.

Brilliant colors of flora and fauna seen through shafts of sunlight were a photographer's dream, and Kitarna couldn't let it go to waste, snapping shot after shot with her small camera.

It may have stopped raining, but the humidity sucked her energy. Her wet shirt clung with perspiration. Narrow rays infiltrated the canopy, but the mosquitoes had descended with a vengeance, buzzing around her bucket hat. She'd need to make up some more repellant if they weren't rescued soon.

"Jack, why haven't we heard any helicopters and search planes?"

"I don't know. They should have been here at first light."

"Wait up." Victoria overtook Roscoe and Alex, pushing Kitarna aside in her haste to get to Jack. "Can I have some of that stinky repellant? The mosquitoes are driving me mad."

"Kit gave you some last night, in the specimen jars."

"Oh, right." She dug in her tote bag and brought one out. "Thanks."

He turned his back on her. "You got any more, kitten?"

"Some." She dropped her rucksack and rummaged. While the other ladies shared repellant with their partners, she passed Jack a jar to share with Ahmed and Roscoe then walked over to where the young boy sat on a log, his cap pulled low.

"How are you doing, Alex?"

"Good. You're pretty. My mommy has green eyes too."

"Does she?" She smiled at the child. He had a sweet little face. "And I guess your daddy has brown eyes."

He looked down, staring at his fingers clenched around the bamboo stick. "We don't talk about him because he's a bad man."

"Oh." There wasn't much she could say to that. Raising the boy's chin, she smoothed the gel on his cheeks then moved to his ears. They were both pierced, which suddenly made sense. "Alex, you're a girl!"

"Shush." She pressed two fingers to Kitarna's lips. "It's a secret."

"But..."

"Alex, it's time to go," called Roscoe.

"I'll just do his ears." Kitarna shifted closer. "Sweetie, do you need help?"

Alex shook her head. "I'm happy Jack stole me. Now he can't smack my face if I cry for Mommy."

"Who? Jack?"

"No, my grandfather. He's mean and ugly, and has scary men working for him. If they find me, they'll take me back to the village."

It took effort for Kitarna to clamp down her panic. Suddenly, their situation made sense. Jack and Roscoe had kidnapped this child from a man who hit little girls, and engaged the mercenaries hunting them. Furtively, she captured a photo of the little girl then one of Roscoe and Jack as they spoke with Piers. "Alex, where's your mom?"

"In Florida, but Roscoe is taking me home to her."

*This is so confusing.* "So why were you in a village?"

"When I first came here, I stayed in a big white house with walls around it, and guard dogs, and men with guns. After a few weeks my bad grandfather brought me to the village. I ran away, but kept getting lost in the jungle. The natives were nice, and they always found me and brought me back."

She grasped Kitarna's hand. "My real name is Alexandra, but you can call me Lexi. And now that you know my secret, you can't tell anyone."

"I see." Taking a deep breath, Kitarna schooled her expression to cool indifference before turning, but judging by Jack and Roscoe's narrowed eyes, she hadn't succeeded.

~ 11 ~

Roscoe gave Kitarna a black scowl before placing his hand on Lexi's shoulder. "Stay with me, Alex."

"I want to walk with Kit. We're friends."

Avoiding his eyes, Kitarna fell into line behind Brett only to be whipped in the face by a wet branch he let fly. "Hey, I'm right behind you."

Brett's grunt had her raising the stick, but walloping his sorry ass would only lower her to his level. It irked her to see Victoria and Marley up front behind Jack, but maybe some distance would be a good thing, now she'd added kidnapping to his list of misdemeanors.

A small hand slid into hers. "Kit, did you know jaguars like water and are really good swimmers?"

"Hmm. Do you want to know one of my secrets?"

"Yes."

"I used to swim every morning for years and made the National Freestyle Squad. My coach said if I kept training, I had an excellent chance of making the National Championships, and maybe one day the

Olympic Games. But I didn't want to train every day. I wanted to learn about plants and how they affect our planet."

"Why?"

"Because plants and trees are vital to all life on earth. They make the oxygen we breathe. Rainforests are unique combinations of flora and fauna that depend and look after each other. That's why it's called an eco-system. The Amazon and rainforests all over the world are the lungs of Earth. Without them we would die. That's why it's so important we preserve out rainforests and stop chopping down the trees."

"How come you know so much about it?"

"I'm a botanist, I study plants, especially those found in rainforests. So many can be used for sickness and healing. I want to discover more. That's another secret, so you can't tell anyone I'm a botanist."

"My lips are zipped. There's a forest near our house in Florida. Roscoe and I take our dog for a walk through it every afternoon, but Mommy makes Rudolf sleep in the garage at night so he doesn't chase possums."

"So, you normally live with Roscoe?"

"Yes, he's my good grandpa. Stella lives with us too. She's my grandma. We moved there when I was three, because my dad hurt Mommy, but he's in jail now."

Things were starting to make sense. They lived in Florida, so that explained their connection to Jack, but what was with the kidnapping? She yearned to know more from Lexi, in case the little chatterbox was in danger. "How old are you, sweetheart?"

"Eight, but I didn't have a birthday party because I was stolen the day before it."

"In that case, once we're rescued, we'll have a party for you."

"Yay. I hope we see dolphins. Did you know the Amazon River is over four thousand miles long?"

"Yes, but there's lots of other rivers and estuaries running into it." Kitarna pushed a fern aside. "I'm guessing you didn't see any dolphins on your boat cruise?"

"No, Jack sneaked into the village at night time. He piggy-backed me to the river, where Roscoe was waiting on a boat. I couldn't see anything in the dark, and after a few hours I fell asleep."

"Alex, concentrate on where you're walking," called Roscoe. "Use the stick to clear the way, so you don't stand on a snake."

"Yes, Roscoe." Lexi whacked the leaf mulch. "There are anacondas here and a yellow snake called an eye-lash viper."

Kitarna shivered. "It's very poisonous, a guide showed me one a few years ago."

"Wow, you're so lucky. We did a project on rainforests at school, and I got forty-eight out of fifty. Roscoe and Stella helped me a bit. That's how I know so much about the Amazon."

"How come you call your grandparents, Roscoe and Stella?"

"Everyone does, even Mommy. I'm hungry and I miss Stella's cooking. The natives eat snakes and monkeys and birds and bugs, but I wouldn't. I only ate the fish and vegetables and fruit."

"How long were you in the village?"

"I don't know, but I cried every night."

"No more talking," snapped Roscoe, catching up to them.

Kitarna glanced back to the end of the line where Piers had stopped to help Juliette over a trunk. They'd taken charge of the first aid satchel last night while Jack cut palms. Any cuts or scratches had been treated with antiseptic and covered. Ahmed had argued with Brett on the necessity to prevent parasites or infectious bacteria entering their bodies.

Up ahead the rest of the group gathered about Jack. He stepped away from them and strode back. "I hear a waterfall, so if it's safe to stop there, we'll take a break and quench our thirst."

"Okay, do you want me to pick some fruit?"

"Only if you know it to be safe. We could all do with food in our stomachs, but don't leave the group. From now on we go everywhere in pairs."

"Sure." She watched him stride back to the others, and like sheep they fell into a line behind him, Victoria and Marley right on his heels.

Conscripting Lexi, Roscoe and Robert, Kitarna directed them to pick figs, mangoes and a bunch of ripe bananas. Fruit would keep them going, but they'd need something more substantial if they weren't rescued soon.

The steep and narrow waterfall made their descent slow and arduous. As they picked their way over spongy grass and slippery boulders, she welcomed the fine mist, a cool reprieve from the humidity.

The water cascaded into a rock pool at the bottom, surrounded on either side by maidenhair ferns. It reminded her of a mystic place in an enchanted forest, which wasn't far from reality. She gave her camera a workout.

After quenching their thirst, most of the others hoed into the fruit then sat around resting or chatting. Brett and Marley had moved well away and appeared to be having a whispered argument. Seeking solitude, Kitarna stripped down to her bikini. Taking some figs and a mango, she sank into the cool water and swam to the far side of the rock pool.

Finding a submerged ledge, she sat licking mango juice from her fingers.

Jack swam across, his huge shoulders and chest claiming her attention. "Hi."

"Don't tell me you're bored with your devotees already?"

Grinning, he ran his hands up her outer thighs. "You're not putting much effort into protecting me, darlin'. Those two women are clinging like leeches."

"Try dousing them in salt. Leeches hate it." It was hard not to react to his touch.

His lips kicked up. "Kiss me."

"No. Lexi told me you kidnapped her. Why?"

"Damn." He sighed and braced his hands on the ledge either side of her bottom. "Five months ago, the kid's South American grandfather sent two men to Florida to snatch her. They bashed her mother unconscious and left her for dead."

"That's dreadful. What about Lexi's father?"

"He's in jail. Six years ago, his wife, Tess, discovered he belonged to a drug cartel and confronted him. As a result, he isolated her, cutting the phone line and confiscating her keys and credit card. Tess became a virtual prisoner, until one night when her husband got high on drugs. She escaped with their two-year-old and went straight to the FBI. In return for her testimony, she and the child were provided with a safe place to live."

"Not so safe, obviously?"

"No. Tess's husband skipped the country, but was extradited. Tess gave evidence, which is why we think they attacked her. She spent three weeks in a coma then woke to discover her daughter gone. Tess's ex-husband insisted he had nothing to do with it, and the police had no leads."

"How did you get involved?"

"An undercover operative contacted Roscoe and gave him the kid's location. He cautioned there'd be no help as a joint operation existed between the US and Brazilian Governments to shut down the drug cartels in South America."

"I still don't see your connection."

"I worked for Roscoe's brother at the timber mill. And I wasn't just a soldier. I was...a sniper in Australia's Special Air Service Regiment."

"A sniper?" *Oh God, I'm infatuated with a man who gets paid to kill people.*

He looked out over the waterfall. "At first, I refused the job, but Roscoe wouldn't let up. He brought Tess to see me. She begged me to save her baby."

"I guess I would do the same thing if it had been my little girl." Kitarna swished her hands through the water. "Is there any chance the grandfather knew Lexi was on the plane?"

"If he doesn't already, he will soon. I'm pretty sure we've landed in a region under his control."

"You're kidding?" How much worse could this get? A man called *El* Jaguar was hunting Bernie, and Jack had kidnapped the granddaughter of a drug lord who just happened to control this area. They probably knew each other.

She gripped his shoulders. "Do you think the grandfather is responsible for bringing the plane down?"

"Maybe. It's after twelve and we haven't heard one plane or helicopter, which suggests no one knows our location, except those mercenaries."

"But planes have transponders."

"They can be turned off, and as we were flying low, we probably dropped off the radar near Tefè. The search parties are most likely looking in the wrong place."

How long would the authorities search before giving up and breaking the news to the next of kin? Lexi's mother would be devastated, and Kitarna's parents—who had no idea she'd hitched a ride with Bernie—would be hit with a double whammy. Rescuers wouldn't know most of the passengers were alive, and fighting to stay that way.

"Jack, what are we going to do?"

"Survive, darlin', but right now..." He lifted her off the ledge, closing his arms around her, trapping her against his chest, "I need that kiss."

He took possession of her mouth like a Viking returning from months at sea to the only woman he craved. How she wished she could be that woman, and he that Viking. *No, not a Viking. They were probably the very first assassins.*

"There's no time for that nonsense, we need to keep moving," called Roscoe.

Jack eased away, his hands sliding down her hips. "I'm claiming a rain-check tonight, after we make camp."

She looked over his shoulder to the nine people on the other side of the rock pool. Juliette, Piers and Lexi were in the water splashing water at each other. Roscoe, Brett, Robert and Ahmed were on the rocks scowling. Victoria and Marley sat on the pool's edge, positively glowering. "Your two leeches may have something to say about that."

"Bad luck. I'm only prepared to share my hammock with you."

"What about your body?"

"That's yours too, kitten, when we reach Manaus."

She watched him swim back, then climb out, transfixed by the corded, rippling muscles, from his shoulders to his calves. His waist tapered in to narrow hips and a tight butt encased in black briefs. *Hail Tarzan, King of the jungle.*

She swam to the rock where she'd left her clothes. No wonder Victoria and Marley were sending her death stares.

Dripping from head to toe, Lexi stood peering into a fern. "Hello, pretty little frogs."

"Don't touch them." Kitarna surged out of the pool, hobbling over uneven rocks. She pulled Lexi away from the fern. One frog glistened red with black spots, just like a lady beetle. On the fern next to it, sat an iridescent-blue frog with black spots. "Sweetie, come away. They're dart frogs, and very poisonous to touch."

"How can frogs be dangerous?"

"These ones excrete poison that paralyzes unwary predators. It's the dart frog's protection against being eaten. There's also a bright yellow one, called the golden arrow frog. It's supposed to be the deadliest ever discovered, and harbors enough poison to kill ten men."

Lexi sighed. "Next you'll tell me butterflies are dangerous too."

"Some butterflies here in the rainforest *are* poisonous. It's best not to touch any."

The little girl's eyes widened. "I can hardly believe it. What about that butterfly? I can see right through its wings."

Kitarna looked up to where the delicate little creature hovered. "That's a glass-winged butterfly, the Spanish call them *espejitos*, meaning little mirrors. They are not poisonous."

"So which ones are?" Jack asked from behind her.

"The monarch and morpho and pipevine swallowtail. I told you about them on the plane. As caterpillars, they eat poisonous plants, and so are poisonous as adult butterflies. The birds learn not to eat them."

"That's so cool," cried Lexi. "Do you know about monkeys too?"

"Not a lot, but while we're waiting to be rescued, we can attempt to name all the ones we see."

"I know lots about animals in the Amazon because of my project. My favorite is called a kinkajou. It's a cross between a cat and a raccoon, but lives in trees and loves fruit. I'll teach you about rainforest animals and you can teach me about botanist stuff."

"It's a deal."

"And can you take a photo of this butterfly and the frogs? My friends will never believe me otherwise."

She grinned at Lexi. "Of course I can."

"Check out the stick insect." Jack slid his arm around Kitarna's waist and turned her slightly, pointing at the black and yellow insect. "It's nearly as long as my boots."

Heat rushed into her cheeks. Thinking about his boots or that other part of his anatomy was not a good idea. She dug her elbow into his stomach. "I'm sure there are lots of things as long as your boots, and lots of things that are *not*."

He laughed then whispered in her ear. "That offer's still open, anytime you want to check for yourself."

She refused to make eye contact or give him further ammunition to use against her. "I need to get dressed and take some photos for Lexi. We should look out for a *bixa...*" *I must stop using botanical names.* "Lipstick tree. We are going to need lots of seeds to make enough insect repellant for everyone."

"Especially a *big* guy like me." He winked at her. "I'll even allow you to coat me all over."

# ⟿ 12 ⟾

Jack resumed the steep climb downward, staying close to the cascading water to mask their descent and take advantage of the fine cool spray. He'd positioned Piers at the rear of the line with a rifle. Coming forward was Juliette, Ahmed, Marley and Brett. Roscoe had the middle, also armed. He followed the kid, Victoria, Robert and Kit. With luck the terrain would prevent Victoria from overtaking.

Marley had backed off, but Victoria seemed to think her Marilyn Monroe looks and generous assets far outweighed Kit's fine-boned beauty, or the kindness she showered on a traumatized child. He'd never met a woman who snagged his interest so profoundly, or held such sensual magnetism. Her gentle caresses, soothing whispers, and ethereal kisses, given to a fractured man to ward off his nightmares, were a balm to his tortured soul. Yet he'd been too embarrassed to admit it. The horror he lived with nightly would repulse her.

*Best case scenario, I have a couple of days to make*

*a lifetime of memories before I get the hell out of her life, and go buy my shack.* It would be cutting things fine, but he was determined to give Kit something special to remember him by.

Even with the cooling spray, by the time he reached a fast running stream at the waterfall's base, he was drenched in sweat. The oppressive humidity made breathing hard. The others would need a rest.

"We'll stop here for ten minutes." He checked his compass. "The stream is flowing north-east, but should lead us to something larger. Keep your eyes open for snakes and caimans."

"I'm just glad we've reached flat ground." Kit dropped to her knees and began scooping water into her mouth.

He searched their surroundings for a minute before following suit, dunking his head and shoulders into the stream, the cool bite a welcome reprieve.

The kid pushed between them and copied him, then sat back and giggled. "I've always wanted to do that." She turned to Kit. "Can I walk with you? It's boring back there between Roscoe and Robert. They don't know anything about plants or butterflies or what those pretty gold monkeys are."

Kitarna laughed. "They're golden lion tamarins. You can walk with me, if it's okay with your grandpa."

A grunt came from behind Jack, and he looked over his shoulder at Roscoe. "I can keep an eye on the kid if you want."

"Why do you always call me *'the kid'*? My name is Lexi...I mean Alex."

Jack climbed to his feet, avoiding her questioning eyes. How did you tell a child using their name brought them emotionally close? Gave them an invitation to seek you out—make you care, or divulge secrets like she had with Kit.

It might not be a war-torn country, but the parallels were mindboggling. It wasn't the kid's fault she'd been kidnapped, or the plane brought down, but she remained the granddaughter of a drug lord, and probably why the mercenaries were after them. One little girl could mean death to so many. Just like before.

Walking away hadn't been an option. Not once Tessa showed him photos of her little girl and begged his help. He'd done the right thing, this time.

Kit touched his arm. "Are you all right, Jack?"

"I'm fine. We should keep moving."

He shouldered his rifle and set off, leading them alongside the stream. An hour later, he halted, holding up his hand as the pungent whiff of cigar smoke reached him. He waved everyone down then crept to the next bend, where the stream entered a large waterway. It had to be the Putumayo River.

"Shit."

No more than ninety feet ahead, two armed mercenaries squatted on the boarded platform of a wharf. They had a perfect view of the river in both directions and an estuary leading off to Jack's right.

He'd been here two days ago. The realization was a kick in the guts. He knew this place. That wharf edged a dirt track leading to a native village before winding up into the thick terrain. He hadn't realised an airstrip lay on the top of the mountain. It certainly wasn't marked on any map.

Without a boat and the cover of darkness, they

were trapped in an area of intricate waterways and isolated islands. They needed to conceal their tracks or the mercenaries would find them.

What a clusterfuck.

Retracing his steps, Jack told the group what he'd seen. "We have to cross the stream and work our way through jungle to a small river that runs into the Putumayo."

"How do you know where we are?" said Robert.

"I recognized the wharf from a fishing trip several days ago."

"*This* is the place?" The alarm in Kit's voice drew several frowns.

He caught her gaze. "Yes, this is where I came fishing."

"Oh, right."

"Roscoe!" The kid launched herself at her grandfather.

"Shush, Alex, it's okay. We know the way home from here."

Jack refilled his hydration pack. "Let's go. Try not to make any noise." He led the way, this time over rocks and sometimes through knee-deep water, in an attempt to mask their trail, constantly listening and watching for any sign of natives or mercenaries. Ironically, the natives were probably better at invisibility than him, which didn't bode well.

He stopped where there were plenty of rocks and overhanging branches. Looking up, he studied the line of a tree closest to the bank. The thick, heavy, wide branches intertwined with the other trees creating a tightly meshed forest bridge. They'd be able to work their way across the stream without leaving footprints. He scoped the branches for snakes. "Okay, folks, we're going up."

It took a bit of maneuvering, but eventually he got everyone up into the trees, and across the stream via the network of wide branches.

Hunger clawed at his belly, when an hour later they reached another shallow stream. Darkness would fall in three hours and they needed to find food and shelter, or he'd have a mutiny on his hands.

"I can see fish." The kid hopped from foot to foot. "I wish we could catch them. I'm starving."

"We can." Kit pulled at a vine. "This is an *ayori-toto*. If we beat the vine until it separates into fibers, the sap will daze fish, so they float to the surface."

"Let's do it." Jack broke off a small branch then bashed the vine. Once he had it flattened and seeping, he jumped across rocks to a deeper hole and swept the vine through the water.

The others crowded to the edge of the stream, watching with anticipation.

"I see one." The kid squealed. "Now we won't be hungry anymore."

Another two floated to the surface and Piers waded out to retrieve them. Within minutes they had eight good-sized fish and an eel.

"Great idea, kitten." Jack dropped his pack and pulled out firelighters. Squatting, he began scaling and gutting the fish, while Roscoe took control of starting a small fire and cutting banana leaves to wrap the fish and eel in.

Kit dropped a handful of red pods similar to chili peppers beside Jack.

"What are these?"

She grinned. "*Zingiberales*. It's the Amazon's version of ginger. It will spice up your fish. And some Brazilian nuts. We can cook them too."

He studied her vibrant eyes, alive with eagerness. "How come you know so much about rainforest plants?"

She lowered her head, shielding her eyes from him. "I'm interested in things like that. Do you need help?"

"No, I'm good."

"I'll see if Lexi wants a toilet break." She tilted her chin toward Victoria. The woman hadn't taken her eyes off him all day. "I think a leech is about to latch on to you."

Damn it, not again. "In that case don't take too long and for God's sake, Kit, be careful."

She strolled over to the kid who quickly slid her hand into Kit's. Jack kept a close eye on them as they pushed their way into a clump of giant ferns. As soon as he had the fish wrapped and packed under a rock bed in the fire, he picked up the rifle and went in search of Kit and the kid. He estimated they'd been gone long enough.

He found them straddling a fallen limb under a tree. The kid busy braiding Kit's hair and chattering.

"Why is the tree all by itself?"

Kit aimed her camera upward. "Because it's a swollen thorn acacia. Ants make their homes in those enormous thorns, and in return for their lodgings, the ants eat through leaves and strangling tendrils, or plants that get too close."

"You know so much about plants."

"She certainly does." Jack wandered over and knocked off some thorns. "These will come in handy if we need to catch fish in the river. Attached to my para cord, the thorns will make great hooks."

"Now *that* is good thinking." Kit's flirty grin fired a direct hit to his groin.

"When I grow up I'm going to be a botanist and know everything about plants." The kid turned a brilliant smile on him. "I can live in a rainforest."

He nodded. "My brothers and I spent our childhood playing in a rainforest back in Australia. It wasn't as dangerous as the Amazon." He looked about. "We should return to the others. The fish will be cooked by now." Slinging the rifle over his chest, he followed them back to the fire to discover three newcomers had arrived.

The female flight attendant, a young Spanish guy and a plump, white-haired lady sat on the ground stuffing their faces with the figs.

Roscoe ambled over to Jack. "I found them stumbling through the forest like a herd of drunk elephants. That the mercenaries didn't hear them is a wonder to me. It's been a complete waste of time hiding our tracks."

"Nothing we can do about it now, Roscoe. Once we've made camp, we'll build a raft and cross the river at first light."

Roscoe scowled. "Why don't we let the current take us down river tonight?"

"The mercenaries will be patrolling the rivers. It's risky enough making a short crossing this close to the crash site. What do you know about these three?"

"The young guy is a college student called Gabe. The older lady is Doris, and upset that she can't find her friend, and the flight attendant is Solana. They left the road and took a well-worn path through the forest, which led to a wooden bridge that crossed to this side of the stream."

Jack ambled over to the newcomers to hear Kit interrogating them.

"Doris, where did you last see your friend?"

"I ran into the jungle when you yelled that trucks were coming. Kerrie and I became separated. Later, I heard a woman screaming, but couldn't find her. When I reached the road again, I met Gabe and Solana."

Kit turned to the other two newcomers. "Are you sure you didn't come across any other passengers, alive or dead?"

The young guy looked down. "We did find the elderly man whose wife died on the plane. He'd been shot and lost a lot of blood. Before he died, he said the soldiers were searching for a young woman with dark hair and unusual eyes."

"Oh no." Kit turned straight into Jack's arms, her lips trembling. "Why is this happening?"

He held her close, stroking along her spine as he went through his memory. There had been a young woman on the plane with unusual eyes. And he'd seen her later, climbing over the tree that had squashed the middle of the plane. She'd looked directly at Kit before shaking her head.

Could *she* be the elusive Bernie? If so, what was her connection to Kit, and why would the mercenaries want her? Had the plane been brought down because of that woman and not because of the kid? He needed answers, but not with all these witnesses. It would have to wait until later. "Let's eat. It's almost five and we have a long way to go."

After satisfying their hunger, they trekked on to the river, its width wider than he'd anticipated. The humidity became suffocating and by the look of the gathering purple clouds, they would likely dump their contents any minute. He set the others to collect palm fronds and clear an area away from the river then went to inspect their surrounds.

Standing on the muddy bank, he grimaced at the steep drop to the water. On the opposite bank, as still as dead wood, lay a couple of caimans. He would need to find a better place to launch the raft.

"I'm not interested." Kit sounded agitated. She stood maybe twelve feet to Jack's left behind a thorny thicket of strangler vines.

Jack frowned. *Who the hell is she talking too?*

"Come on, Kitty. Marley and I are finished. I'm a free man and I'm coming into a lot of money in the next few days. Your boyfriend is nothing but brawn. Robert saw him slit a soldier's throat and stab another in the heart. Doesn't that sicken you? Wouldn't you rather live the high life with me, Kitty?"

Jack surged forward, the thorns scratching his arms.

"Don't keep calling me that. I'm not interested in you or your money, and Jack is more man than you will ever be. Leave me alone."

"You stupid bitch. I'm just as good as him."

Brett grabbed her, but before Jack could untangle his body from the last of the clinging vines, Kit brought her knee up and got the dumbass in the gonads. Brett gasped then swung his fist, hitting Kit in the shoulder and knocking her backward. She gasped. A second later came an almighty splash.

~ 13 ~

"You fucking idiot." Jack shoved Brett aside and leaned over the bank. It dropped away steeply, but there were exposed roots above Kit, who wallowed about, trying to get a footing. He glanced across to the opposite bank. The two caimans were up on their stumpy legs and on the move. "Grab the roots, kitten."

"Jack!" She made a lunge and missed, tried again and missed.

"Come on, darlin', grab on and climb."

"I'm trying. They're slippery."

"Come on, girl, push off the ground," called Roscoe, running to Jack's side.

"Alligators!" screamed Marley. "Quick, Jack, get her out."

He wrenched a vine free and dropped it to Kit. "Grab this and I'll pull you up."

She looked over her shoulder. "Where are they?"

"Don't look, kitten, just climb."

"Why don't you shoot them?" called Solana.

"Shots will give our position away," muttered

Roscoe. "And so will Marley's bloody screeching. Somebody keep her quiet."

Jack kept calling down, but Kit couldn't maintain her grip and her feet kept slipping from under her. Frustration ate at him. The caimans were half way across the river. It didn't help that she kept looking behind, her gaze riveted on the two dark shapes moving steadily through the water.

"I can't get up."

"Yes, you can."

Kit gripped with both hands, scrabbling with her sodden boots, making it up four or five feet. The vine snapped, and she plummeted into the water along with his heart.

She came up sputtering. "Jack, tell Bernie this isn't her fault, and you aren't to blame either. I'd rather die this way than be captured by those horrible men."

"You're not dying today, kitten." His heart thumped erratically, but years of training kicked in as he swung the rifle high. As steady as a rock, he scoped the nearest caiman, pumping five bullets into its head before the mongrel sank beneath a ring of bloodied water. He sighted the scope for the second caiman and passed over a lone native, standing in a canoe near the opposite bank. *That's all we need.*

"My name is Kitarna. Kitarna Ashford."

*Now she tells me.* He scoped the other caiman. Too close.

The kid kept screaming for him to do something. He'd grown up in an area inhabited by crocodiles bigger than this caiman. He'd even helped his father and brothers catch and move several, but he didn't have a cage. He threw the rifle to Roscoe.

"No!" Kit's petrified scream fueled his resolve. She hadn't done a bad thing, whereas his black and battered soul taunted him.

Hoping he'd judged correctly, he took a running leap, executed a somersault-twist and landed right on target. The impact knocked the air from his lungs, but he managed to lock his arms around the beast and keep his face glued to its neck, away from those deadly jaws.

The caiman took him into a death roll, its strength far greater than his. A week ago, he might have accepted his fate, but not now. Lungs screaming for oxygen, Jack reached for his knife, driving it up through the animal's jaw, into its brain.

Death came instantly.

Letting the beast sink to the murky depths, Jack kicked and clawed his way to the surface, sucking in air, his strength spent.

Another caiman latched onto his pack and yanked. Jack didn't have enough energy to fight, and could only hope Roscoe shot the bastard before it took off his head.

The attack or shot didn't come; instead he continued to be dragged toward the bank. Gathering his mettle, he looked behind. *Jesus!*

It wasn't a caiman dragging him off to wedge in a hole beneath the rotten tree roots, but Kit, swimming like a champion, hauling him to the bank. He rolled and found the riverbed under his feet, but before he could open his mouth, she slogged him in the arm.

"Are you crazy? Who in their right mind wrestles a bloody caiman? What were you thinking?" She hit him again.

"Darlin', I'm glad to see you too." He pulled her into his arms and held her.

"For Christ sake, get out of the damn river before any more caiman think to snack," yelled Roscoe. "I've secured these vines around a tree, now climb the wretched things. We need to get out of here before the whole damn mercenary army descend on us."

Releasing a ragged breath, amazed he still lived, Jack picked Kit up, tugging her legs around his waist. He caught hold of the plaited vines and climbed, one hand after the other. His tendons screamed, but he'd been given another lifeline, and he wasn't going to waste it. Looking up he noted all but Brett leaning over the bank calling encouragement.

Piers and Roscoe pulled Jack the last few feet. He collapsed on the ground, still holding Kitarna in his arms. "Thanks."

"I can't see any bites." Piers ran his gaze over them. "How the hell did you both end up in the river?"

"Brett doesn't take rejection well." Jack clambered to his feet then helped Kitarna up. "I'm going to wring the bastard's scrawny neck."

Kitarna clutched his arm. "Leave it, sweetheart. He's not worth it."

*Sweetheart. She called me sweetheart.*

"You're so brave, Jack." The kid hopped from foot to foot. "That's the scariest thing I've ever seen."

"Me too, Lexi." There he'd done it, for better or worse. The kid had worked her way under his skin, just like Kitarna. "After that excitement, we better get to and build a shelter." He took the rifle from Roscoe, scoping the opposite riverbank. "We need to set up a watch."

Roscoe moved closer. "You saw the native?"

"Yeah, but he's vanished now." Jack checked for eavesdroppers, but the group had moved well out of hearing, most heading back to camp. Kitarna had walked over to the thicket to retrieve her rucksack and now had an arm around Lexi waiting for him and Roscoe to join them. "Whether the native is curious, or a threat remains to be seen."

Jack stripped off his shirt and got straight to work, cutting bamboo, balsa saplings and palm fronds. He tore the frond stems into thin fibers then handed them around. "Start plaiting, we need a dais and roof to keep out crawlies and rain."

He found four saplings close enough to build a platform between, and far enough from the river not to be seen. He used the machete to hack notches out of the saplings then showed Piers and Ahmed how to anchor shortened balsa lengths for the platform's frame. The bamboo he had them tie across the balsa as flooring.

Roscoe must have sensed Jack's simmering fury, as he sent Brett with Robert to keep watch over the river, while he and Gabe built an A-frame roof.

Kitarna, Juliette, Lyn and Lexi pitched the tent then began weaving palm fronds between the bamboo walls. The dais also had a bed of palm leaves. It would sleep no more than seven, but they had the tent and three hammocks with waterproof flysheets.

Glancing around, Jack found Victoria, Marley and Solana sitting side-by-side on a log, watching him. He'd much rather they lifted a finger to help build the shelter. The only reason he'd taken off his shirt was after the dunking it didn't smell of sweat, and as he intended sharing his hammock with Kitarna, he'd like to keep it that way.

He helped Roscoe hang the hammocks and attach para cord above to throw waterproof sheets over. They hooked their packs underneath to keep them dry.

Although Kitarna hadn't said a word since telling him to ignore Brett, she hadn't stopped working. He wandered over to where she rubbed the stinky gel round the base of the platform's four supporting trees.

"How you doing, kitten?"

"Still a bit shaky. Thank you for coming to my rescue. At this rate, I'll be in your debt for years." She gave him a half-hearted smile. "Our shelter looks great."

"Kitarna, you're with me in my hammock. And, darlin', you don't owe me anything. I jumped on that motherfucker because I couldn't bear the alternative." A raindrop hit his nose. "It's about to bucket down. Hang your rucksack and boots at the end of the hammock and jump in. The mosquito net will keep the little blighters away. I'll join you once we've built the raft."

"Won't the mercenaries search for us after hearing the rifle shots?"

"We're a long way from the wharf and my shots would be distorted by the jungle, but I did notice a native across the river."

"He might not have anything to do with the mercenaries."

"I hope you're right, kitten. Fortunately, we're in for a downpour. That will cover our tracks and keep the mercenaries at bay."

She grimaced before trudging to his hammock, her shoulders bowed, and her head bent. She was barely keeping it together and had to be in shock. He silently cursed. After her close encounter with the caimans, coming to his rescue took a lot of guts.

Jack cut sufficient balsa and bamboo for a raft big enough to carry ten people. They would have to make two trips. Piers, Roscoe, Ahmed and Gabe joined him, eager to help.

With the raindrops increasing, Roscoe sent Lexi to bed. Marley and Solana climbed up into the A-Frame, and Victoria disappeared into her hammock. Juliette took Doris inside the tent with her.

"We need to lay the five thickest lengths of balsa together and leash ten thinner ones on top, but crosswise, then layer that with bamboo." Jack handed Ahmed the roll of para cord. "Use this for the base, while I make up more plaited twine for the rest."

"How do we steer it?" called Gabe.

"I'll cut more bamboo and lash it together for paddles and a rudder. We'll use the fly-sheet as a sail. We can't stay on the river, so once we cross, it's back to trekking."

They worked as a team, close to the river on a lower bank, until the heavens opened. Jack sent Roscoe and Piers to their beds, but Ahmed and Gabe stayed until the paddles and rudder were finished. They helped secure the raft in case the river rose.

They walked back into camp as Robert and Brett stumbled from the opposite direction. By their giggling and uncoordinated movements, they had to be high.

Striding over, Jack blocked their path. The sickly

sweet smell of marihuana hit him. "You miserable bastards. You were asked to watch the river. Instead you put all our lives at risk to smoke fucking joints. I should have left you both where I found you." Clenching his fists, he turned and marched away before he knocked some sense into them. Venting his anger would only inflame matters.

"I will take the first watch," offered Gabe. "A few hours are the least I can do."

"I'll come with you," offered Ahmed. "Roscoe told us what happened at the river. "You need a good night's sleep. Piers wants to take a shift too, I will wake him and Roscoe at twelve o'clock. Brett and Robert can take the last shift."

"Thanks. Take my rifle, but I want it back. We need to be on the river by five, so let Robert and Brett know to wake us."

Ahmed nodded. "I shall pass the message on. And...I wanted to say, you are very brave, as is your wife."

"She isn't my wife. But you're right, she is brave."

For a moment Ahmed looked horrified. He shrugged. "You should make her your wife."

Jack turned away, heading back to the shelter, his thoughts grim. *She wouldn't have me if she knew what I've done, and I'd never ask.*

$$\sim 14 \sim$$

Sleep refused to come. The second she closed her eyes, flashes of Jack and the caiman spinning over and over, rose to torment her. Her anguish and inability to act as the large reptile thrashed about, snapping its massive jaws...and the blood.

Jack could have died.

As for Brett—the bastard had no right to accost her or any woman like that. Marley would be better off without the sleaze.

Thunder rumbled over the steady fall of rain and bird chatter. Where was Bernie? *Please God, let there be someone like Jack to protect her.*

Kitarna scrubbed at her eyes. It wasn't as if they'd seen any tracks to show other passengers had come this way. Gasping, she sat upright. "Oh God, I haven't been looking. I'm such a twit."

As children, Bernie had pretended to be the World's best archeologist and Kitarna her loyal assistant. How many times had they discovered ruined temples in the grounds of their parents' estate? Indiana Jones had nothing on Bernadette Ashford. It used to amuse the gardeners no end. And Bernie always left markers for Kitarna to follow. But would she remember something they did so many years ago?

*First thing in the morning, I'm leaving a marker only Bernie will recognize.*

She lay down again, curling onto her side, her thoughts drifting to Jack. She'd eavesdropped on his deep drawl as he guided the men in building the raft. He had the survival stuff covered. His years in Special Forces would account for that, but why did he have to be a sniper? If he hadn't been a sniper, she'd be dead.

No matter that he'd saved her life twice now, he would never be good enough for her parents. They'd be extremely grateful of course, but an ex-soldier-sniper would not be welcomed warmly into their social circle, composed of diplomats, philanthropists, tycoons and royalty.

Although divorced fourteen years, her parents and their subsequent spouses deemed Kitarna's passion for plants a whim, to be indulged until she accepted her rightful position as wife to the right kind of man.

Only Bernie supported her dream to study rainforest plants and have a large garden and hothouse to fill with her subjects. The only thing that could top it would be to meet a man who absolutely adored her and wasn't afraid to show it. A man who supported her work, and cherished family time above all else, unlike her parents, who *still* spent their lives attending or hosting dinner parties and social or political events.

No way would she have a nanny supervise all

aspects of her childrens' lives. As for boarding school—not happening. If it hadn't been for Bernie and their adventures, Kitarna would have led a boring, unimaginative life.

Her brain switched gear again. *What is Jack's true interest in me?*

He wasn't like Jeff; dating her in the hope her mother and stepfather would assist his diplomatic aspirations, or any of the men her parents had introduced. Jack wouldn't give a toss that she spoke three languages, or had been groomed to be the perfect hostess. He was a rough diamond with a wicked sense of humor and so brave.

Lord, the strength it must have taken to hold onto that caiman, and then climb up the vine carrying her weight as well as his saturated pack. Earlier she'd heard Jack censure Brett and Robert, the ice in his tone so foreign to the warmth he used with her.

Under the waterproof flysheet complete darkness reigned. The rain had gradually grown to a heavy downpour, thunder crackled and boomed constantly, but had no effect on the trilling crickets or croaking frogs or birds chirping and screeching.

Something knocked the hammock, rocking her slightly. She was too high for wild boar or *capybara*, but what of deer or jaguars? A rustle came beside her then a muttered oath. "Who's there?"

"It's me, kitten. I need to get out of these wet pants. It's that or soak you through."

Oh boy, he had a surprise coming. This may be the most stupid thing she'd ever done in her life, but being hunted by mercenaries, almost dying, and wondering if you would even survive the jungle had a way of changing a person's priorities.

He parted the mosquito net and rolled in beside her, his weight pitching her across his wet body. Instantly his arms came around her. "Jesus, kitten, where are your clothes?"

"Drying, and who knows what tomorrow will bring. We should make the most of every opportunity."

"I'd like nothing better, darlin', but we're in a bloody hammock."

"Don't you know a way?" Wishing she could see his face, she ran her fingertip over the taut muscles of his bicep, hoping her touch had the same effect as his caressing hands on her backside.

"S'truth, I've already got a hard-on from being this close to you, and it's going to keep me awake all night. Believe me, I would like nothing better than to bury myself inside you, but we're both exhausted and you're vulnerable. When I make love to you, it's not going to be in a hammock."

She groaned. "I finally meet a man I'm itching to have sex with and he isn't interested. Do you have any idea how much nerve it took to take off all my clothes?"

"I didn't say I wasn't interested, Kitarna. Just that this is not how I planned your seduction. I want that bed we spoke of and I want to be able to see you."

"I guess so, but if either of us die before the event, I will never forgive you."

His deep chuckle vibrated against her cheek. "Tell me about Bernie. From what you said at the river, I assume *she* is the young woman I saw you with at the airstrip, and the woman the mercenaries are looking for?"

Kitarna tried not to stiffen, but he'd taken her by surprise. All her insecurities came flooding back. Silence was a friend who never betrayed, but Jack had his own troubles with Lexi's drug lord-grandfather. And she needed to trust someone. "Bernie is my sister. She's an archeologist and her old professor invited her here to work on a newly discovered dig. We were supposed to meet our guides and head into the jungle yesterday, but our father rang from Florida, warning us to get out because someone called *El* Jaguar was after Bernie."

"You're from Florida?" He sounded as astounded as she'd been at the tree. "You don't have an American accent?"

"I was born in America, but my parents separated after my eleventh birthday. My mother is English. She took us to her parents in England. Sadly, my grandparents couldn't cope with two boisterous girls, so we were dispatched to boarding school. Our mother remarried and moved to France. Charles is an attaché at the Embassy in Paris. So our holidays were divided between the US and France, or wherever our assigned parent and their spouse happened to be."

"Poor little rich girls."

Kitarna pushed away. "That's unfair. Money didn't stop us being lonelier than most children. Our parents were rarely home, so they were never there to put me to bed, or wipe my nose, or teach me to ride a bike." A sob caught in her throat. "Bernie is four years older than me, and she did all those things. Her fantastic bedtime stories and the adventures she took me on, is still taking me on, are what I suspect parents are supposed to do, and which I will make damn sure I do with my children."

"Shush, I didn't mean to upset you." He drew her against his warmth. "Tell me about your latest adventure. Why would this Jaguar be after your sister?"

"We don't know. Dad's words were hard to make out because of the static. We tried to ring him back, but couldn't. The receptionist said the lines had gone down."

"Or, someone had them disconnected. Why isn't *El Jaguar* after you too?"

"He probably doesn't even know I'm here. Our parents didn't even know. Bernie received permission to bring me along two days ago. Her professor agreed to let me indulge my botanical studies, but stipulated I wasn't to enter the dig site."

"Botanical studies?"

*I won't have any secrets at this rate.* "I have degrees in environmental science and botany. My chosen field is the rainforests of the world, and how they can help us."

"So not a butterfly enthusiast?"

"I like butterflies." She ran her fingers down his chest to his hip, smiling when a shiver rippled under his skin. "And I like big strong men who perform acrobatic twists to wrestle a caimam for me."

"That's a one off, I assure you."

She yearned to explore further, especially as he had her firmly planted against his side, stroking her spine and bottom in sensual, circular swirls. It seemed only fair, and by the tension riding his body, he would welcome her touch.

She pressed a light kiss to his shoulder. "There's something else you should know about me." She tiptoed her fingers across his belly.

"Wha...What's that."

"I have an inquisitive nature and thirst for knowledge." She swept her hand downward, bumping into a substantial obstacle.

They both jumped sending the hammock swinging wildly. She released her breath, aware he held his, waiting to see what she'd do, which wasn't the least helpful. Fine, she'd wing it. Closing her fingers around the thick column, she slid upward to the rounded head. Having never touched a man's appendage, it came as a delightful revelation to touch velvet-encased steel. She *wasn't* surprised to find him well-endowed.

"You've got my attention, kitten. What are you going to do with it?"

"Let me see." She reversed her stroke, thrilled when he groaned. She knew the theory behind a hand job. It was the practical she lacked expertise in. By his muted sighs and groans as she experimented, it wouldn't take long to master.

He wrapped his hand around hers, tightening her grip, slowing her pace. "So good."

He slid his hand between her thighs, pushing a finger inside her, to thrust and stroke, distracting her. She tried pushing his hand away. He wouldn't budge.

"Jack, I can't concentrate when you're doing that."

He chuckled. "Let me do this, then I'll show you how I like it."

"Aren't we going all the way?"

"Not tonight, darlin'." He pushed her legs wider and proceeded to give her an explosive orgasm. Thankfully the thunder drowned out her moans of ecstasy. And once she'd recovered, Jack let her have her way with him.

~ 15 ~

Kitarna woke alone, and to the most colorful language she'd ever heard. Scrambling into her bikini and tank top, she reached through the mosquito netting and pulled down her damp cargo pants and shirt. Were mercenaries coming?

It wasn't just Jack letting off steam. Roscoe and several other men were hot under the collar. Socks on and wet boots laced, she slid out of the hammock and ducked under the flysheet.

All the men, except Brett and Robert where standing in the steady rain, soaked to the skin, fury vibrating from each of them as they looked toward the river. Across the small clearing, Robert sat on the edge of the shelter, his head bowed. Behind him, she could see Solana rubbing sleep from her eyes.

"What's happened?" Kitarna darted across the ground, jumping left and right to avoid landing in mud puddles.

Jack turned and just for a second his eyes softened

before he grimaced. "Brett and Marley stole the raft, my pack, the machete and a rifle."

"You're joking?"

"No, I'm not. The raft is beached on the opposite side of the river and without the machete we can't build another one, nor can we go back. Our way forward isn't filling me with joy."

She didn't like the sound of that. "What are you planning, Jack?"

He looked up. "We pull down strangler vines and weave them together. I'll swim across the river, tie it to the raft, and you all pull it back while I steer."

"That's madness."

"That's what we've been telling him," said Victoria. She sat on a log under giant palms, next to Juliette and Lexi. "We need Jack to protect us, so someone else has to go."

"You could swim across, Kit," cried Lexi.

"No, I can't."

Jack shook his head. "I'll do it. Caimans are territorial, so now those two are dead, hopefully there shouldn't be any others close by."

"But Kit's a champion swimmer," called Lexi.

"What does she mean, you're a champion?" asked Solana.

"Kit made the National swimming team," boasted Lexi. "And, they wanted her to try for the Olympics, but she likes plants too much."

"That's perfect. You could do it no problem," cried Victoria.

"No." Jack began unlacing his boots.

"Come on, Kit. It can't be more than five hundred feet." Victoria's insistent cajoling aggravated Kitarna.

"Leave her be," called Jack. "I'll get the raft."

"We should put it to the vote," snapped Robert. "Who thinks Kit should go?"

Jack flew at Robert, slamming him against a tree. "Kitarna has supplied us with food, helped build the shelter and shared her clothes and repellant. What have you done?"

"I've been on watch with Brett."

"Bullshit. You were as high as a kite. I suggest *you* make the swim and stop harassing Kitarna. She's done more for the group's wellbeing than anyone."

Lexi's eyes filled with tears. "I'm sorry. I just want to go home to my mommy, and I don't want my bad grandfather to kill Roscoe and Jack."

"Who is your grandfather?" asked Juliette.

"*El* Jaguar."

Solana gasped. "*He's* your grandfather?"

Stunned, Kitarna turned to Jack.

He held his hands wide. "I didn't know he went by that name."

They were running from the same person. Heart thumping hard, she glanced at Solana. "You've heard of *El* Jaguar?"

"Most people in this region have, but if this is *El* Jaguar's grandchild, you must give him up immediately, or you will die terrible deaths."

"Who is *El* Jaguar?" Victoria demanded.

"A notorious drug lord who controls this region by intimidation and cruelty," said Roscoe. "Five months ago, he sent two men to our home in the US. They bashed my daughter unconscious and kidnapped Alex. Jack and I are taking the child home."

"Are you crazy?" cried Solana. "*El* Jaguar will skin you alive."

"Not if he can't find us." Lexi hung her head.

Hands fisted, Kitarna battled her rising terror. She wanted to run and hide. Why should she be singled out to swim across a river teeming with deadly creatures? Her mind raced, fear adding to her desperate need to survive.

If they stayed here, or turned back, *El* Jaguar would capture them. He must have brought the plane down with the intention of ransoming Bernie. By now he probably knew both sisters where on board. Not to mention his granddaughter. Her gaze settled on Lexi's tear-filled eyes.

"I'll swim across with the rope." Clenching her trembling hands, she turned to Jack. "Please keep your eyes on the banks and shoot anything that moves."

"You don't have to do this, kitten."

"It seems I do, but knowing you're watching over me will help."

"You're the bravest woman I know." He hugged her briefly then began ripping down a mountain of sturdy strangler-vines from the surrounding trees.

She helped him roll it in coils, watching as he used the knife to slice the ends into thin fibers. He showed her how to plait them together.

The rain continued to fall as they worked under the watchful eyes of a family of gray and yellow squirrel monkeys, who were much more curious than frightened. The rest of the group packed up camp or picked figs for breakfast.

"Now for your tow rope." Jack grabbed the para

cord he'd used to support the waterproof flysheet. "I'm going to make you a belt to loop through the vine. Once you get to the other side, secure it to the raft so we can pull it back."

"Don't forget to bring my gear."

Kitarna stripped down to her bikini then squashed her clothes into the rucksack. She braided her hair and tied her boots to the rucksack's shoulder straps. Almost seven o'clock, the moment had come. Her heart pounded, and puking was a real possibility as she broke out in a clammy sweat.

"Here, you need this." Jack held out an empty hand.

"What is it?" She placed her hand in his, squealing when he pulled her into his arms. He kissed her soundly.

"I'll be with you every step of the way, darlin'."

For several minutes, she squinted at the opposite bank through the rain, but saw no sign of caimans. Taking a deep breath, she closed her eyes and visualized the edge of her English grandfather's reedy, fish-filled ornamental lake.

She dived in, kicked hard and surfaced, automatically going into her stroke, rolling her head—breathe, two strokes, breathe. The current wasn't as strong as she'd expected, but the cord around her waist became an irritating reminder of her perilous situation. *I'm in Grandma and Grandpa Carlisle's lake. Stroke, stroke, breathe.*

Something smooth slithered past her leg. "Argh." Treading water, she searched the surface, her heart racing. *Must have been a fish.* She looked back to the bank, so far away, and the group of people watching.

The current had pulled her slightly left of where she wanted to be. She sank a little, taking in a mouthful of water. Choking and spluttering, she searched the banks, half expecting to see a caiman raise its head at the ungodly noise.

*Got to keep going.* Facing forward again, she caught a flicker of movement—a native, standing in a canoe, under overhanging vines, a long spear in his hand. *This is just not my week.*

Maybe she had time to get on the raft and be pulled to safety before he harpooned her. Desperation gave her strength. Changing direction slightly, she resumed swimming. *Stroke, stroke, breathe.*

Reaching the opposite bank without being eaten, bitten or speared re-energized her aching muscles, propelling her through the sucking mud to the raft. The native hadn't moved, yet had become completely hidden from her position. Maybe curiosity kept him here and he had no intention of betraying them.

Quickly, she secured the lasso to the raft. The others pulled, she pushed, until it came free of the mud with a loud glug, and shot out into the river. A quick glance to her left reassured her the native had made no move to attack. Maybe he'd never seen a pale-skinned woman swimming in caiman infested waters. *Maybe he thinks I'm a figment of his imagination.*

Climbing the sloping bank, she expelled a shaky breath and for a minute watched Jack and Roscoe hauling the rope. The others were gathering their belongings, ready for their much easier passage across.

Along to her left were several *bixa Orellana* trees, laden with spiny red fruit. She might as well gather the seeds to make up repellant. While she waited, she could crush the seeds. Working quickly, she collected a horde of fruit, piling it on the ground under a canopy of thick branches.

A lone emperor tamarin lounged on a branch above, sheltered by the canopy as he groomed his long white mustache. His big brown eyes observing his odd visitor with a bored casualness.

Squatting under a large fern, Kitarna used a sharp, flat rock to split the fruit open then scraped out the seeds. Her mind strayed to Jack and his deliberate, slow seduction last night, his long, drugging kisses, and his magical fingers.

*Now wasn't the time to think about that.* He had to be weakening though. She would have her way with him tonight for sure. This morning he'd kissed her in front of everyone, for the second time. That reminded her of the spite she'd glimpsed in Victoria's eyes. The blonde's beauty and curves probably had men falling at her feet, but she fancied Jack, even though he'd made his preference clear. So maybe like Kitarna, Victoria couldn't fathom his interest.

She scraped the crushed seeds into a pile then stretched and checked on the others. They were on the raft and making their way over.

A moan had her whipping around, Kitarna checked on the native. He'd either gone or remained hidden under the vines. "Who's there?"

"Help me."

The weak plea had her scrambling to her feet. She glanced over her shoulder, through the rain. The others were intent on paddling and avoiding the billowing flysheet. No one looked her way.

Clutching the rock in her fingers, she crept forward, pushing aside plants, careful not to put her bare feet on something sharp. An infected cut was the very last thing she needed, besides being eaten by a caiman or speared by a native, or caught by the mercenaries.

A rustle slightly ahead to her right.

She jumped as a fat lizard shot across in front of her, taking a year off her life. Her gaze fell on the machete leaning against a tree, right beside a body. "Marley!"

Running forward, Kitarna dropped to her knees. Marley lay shaking and foaming at the mouth, the stench of vomit and excrement surrounded her.

"Did you eat something or get bitten?" Kitarna searched for any sign of a bite.

"No." Marley's eyes rolled, seemingly unable to focus. "Where's Brett."

"He's gone." A shudder racked her thin body. "Gave me laxatives to get the capsules."

*Capsules?* "Are you saying you were carrying drugs inside you?"

"Eighty capsules. Cocaine. One must have broken."

*Oh God, they're drug mules.* "I'll get help."

"Terrible chest pain, keep passing out."

"The doctors will be here in a minute." Kitarna rolled Marley into the recovery position than ran, leaping over sticks and tussocks, shoving ferns aside. She raced down the bank and into the water, waving her arms over her head. "Hurry! Marley needs a doctor urgently."

They heard her and the four men paddling increased their speed. Not knowing what else to do, she ran back to Marley, who had lapsed into unconsciousness.

Kitarna called her name, trying to wake her, as well as give the others their location.

Several minutes later, Jack, Piers and Juliette ran into the clearing.

"What happened?" Piers went down on his haunches, Juliette followed.

"She had cocaine capsules inside her, and thinks one broke. Brett gave her a laxative and he took the capsules and ran off." Kitarna burst into tears.

"Shush." Jack put his arms around her. "If Marley is a body-packer and the cocaine got into her blood stream, there's nothing we can do for her."

"Don't say that." She leaned against him, sobbing as she watched Juliette and Piers examine Marley.

"Pulse is feeble and erratic," murmured Juliette.

"She said her chest hurt," cried Kitarna.

Piers shook his head. "I'm not surprised. The cocaine would have spread through her body, leading to vasoconstriction, increasing her blood pressure. Heart attacks are common in these situations. There's nothing we can do for her."

"We have to do something." Kitarna clutched at Jack's shirt. "I need my book. Maybe I can make up a herbal remedy?"

Juliette stood. "Her heart has stopped beating."

"No." Kitarna sagged.

"I'm sorry, darlin'," murmured Jack, holding her tight. "We'll wrap Marley in a space blanket and bury her. That way the authorities can return her to her family."

She hiccupped against his shoulder. "Brett might have swallowed drugs as well."

"Probably."

"He told me he expected to come into a lot of money in the next few days."

"Drug trafficking is big business here. Marley just paid the ultimate price."

"What's the emergency?" Victoria called, stalking into the clearing. Solana and Ahmed were behind her. Their gazes dropped to Marley's still body.

"Stay back." Jack gently steered Kitarna toward the trio. "Marley was body-packing cocaine capsules. One must have burst today and entered her blood stream. Victoria, take Kitarna to the river, she's cold and in shock. Send Gabe back with a space blanket."

Numbly, Kitarna turned from Jack's protective warmth. Violent shivers racked her body, so much so, that her legs threatened to give way.

"I've got you, honey." Victoria's arm came around Kitarna's waist. "This has been a shitty few days, but a rescue team will find us soon. Hey, you look a bit green—give me fair warning if you want to puke."

Kitarna glanced back at Jack. How did he know so much about body-packers?

$$\sim 16 \sim$$

Using sharpened bamboo and the crude oars, the men helped Jack dig a grave. They lowered Marley's sheathed body into it and covered her. A somber group stood around the grave, heads downcast and faces drawn. Only Lexi remained oblivious to Marley's traumatic death. Roscoe kept her well away, searching for fruit.

Relieved to have the machete back, Jack fashioned a cross and wedged it deep in the dirt. He stood back as Kitarna, teary-eyed and coated in red dye, draped orchids over the grave. A touching gesture by the woman who'd woven her way through his walls.

The rain had stopped. They had to keep moving. Jack strode back to the river and waited for the group to assemble. "It's eight-thirty. We have a full day of trekking ahead, so best get to it."

"We're surrounded by jungle," called Gabe. "Wouldn't it be better to stay here?"

"No. We're heading east for the Putumayo River. Once there, we build another raft and travel by night.

We can't risk meeting mercenaries. I estimate it will take three or four days to reach Santo Antonñio do Içá."

"Oh no, your shack!" Kitarna gripped his fingers. "Will the seller hold it for you?"

Jack clenched his teeth. "I still have two days." Releasing her hand, he picked up the rifle and machete. "Time to move out."

"I just need to do one thing." She looped a garland of bright orchids from a branch then crouched on the bank arranging rocks in a row.

"What are you doing?"

"Leaving signs Bernie will recognize. Hopefully she'll see the orchids and know I'm alive and safe. It's a game we played as children."

The chances of her sister seeing it were slim, but he kept his mouth shut and waited then led the way, only stopping for fruit or toilet breaks. He called a halt at twelve-fifteen, and only because they'd reached a wide river.

"This has to be the Putumayo, but we're still too close to that wharf."

During the morning, Kitarna had told him about the native watching her swim across the river, but as mercenaries hadn't descended, he could only assume the native meant no harm.

Looking along the banks on either side, he spotted several snoozing caimans and a family of capybara. There were also tracks belonging to wild boar, but no human footprints. Without a compass, Brett would be going in circles. If he had reached the river, he didn't have a machete to build a raft, so he'd have no choice but to swim, or go back for the other raft. He wouldn't realize until he got there that Jack had dismantled the raft to reclaim his para cord. Brett could also be somewhere close with that rifle.

Kitarna touched his arm. "What are you thinking?"

"That it's not safe to swim across this river, and it's not safe to stay here." He turned to the others. "All right, folks, we need all hands on deck to build another raft."

Other than a groan from Victoria, everyone pitched in, gathering palm fronds and strangler vines or carrying the bamboo and balsa saplings he cut. Finally swamped by exhaustion, he let Ahmed take over the chopping. At all times, they stationed a lookout near the river and another covering their backs.

Hunger pangs stabbed at Jack by the time he cinched the last knot. Their raft, bigger and sturdier than the first, should carry the twelve of them safely. The rain had eased to a drizzle, which the canopy mostly blocked. He wished he had his pack and the thorns, because sweeping sappy vines through a deep river wouldn't work. "Let's cover the raft so it's not visible and find something to fish with."

As soon as Jack was satisfied the raft lay hidden, he looked for Kitarna. She sat on a fallen tree with Gabe, their heads together, both intent on whatever they were discussing. A spike of jealousy hit, but then Kitarna glanced up and gave him a smile, its radiance showering him in a glow of warmth.

"You two are looking serious. What's up?"

Gabe moved away to make room on the log. "I suspect the girl and her boyfriend were body-packing for an arm of *El* Jaguar's cartel. My uncle told me there is a drug manufacturing plant deep in the jungle."

"Hold your tongue, Gabe." The flight attendant stalked over and glared at the young man. "If you value your life and the lives of your family, you will not speak of such things."

"Solana, *El* Jaguar is out of control. For years the people here have turned a blind eye or paid protection money to his mercenaries. My father is a farmer and he is expected to supply part of his crop to feed *El* Jaguar's workforce. I am lucky that I attend college in Manaus, but many young people have disappeared, never to be seen again."

"You cannot discuss him." Solana looked at Jack. "*El* Jaguar has ears and eyes everywhere. By now he knows every passenger's identity, and he will know you have taken Alex. You are endangering all our lives."

"He won't catch us if we all work together." Jack unwound some para cord. "Kitarna, have you seen any of those thorny trees around here?"

"There's one further along the river."

"Good, we need to make fishing lines. Show me where it is."

"Follow me." She led him along an animal trail to the heavy-branched tree. Together they collected thorns and dug for fat worms.

Half an hour later, Jack and Gabe had caught four huge fish, more than enough to feed the group. Once they were cooked, everyone sat on logs they'd dragged close to the small fire.

Jack looked at the newcomers, sitting side by side. "You three want to introduce yourselves?"

The white-haired lady licked her fingers. "I'm Doris. I'm sixty-five, a widow from Canada. This is supposed to be a trip of a lifetime with my friend, Kerrie." She sniffed. "Lord only knows what's happened to her."

The young guy beside Doris patted her hand. "I'm Gabe, I'm twenty and I study accountancy in Manaus." He turned to the flight attendant.

"*Sí,* I am Solana from Sào Paulo de Olivença. I have worked for the airline for ten years."

Jack figured her to be in her early thirties. The conversation turned to Marley and Brett, where everyone agreed they hadn't seen either eating over the last two days.

"That's because they couldn't risk pushing the drugs through their bodies," said Piers. "It's common for body-packers to swallow anti-diarrheal medicine."

Lexi came skipping over then stopped, an expression of horror on her face. "Victoria, you've got one of those black worms on your neck."

"What? Get it off." Victoria jumped up flicking at her skin.

"It's a leech and if you pull it off, it will only bleed more." Kitarna rummaged through her rucksack, pulling out a small container. "Salt makes them drop off. I'll put some antiseptic on it. Best to cover it with a bandage to keep bot flies off."

"Thanks." Victoria stood still as Kitarna dispatched the leech.

"I've got a mixture of salt and eucalyptus oil. If you sprinkled it over your hat, boots and around the bottom of your tights, the leeches won't come near you."

Observing the scene along with the rest of the group, Jack saw the considering glance Victoria cast Kitarna. Most of them already looked to her as if she were their medicine woman. All except Ahmed, who kept his distance, and Solana, who Jack had caught watching Kitarna with a strange calculation in her eyes.

They ate every morsel of fish and fruit then after a thorough search of the banks, Jack gave the order to board the raft and cast off. He could only be thankful for the break from rain. There'd been no sign of Brett, but the bastard could be somewhere close, so they needed to cross the river, no matter the risk.

As they paddled away, Jack noticed Kitarna had left another garland of three orchids for her sister. As the leader in their childhood games, he hoped Bernie had the ingenuity of her younger sister. He flicked Kitarna a sidelong glance. The bond she shared with Bernie had to be envied. It drove home how empty he'd made his life.

A flood of memories swamped him. Coming from a working-class background, there'd never been surplus money, but always plenty of wholesome food and laughter. His parents had been a big part of his and his brothers' lives, even to the point of building their eco-tourism business with the hope all three boys would one day run it together.

Guilt fell heavily on his shoulders. His close-knit family couldn't comprehend the downward spiral his life had taken, or the distance he'd created since leaving the army. But he'd been unable to unload his demons on the people he loved. The disappointment in their eyes had been unbearable. And so, he'd walked away.

A warm breeze caught the flysheet, making the six oarsmen's slog a little easier. Kitarna had insisted on manning the makeshift rudder, wanting to contribute. Jack's admiration grew. She kept stepping up, allowing nothing to keep her in the doldrums for long. He'd never met a woman to equal her courage or fortitude.

Three small caimans slid into the water, but kept their distance, along with a lone native in a canoe. Other than a coral snake—more frightened by them than they were by it—nothing came close. They'd all kept shooting nervous glances toward the bends in the river, fearful a boat of mercenaries might come from either direction.

They ran aground well away from a snoozing caiman then dragged the raft under cover. The rain came back with a vengeance, so Jack forged into the jungle a short way, using the heavy canopy to keep them reasonably dry.

"I know you're all tired, but we have a decision to make." He squatted on his haunches and waited as the others gathered in a circle, mimicking his stance. Kitarna and Lexi took up their now habitual places either side of him. "You may not have noticed, but the native is a different man to yesterday."

Everyone gasped.

"They could be tag teaming, but that doesn't necessarily mean they're from the village *El* Jaguar controls. And, if they are, it will take time for them to relay information." He glanced at his watch. "It's now almost fifteen hundred and possibly another few hours through jungle to the next curve in the river. We can trek, but it will be dark by the time we reach the river, and we would need to build another raft. Or, we split up. Four of us men take the raft around the river while the rest of you stay out of sight and hike."

He looked to Kitarna. "You're the best person to lead a party through the jungle. We would meet up under cover of darkness. What do you think?"

"You can't put this responsibility on a woman," called Ahmed. "Two men are not enough to protect them from mercenaries."

"We are more likely to meet mercenaries on the river than in the jungle." Jack hadn't taken his gaze from Kitarna. "It's your decision, darlin'."

"I'd rather we stayed together, but what you say makes sense. I'll do it."

"Good." Jack looked at Roscoe. "If you and Piers go with the ladies, I'll chance the river with Gabe, Ahmed and Robert. Without the extra weight we will move quickly and hopefully catch a few fish on the way. If we come across trouble, it's every man for himself."

"Why can't we all risk the river?" asked Victoria.

"There is an eight-year-old child with us, and I didn't think *you* wanted to swim through caiman infested water?"

"You're right. I'll hike."

He glanced around the worried faces. "Does everyone agree?"

Robert looked nervous, but nodded. The others gave verbal agreements.

Jack stood. "Don't wander too far from the river. I'll give Roscoe my compass to keep you on track."

"No need," said Kitarna, standing and coming to his side. "I've got one in my rucksack."

He couldn't help but laugh. "Of course you do."

She stretched up and kissed his cheek. "Stay safe, and listen for my bird whistle. I don't want to lose you."

"You take care too." He closed his arms around her, holding her tight, knowing their time together limited, but wishing he could keep her forever. Her words could mean everything and nothing.

<h1 style="text-align:center">❧ 17 ❧</h1>

Watching Kitarna walk away had Jack second-guessing himself. He didn't like splitting the group, but thanks to incredibly good luck, they hadn't been caught yet. He crossed his fingers their luck would hold. The mercenaries had to be patrolling the Putumayo River. Without roads, it offered the only route to safety.

The mercenaries were thin on the ground, chasing passengers in every direction. They likely hadn't expected anyone to make it to the river or build a raft. Why were the Ashford sisters so important to a drug lord? Had they got into something over their heads?

"Right, fellas, let's grab some worms for the lines and get on the water."

"Wait," called Ahmed. "A boat is coming."

They took cover, hiding behind trees as a fishing trawler chugged past, black smoke bellowing from its chimney. They heard a plane flying low, but couldn't risk going out in the open. Several minutes later, a barge appeared from the opposite direction, loaded with goats and crates of chickens. Finally, after twenty minutes of mentally urging the watercraft to speed up, Jack gave the all clear. They dragged the raft from its hiding place, hoisted the flysheet and boarded.

With two on each side, they paddled hard, moving along as fast as the current would allow. The sail helped and, except for the occasional scramble to pull in a fish, they made good time, navigating several miles of the long, sweeping bend.

The river and banks were alive with wading birds, flying fish, the occasional caiman and scurrying lizards. The unceasing chatter and screeches from within the rainforest had become a familiar constant, and well able to disguise approaching boats, but luck stayed with them.

Sweat poured off Jack as he ploughed his paddle through the water, continually checking ahead and behind. Judging they were now opposite where they'd started, and hopefully close to where the others would appear, he called a halt.

"This will do us, lads. Head for those low-lying branches."

They pulled the raft onto the bank. After securing it, Jack cut branches and ferns as camouflage. "It will be slow going through the jungle, so we have a couple of hours before the others get here. Take a break while I clean the fish. Once we've all eaten and it's full dark, we'll hit the river again."

Jack prepared the fish and packed it under rocks in a campfire, ready to light when the others arrived. It hadn't rained for a couple of hours and everyone would need drinkable water, so while the other men rested, he scouted the area and found a clump of bamboo, which would hold more than enough fresh water for everyone.

He heard Kitarna's bird whistle earlier than he'd expected and slightly north of his position. He squashed the burn of unease. If they were in trouble her whistle would pierce the quiet in frantic bursts, not well-spaced intervals. It was now eighteen hundred hours and they had an hour before dark. Time enough to eat and rest before taking to the river.

Preferring not to be shot, he called out. Kitarna looked tired, but gave him a spontaneous smile before walking into his open arms. She squeezed him tight, lifting her face, and it seemed the most natural thing in the world to kiss her, so he did. "No, problems?"

"We saw a family of spider monkeys, an iguana, and a huge spider, which gave us a fright, but none of them bothered us."

Lexi tugged at his shirt. "I saw a beautiful Toucan and lots of pretty parrots."

"Great." He glanced at Roscoe. "I've got fish ready to cook."

"Wonderful. We collected some bananas and Kit found us a little water in bromeliads, but we could do with a decent drink."

"I've got that covered." Winking at Kitarna, he led them back to camp then lit the fire. "There is a clump of bamboo close by, which will be full of water. Once I cut them water will gush out. It's this way."

Everyone stood patiently as he cut and passed each a stick of bamboo. Soon everyone slurped and guzzled the water, a good sign of how thirsty they all were. They trooped back to the campfire where Jack set up a watch and they ate the fish and bananas. Several boats passed, going down river, but no one onboard showed any sign of seeing them or smelling the campfire. The cool breeze kept most people inside the wheelhouse, and engine fumes more than likely blocked the smell of fire and baking fish.

Once Jack deemed it safe, they uncovered the raft, hoisted the sail and spread the three sleeping bags out in the center. "We need to stay close to shore in case a boat comes along, and we'll have to take turns sleeping and paddling. So, get as much sleep as possible."

"Do I get to paddle too?" asked Lexi.

"No, you're in charge of the rudder and lookout for the next two hours."

"Yay."

He lifted her onto the raft. "The rest of you hikers can have a two-hour sleep, before taking a turn on the paddles. Doris, you'll be on the rudder and lookout for the rear. After two hours, you wake the first crew again. We continue like that until daylight then we make camp and sleep for a few hours. All agreed?"

Everyone nodded.

"Let's go." He lifted Juliette then Doris, Solana and Victoria on board, irritated with the flight attendant and blonde's prolonged embraces.

By Kitarna's narrowed eyes, she'd witnessed the women pressing their breasts against him. He held out his arms to lift her across. She gave him a mutinous glare before accepting Robert's hand.

The blast of possessive jealousy came out of left field, knocking years of discipline flat on its face. Blinded by his aggravation, Jack bent forward and swept Kitarna into his arms, leaving Robert gaping like a stunned mullet.

Jack stole a brusque kiss before depositing her on the raft and bowed. "My lady, your carriage awaits. I serve only to please *you*."

She raised a delicate eyebrow then ran her tongue over her lower lip. "I look forward to that, and in returning the pleasure two-fold."

His blood shot south, leaving him lightheaded. His need to kiss every delectable curve, lick every erogenous inch, and bury himself deep inside her consumed him faster than a tornado tearing through Kansas. At this rate, he'd have to jerk-off first, or he'd take her too fast.

How long they stood, locked in each other's eyes, he didn't know, but Roscoe clearing his throat refocused Jack's priorities. Everyone was in position and waiting.

"Right." He jumped aboard and took up his paddle, his ruffled senses sidelined when Kitarna asked Victoria, in clipped tones to move it, or lose it, before curling up under the netting of his hammock. His kitten had flexed her claws, but would she go into battle for him?

He swiped at the haze of mosquitoes. They'd been pestering him all day, along with the flies. If it hadn't been for Kitarna's red dye, he and the boys would have gone mad. Even Victoria had spread the mixture over her face. As a group, they looked like a band of Indians on the warpath. All they required were feathered headbands and they'd be set. If they made it out alive, the photos Kitarna kept taking would be worth a mint.

The evening passed slowly. After two hours, he woke the next crew then crawled into his flattened hammock. Lexi squirmed in beside him, cuddling up like a koala. He wasn't comfortable with the protectiveness this little girl evoked, or how she attached herself to him, but a look from Roscoe and Kitarna had him surrendering. They both needed to know Lexi remained safe while they paddled. He closed his eyes, hoping for a dreamless few hours.

He didn't stir until Kitarna nudged him. "Wake up, my lion, it's your turn."

"Hmm, kiss me first."

Her lips gently touched his. "Don't wake Lexi. It's midnight and I've tied a cord to the rudder to keep it in position."

"Good idea." He carefully eased out of the hammock, holding the netting up so she could slide in. "I didn't hear engines, so I take it you saw no river traffic?"

"No, but lots of caimans and a couple of otters. Wake me in two hours."

He did. At four, she woke him again. He and the boys paddled hard for an hour. As the sky began to lighten, Jack noticed a narrow estuary off to their right. They paddled up the channel until six-foot-wide water lilies surrounded the raft.

Masses of sweetly scented orchids hung like drapes to trail in the water. Above and around them the dayshift of birds and monkeys had woken. Hummingbirds in an assortment of colors flitted everywhere.

They were well hidden from the main river, so leaving the others sleeping, Jack got Ahmed, Gabe and Robert to stretch their aching muscles then he used Kitarna's trick, sweeping the inlet with crushed *ayori-toto* vines. Within minutes, they had enough fish to feed the group.

Ahmed came back with wild figs and ginger bracts, edible food Kitarna had introduced them to. "I've found a waterfall not far away. I think everyone would appreciate washing away the sweat and refilling drink bottles."

"You're right, thank you, Ahmed." A shower would make the world of difference and Jack knew exactly who he'd take with him.

The smell of ginger-baked fish soon woke the others and once they tasted it, they were full of praise. Kitarna smiled at him and he loved her for it. The thought sent shock waves through him, as if someone had dumped a bucket of icy water over his head. *I'm not in love. Christ, I barely know the woman.*

With two lookouts, rotating hourly, everyone made the most of catching up on sleep. They spent the rest of the morning lazing about, getting to know one another or collecting fruit and visiting the waterfall in pairs.

Jack made sure he and Kitarna went last, as he wanted time alone with her. The crowd of red and blue parrots congregating in the surrounding trees didn't count.

"Oh, this is lovely." She ran ahead, stopping to gaze up at the cascading water. "Juliette said there is a small cavern behind. Let's investigate."

Piers had told him the same thing. "I'm right behind you." Her innocent excitement came as a refreshing balm to his jaded senses.

Climbing up the rocks, he ducked behind the screen of shimmering water and kicked off his boots. In the mellowed light, it took him a moment to find her. Spellbound, he memorized every curve of the naked nymph smiling at him from under a curtain of gushing water.

# ～ 18 ～

Her sexy body captured his attention. Her beautiful smile captured his soul.

"Why are you standing over there? Come here, my shy lion."

"Not shy, darlin', just getting my hormones under control so I don't eat you alive."

"I'm not scared."

"You should be. I'm ferociously hungry." He whipped off his clothes and plunged under the waterfall. Her gaze dropped. She gasped, but he didn't give her a chance to air her concerns. They'd deal with that later. For now he needed to be sure he wasn't dreaming.

Lifting her against his chest, he claimed her mouth, as he meant to claim every inch of her.

She clung, her hands in his hair, her legs locked round his waist, kissing him with the same wildness he couldn't hold back.

Sliding his hands down her slick spine, he cupped the smooth contours of her bottom, stroking then clinching each sweet cheek. Her high, plump breasts pressed against his chest.

"Darlin', I'm too desperate to wait for a bed. I need you now."

She laughed huskily. "Then take me, my handsome lion."

He kissed her again, long and deep, his tongue dueling for supremacy, while he slid one hand under her butt-cheeks, to sink a finger deep inside her. "So wet."

"Do it." No shy little kitten now, she arched against his engorged erection, her gasps and moans swallowed by the plummeting water and rowdy parrots.

Fighting free of his mouth, she pulled herself higher until his cock nudged her mound. Her breasts were right there, begging for his attention. He swooped, taking a rigid nipple with his mouth and suckling, pushing another finger inside her and thrusting until she quivered. "Come for me." He sucked harder.

She cried out, shuddered and contracted round his fingers. Her eyes in hazed passion. With his fingers still inside her, she collapsed against his shoulder, trembling and panting. "I'm going to lock you up and keep you forever."

*Yes please.* Speaking became well and truly beyond him.

Adjusting her slightly, he probed at her entrance, willing her to re-engage, fighting the urge to take her hard and fast. She was tight, but so very wet, and he couldn't wait to taste her. *Next time.*

Vitality gradually enthused her body until she

lifted her head, giving him her ray of sunshine smile. "I'm in awe." She clung to his shoulders and sank over his erection, further testing his resolve.

He pushed in deeper and she gasped, her fingernails biting. "Am I hurting you?"

"No, it's just so…" She wiggled again. "So incredibly mind-blowing."

Blinded by his overwhelming need, Jack clutched her butt and drove home, her cry of pleasure releasing his inhibitions. Holding her firmly in place, he fed his hunger, thrusting deep and hard, not holding back. She'd be bruised from his fingers and mouth, but chivalry and gentleness were beyond him. He rocked into her faster and faster as his climax built.

"Jack, I'm…" She shuddered and clamped round his cock, sending him spiraling over the edge.

"Kitarna." He went to unlock her ankles, but ran out of time, pumping his seed deep into her body. Light-headiness threatened. He staggered to the rock face, clutching the wet surface before sinking to his knees on the cavern floor.

She'd gone limp in his arms, and it was all he could do to pull out, lie down and drape her alongside him. Long minutes passed before either stirred. Aware someone might come looking for them, Jack sat up and reached for his soaked clothing. "At least we've got clean clothes to put on."

She giggled. "I prefer you naked. Thank you for making it so wonderful."

"It's my pleasure." He passed her wet clothes across. "We should get back."

"Hmm." She sat up and stretched. "I've got delicious twinges everywhere."

Unable to prevent his reaction, Jack pulled her onto his lap for one more drugging kiss then slapped her bottom. "Get dressed."

"I need another shower." She stepped under the deluge again, closing her eyes and lifting her face to the torrent of water.

She was a fantasy come true and Jack could only stare, knowing he'd risk his life to protect her, but conscious she would reject him if she knew the truth.

"Stop frowning, I'm more resilient than I look." She stepped away from the waterfall and squeezed out her hair. "I think I'm falling for you, Jack Callaghan."

Her declaration hit him square in the chest, almost winding him. A sliver of hope welled only to be dashed by reality. "That would be unwise, kitten. This can only ever be a fling." He turned his back and picked up his clothes, the silence behind him deafening. When he turned back, he found her sitting on the rock floor clutching her shirt to her chest, like a protective shield.

Her wounded eyes searched his face. "Why? Neither of us is married."

"Kitarna, there are things I've done that would make you despise me."

"You're pushing me away because of something in *your past*? Don't I get to decide?"

She looked so damn miserable it pained him. "I'm sorry, it's better this way."

"Oh no, Jack. You don't get to say *it's better this way*. My father is the governor of Florida. My stepfather is an attaché at the British Embassy in Paris. I stopped accepting that particular phrase years go. What are you afraid of?"

"Darlin', you're so far out of my reach. I'm not good enough for you."

Her eyes widened. "If you say it's because I've been raised with a silver spoon in my mouth, I'll screech louder than those blasted howler monkeys. Why am I out of your reach?"

"There are things I've done in the army that would horrify you. And something I didn't do caused more death and grief than your tender ears could cope with."

"You underestimate me, Jack. Having someone to listen could be of help to you. Talk to me. Trust me. Let me into your life."

Could he? What did he have to lose? Sitting down beside her, Jack kept his gaze on the shimmering curtain of water. "The army's shrinks couldn't prevent my nightmares, so I resorted to alcohol and anti-depressants. I pushed my family and friends away. If it hadn't been for my ex-Colonel, I might not be here today."

"What did he do?"

"Sobered me up and stuck me on an oil platform in the middle of the ocean. No alcohol and no anti-depressants for three months, just long, sweaty shifts, welding steel beams. Then he arranged a timber-cutting job for me in Florida. It wasn't negotiable."

"What about your family? Don't they miss you?"

"Maybe, but I can't stand to see the pity and disappointment in their eyes. I'm not the son and brother they want."

"Are you sure?"

"Since meeting you, I'm not sure of anything anymore."

"I'll take that as a compliment. When we get to Manaus, I want you to tell me everything. Having spent the last few days with you, I think I know what sort of person you are. I can make up my own mind, thank you very much. I'm not going to let you get away that easily." She dropped her shirt. "Now, kiss me, before I throw myself at a caiman."

"We can't have that." Only she could make him smile at a time like this, especially when she must be hurting at his rejection. He could hope for a miracle, but only time would tell. Dropping his clothes, he lifted her to his chest, kissing her leisurely, learning every naked curve and hollow with his hands and lips.

He laid her gently on top of their clothes, spreading her thighs. Her heady scent gave him a high no drug could match. "You have no idea how much I've wanted to taste you."

"Another first for me," she panted.

"I kind of figured that, kitten. Lie back and let me give you this." He ran his tongue over her soft folds, smiling when she jolted. He thrust inside, mimicking his earlier action, retreating to lick her tart nectar, lapping up her juices and soft moans, as she squirmed and bucked, clutching his hair. He pushed two fingers inside her, rubbing back and forth then closed his mouth over her nub, flicking his tongue and sucking hard.

She shrieked his name, bucked and convulsed.

"Wild cat." Leaning back on his ankles, Jack wiped his mouth and waited. Her eyes fluttered open, a dreamy smile surfacing.

Her breasts rose and fell, the nipples as erect as his cock. "I want you inside me."

He couldn't argue with that, and it was the surest way to appease his throbbing erection. He lifted her across his thighs. "Next time we do this in a bed. Rock is too damn hard."

"Yes, honey." She sank onto his cock, slowly like she had all day and he wasn't about to combust. Hell and Heaven.

Taking control, he lifted her and brought her down as he surged up, sheathing himself to the hilt.

She gasped, grinned, and let him take control, meeting each thrust with abandoned cries. He wouldn't last much longer. Supporting her with one hand, he found her nub and rubbed, holding back until she began to shake. He thrust once, twice, and followed her over the edge, exhaling as he pumped his seed into her.

He'd never taken such a risk with any other woman.

"Darlin', I know it's a bit like shutting the gate after the horses have bolted, but is there any chance we just made a baby?"

"Of course not." Lifting her head from his shoulder she cupped his face in her hands, her eyes locking with his. "I know exactly when I ovulate."

"On the plane, you asked me if I had protection."

A soft blush blossomed in her cheeks. "Safe sex. I didn't know you."

"You don't know me now."

"Yes, I do." Leaning in, she brushed a feather-light kiss on his lips. "I want another shower before we go back." Placing her hands on his thighs, she eased off his cock, the sensual slide, reviving his erection.

Lifting her to her feet, he stepped into the curtain

of water to wash off before pulling on his clothes. "I'll wait outside." If he didn't they'd never leave the waterfall.

"Use some *urucu* repellant. With this humidity, the mosquitoes will be out in thousands."

"Thanks." Scrounging through her rucksack, he bypassed the dress he'd told her to leave behind and pulled out a jar of the red dye. "What makes it so slimy?"

"Fish oil. It's what the natives' use, and thanks to you catching all those fish, I mixed the oil with crushed *urucu* seeds."

"Thankfully it doesn't stink like your other repellant."

He smeared the gunk over his face, neck and arms then, dodging the water, stepped outside. Patches of powder-blue sky had replaced the dull ominous clouds. A family of lanky, white-faced monkeys balanced on limbs above, nibbling figs and hurling them at the chattering parrots. Sweet scented orchids hung from vines twisted about the lowest branches. Gold and fire-engine-red bromeliads encircled the trunk. He hadn't noticed earlier, but everything seemed brighter and louder today. It felt good to be alive, and the mosquitoes gave him a wide berth.

"All done." She popped out beside him, braiding her dripping hair as she glanced around. "It's turning humid again. I hope Bernie remembers me telling her about the *urucu* seeds. It's sometimes hard to know if she's listening."

A terror-filled scream echoed through the forest.

# ∽ 19 ∾

"Mercenaries!" Kitarna twisted left and right, not knowing which direction to run. Her stomach knotting as dread filled her veins.

"Get back behind the waterfall." Jack leaped off the rocks, ducked under a spindly branch then jumped over a crumbling log as he ran toward camp.

"Wait!"

She ran after him, dodging vines and thick clumps of grass. She hadn't heard shots or shouting, so maybe it wasn't mercenaries. Pounding feet converged from all sides. Pushing through a grove of bamboo, she emerged on a narrow, animal trail and almost collided with Ahmed and Gabe.

"Who screamed?"

Gabe blinked. "We thought you did."

"No, I'm fine."

Jack came striding toward Kitarna, a thunderous scowl on his face. "I told you to stay put. Is that too much to ask?"

"Yes, it is." She returned his glare. "We are better off sticking together."

"Over here." Doris stepped out from behind a thick-girthed tree. Her voice shook, her face and shirt covered in blood. "I've been bitten by a snake."

"Snake?" Hoping to scare off any loitering reptiles, Kitarna tramped heavily, following in Jack's footsteps. "Where is it?"

Holding her face, Doris pointed at a mass of bromeliads. "I bent over to admire those beautiful plants and the damn snake struck so fast."

Eying the colorful booms warily, Kitarna hesitated. There were so many venomous snakes in the Amazon, she could only hope it had been a python. Anything else and there wasn't a thing they could do, stuck in the jungle. As Ahmed and Gabe assisted Doris to a log, Kitarna grabbed a stick. She helped Jack search the bromeliads and decaying mulch.

The reptile was almost completely hidden; its tan coils and dark-brown, diamond-shaped markings camouflaged by leaf litter. Snapping a thick twig from the tree, she moved closer, looking for the head. *Not a python.*

Her heart sank. By the craters between its eyes and nose and the horny spine at the end of its tail, it had to be a bushmaster pit viper. One of the most venomous snakes in the world.

"Bloody hell." Jack muttered, shaking his head. "We're going to have to risk flagging down a boat. Doris needs antivenom ASAP."

"Yes." Kitarna cautiously stepped back and hurried to Doris. "How do you feel?"

"Not great, dear. It gave me a nasty fright, but it's

something to boast about when I get home, don't you think?" Her breath came in short, harsh rasps.

Jack passed his stick to Ahmed and crouched beside Doris. "I'll carry you back to camp. Piers and Juliette will take care of you."

"Bless you."

"Wait." Kitarna dropped her rucksack then pulled out a packet of moist wipes. She pressed several between Doris' cheek and hand. "Hold it firmly. The doctors can put antiseptic on as soon as the bleeding stops."

"Thank you, dear."

Kitarna watched Jack lift the woman's considerable weight. Avoiding Ahmed and Gabe's questioning gazes, she led the way back to camp.

Roscoe stood armed and ready by the fire with Lexi and Solana. Robert, Victoria and the doctors formed a small huddle at the raft, ready for flight, but frozen with fear. Everyone gathered in a somber group as Jack laid Doris on a sleeping bag.

"What are we dealing with?" asked Juliette.

"She's been bitten by a juvenile bushmaster." Kitarna removed the blood-soaked wipes from Doris' cheek and a stream of fresh blood poured from the swollen puncture wounds. "The excessive bleeding is a side effect of the venom. Do you have any morphine?"

"It won't relieve the symptoms." Piers opened the medical satchel and whipped out a syringe and wad of gauze. "You're sure it was a bushmaster?"

"Yes. I visited Brazil several years ago on a study grant, and a guide pointed one out to me."

"I'm going to be sick." Doris wiped a trickle of blood from her nose. She fell sideways and retched.

"I've got more wipes." Kitarna crawled over beside Jack, shrugged off her rucksack, and dug inside. "Hold Doris up so I can clean her face."

By the convulsions racking the woman's body, Kitarna figured Doris had only hours. Next her organs would shut down. The snake must have pumped a massive amount of venom into her.

Juliette taped gauze and a pad over the bite. "She's bleeding from the gums and her pulse is erratic. Let's move her inside the tent."

"What's a bushmaster?" asked Lexi. "Is it a poisonous frog?"

"No." Kitarna wiped perspiration from Doris' forehead then stood back as Jack and Ahmed carried Doris into the tent.

"What can I do, Kitarna?" asked Roscoe.

"Take Lexi and collect fresh water. I have some teabags, we could all do with a drink."

"Yes, of course." He took the billycan she handed him, another item she was glad to have brought. Keeping Lexi away from Doris had to be a priority and the tea would help restore their depleting spirits.

"We'll pick some fruit too," called Roscoe.

Peeping into the tent, Kitarna met Jack's gaze. He shook his head as he rubbed Doris' shoulder. "Ma'am, your body is reacting to the toxin, and you might lose consciousness. I promise we'll take care of you."

She squeezed his hand. "Thank you for your kindness, Jack. I pray you all make it back to your families." She closed her eyes. "I've always liked Bromeliads."

Witnessing Doris on the verge of death had a subdued effect on everyone. Most sat around the campfire staring into its flames, while Piers and Juliette kept a vigil over their patient.

Kitarna tried to busy her mind by teaching Lexi and Victoria how to weave sun hats and baskets from palm fronds, while Jack and Roscoe set up watch by the river.

After several hours, Kitarna stood and stretched. "Lexi, let's take some fruit to Roscoe and Jack. The walk will do us good. I'll swap places with Roscoe and the two of you can do some fishing."

"Okay." Picking up her basket, Lexi skipped off in front of Kitarna.

They'd almost reached the river when two boats came rocketing round the bend.

"Get down," called Jack, diving behind a rotting log.

Kitarna lunged at Lexi, knocking her among the coarse tussocks. They stayed hidden as a boats speed past. The uniformed men aboard were armed, but their rough disheveled appearances bore little resemblance to Brazilian soldiers. "Mercenaries!"

Roscoe crawled over. "There's no way we can take to the river during daylight."

"No." Jack sighed. "That's the third time we've seen those boats. We have no choice but to wait for darkness."

Rubbing her elbow, Kitarna grimaced at Jack. "Everyone is hungry and sick of fruit. Is there any chance you can set traps for a tapir or capybara?"

"Maybe. I saw tracks earlier. I'll take Gabe and see what we can find."

"Thank you, Jack."

They walked back to camp then Jack and Gabe set off with a coil of thin vine and a rifle. It might keep Jack occupied, but a change in menu did little to enthuse Kitarna. She'd lost her appetite. At least crushing *urucu* seeds and mixing the powder with fish oil, gave her something to do.

A low flying plane and a helicopter flew overhead, but with the thick canopy they couldn't know if it carried mercenaries or search parties.

Kitarna glanced at the tent furtively. Time was running out. Inside, Juliette watched over Doris, whose heart barely beat, pumping infected blood through her body. Without urgent medical intervention, she would die.

Morale hung at an all-time low, even the birds and monkeys, high in the canopy weren't as vocal as usual.

*We need a miracle.* Kitarna chewed on a fingernail. She hadn't felt this lost since her parents announced they were divorcing. Given no choice, she and Bernie had moved to England with their mother. Leaving Cookie, Martha, Jed and Morris behind had been heartbreaking. They may have been paid to run the house and estate, but to Kitarna and Bernie these people had been family.

Frustration ate at her. Doris needed urgent help, but they couldn't risk the river until dark. Where were the search parties?

She glanced across at Solana, Robert and Victoria sitting on a log, talking in whispers like grounded teenagers. Jack and Gabe hadn't come back from hunting. Ahmed and Piers were on watch out by the main river. Lexi, wearing her new lopsided sun-hat, sat cross-legged beside Roscoe, helping him weave palm fronds into a bamboo frame he'd built. It would go on the raft, protecting them from rain.

The *urucu* seeds would give them some protection too. She sighed. This wasn't the quest she'd set out on. Her need to ascertain her place in the botanical world, to show her parents her true calling, unearthing a plant with astronomical healing powers, had vanished. Now all she wanted was to survive, help Jack get these people to safety and find Bernie.

Closing her eyes, she bent her head. *I vow before the almighty universe, if I survive, I will live my life to the fullest. I will go after my dreams, and let no one else decide my future. I will marry the love of my life and together create a family and home full of warmth and laughter.*

"Well, well, well, isn't this a cozy little scene."

"Brett!" Kitarna recoiled, clenching the rocks until the sharp corners bit into her fingers. An all-consuming fury built in every cell, the inferno surging through her bloodstream as she came to her feet. She turned to face the rotten scumbag who'd left Marley to die. His sneering cockiness tipped her over the edge.

"You vile, disgusting shit." She spat the words out. "There's nothing for you here. Get the hell away from us. If Jack sees you, he'll feed your scrawny ass to the caimans."

"Wow, Kitty, so much anger. I can't think what I've done to deserve it."

"What kind of monster are you?" Raising her hand, she took a step forward, intending to hurl the rock at him.

Roscoe stepped across her path. "You're not wanted here, Brett. What you did is contemptible. Get lost before I take that rifle and shove it up your ass."

Kitarna gasped as Brett swung the rifle up. "Shut up, old man. I'll leave, but only when I've got what I came for. It's been a real bitch waiting for an opportunity like this. The fucking mosquitoes and flies driving me demented, so thirsty my piss burns. I've got enough bullets to kill you all if I have to."

"Give him what he wants," called Robert from behind a tree. "We've got plenty of food and water."

"That's not all he wants." Kitarna narrowed her eyes.

Brett's barking laugh reminded her of a hyena and sent chills spiraling down her spine.

"Clever, Kitty." Brett swung the rifle smoothly from side to side. "Hope your Aussie boyfriend likes sharing, because I can't wait to fuck you. But first you're going to find me food and water. Let's go."

"Wait!" Solana poked her head out from behind a tree near Robert. "We can give you food and water. If you take Kitarna, Jack will come after you."

"He's gone hunting, and by the time he gets back, we'll be long gone. Now, Kitty, are you coming, or will I shoot the kid?"

"Over my dead body." Roscoe ran at him.

"Stupid old man." Brett fired.

Kitarna screamed as Roscoe flew off his feet, landing hard. In seconds, his shirt turned crimson.

She ran to his side.

Lexi beat her to him. "Roscoe, don't die. Grandpa, I love you."

"Kit, you have to find Jack," he whispered, gasping. "He's the only one who can get Lexi home to her mother."

"I will, I promise. Hang in there."

"I'm waiting," yelled Brett. "Who will I shoot next, Kitty?"

"I'll come with you. Just let me stop the bleeding." Her gaze searched the camp. Victoria and Robert were invisible behind their trees. Juliette half crouched at the tent's entrance. "Please, Juliette. Roscoe's losing blood, he needs your help."

"I can't do anything for him."

"Don't say that," Lexi shouted, tears streaming down her face.

Solana ran from her tree and picked Lexi up, who began kicking and screeching.

Kitarna stood, blocking Brett's aim. "Are you mad?"

Ignoring Lexi's screams and thrashing arms, Solana ran for cover.

*At least Lexi is safe.* Kitarna reached for the medical satchel. She pulled out several arm slings and packed them against Roscoe's shoulder, clamping his hand over it. "Try to relax. Jack will be back any minute and he'll know what to do."

"Yeah." He closed his eyes.

Rising to her feet, she glowered at Brett, "You're going to regret this big time."

"Shut the fuck up." He grabbed her arm, his fingers pinching cruelly as he shoved her ahead of him.

Wrenching out of his hold, she trudged off. She had to stay calm and bide her time until Brett lowered his guard. She must escape and find Jack.

<h1 style="text-align:center">❦ 20 ❧</h1>

The day had started out so well, and now two in their group were close to death. The sooner she went with Brett, the sooner Piers and Juliette could work on Roscoe. Leaving her rucksack on the ground, Kitarna faced Brett. She couldn't dally any longer, but she refused to bring anything that would help him in any way. With luck, the mosquitoes would eat him alive. "I'm ready."

He pushed an oar into her hand. "Might as well help ourselves to another paddle." He pointed at the estuary. "I rebuilt our old raft using vines. It's that way."

His hand rested on the rifle hanging across his thin chest. Slung over one shoulder was Jack's open pack with Marley's fringed-bag inside. Deep scratches crisscrossed his arms and legs. Grime stained his baggy shorts and T-shirt. He reeked of stale sweat. Patchy whiskers covered his knobby chin, and the neat dreadlocks of three days ago were fuzzy and matted.

The raft turned out to be four wet balsa-saplings corded together. Hands shaking, she turned to him. "It's too low and narrow. We won't have any protection against caimans."

"It works fine."

"You have blood on your legs, Brett. These rivers are full of piranha."

"Get on the raft and stop your whining."

The second her bottom touched the snarled saplings water seeped over the edges, soaking her cargo pants. The only way to balance the death trap was to sit cross-legged, which allowed water inside her boots. She looked back, hoping for a glimpse of Jack. To her horror, Juliette, Robert and Victoria were running toward the waterfall, maybe in search of Jack, but they'd left Roscoe and Doris defenseless and vulnerable.

Reaching the river mouth, Kitarna heard Lexi screaming then saw her further upriver being dragged along by Solana. *Oh no, they're going in the wrong direction.* Swallowing a sob, she rallied, determined not to show any sign of weakness or distress, as she searched the banks for Ahmed or Piers. They had to have heard the shot. Where were they?

Brett might believe her his meal ticket, but he had a rude shock coming. She'd give him poison berries, or better still, raw yucca root. As long as he didn't know soaking it in water rendered it safe, the hydrogen cyanide would kill him. As for the rest—no way would she allow him to touch her. That privilege belonged to the man she... Kitarna stilled as the truth hit her. *I'm in love with Jack.*

A flicker of movement caught her eye. On the bank as still as the ancient trees around him, stood a native with a long bow. Blue and yellow feathers hung from a plaited cord round his neck, fluttering in the slight breeze. It remained a faint hope, but if the bullet hadn't nicked Roscoe's heart, maybe the native could help save him. She paddled shallowly, darting glances between him and the estuary, praying he understood her silent plea. He didn't so much as twitch before she lost sight of him.

Glancing up at the lowering sun, she grimaced. The sky had cleared, but it would be dark in a couple of hours and if Roscoe died, Jack's priority would be getting Lexi back to her mother, if he knew where to find her.

Kitarna's spirits plummeted. Jack might be in lust with her, but he had his hands full with saving Roscoe and Doris, and finding Lexi. *I'll just have to save myself.*

Brett cackled. "I bet you're wondering how I found you."

She wasn't interested in anything the creep had to say, but their voices might attract attention. "So, you rebuilt the old raft and followed us."

"Yeah, but I stayed well back so *Jacko* wouldn't shoot me. I knew an opportunity would come sooner or later."

His oar splattered her neck in cool droplets. "Start looking for a good place to pull in. You can find food and water, but don't think to trick me. You'll be eating first then we'll have a good time, Kitty."

She patted her pocket, checking for the rocks. She'd stab him in the eyes and run.

"I'm going to tie you to a tree and strip you naked." He ranted on and on, his crudeness and depravity churning the contents of her stomach.

She'd rather dive into the river full of piranhas. She paddled on, her arms aching as the sun sank without any sign of rescue.

Brett tapped her shoulder with his paddle. "Up ahead on the right. It's a good place to land and there's plenty of cover to hide the raft."

Kitarna prayed for inspiration. She considered swimming to the closest bank, but a huge caiman on the opposite bank put an end to that. He could easily swallow her in one gulp. If she tipped the raft, there was a fifty-fifty chance he'd go after Brett. A quick inspection of both banks revealed no other caimans lying in wait. It might be her best chance.

She drew in a deep breath, willing her courage not to desert her. *Oh, no.* Ahead, another caiman blocked their path. She frowned. Not a caiman, a log, but how could it be moving against the current? A dark shadow shifted then two eyes appeared. *Jack.* Her heart swelled. It was nearly impossible to stay still, and not shout for joy, or rocket off the raft, shoot into the sky and splash down beside him.

She shot a glance at the caiman on the riverbank. It hadn't moved, yet watched her with an unblinking black stare. She had to keep Brett's attention away from the approaching log.

"Look!" She pointed. "That caiman is watching us. Ever since you knocked me into the river, I've had nightmares about them."

"I'll shoot the bastard if it moves. Keep paddling."

"It's not that easy to hit a moving target. Did I

mention Jack's a sniper? That's why he hit the other caiman, but it took five bullets to kill it. You want to pray Jack never gets you in his scope." She paddled as slowly as she could, bracing herself for the impact.

"What the fuck?" Brett clambered to his feet, pitching the raft.

Looking over her shoulder, Kitarna's heart stammered. "No!"

He had the rifle up, aimed at the log and fired a shot. She swung the oar, putting all her strength behind the strike. It connected with Brett's knee. He howled and staggered. The raft listed, pitching Jack's pack and Brett into the river.

Dropping her oar, Kitarna grabbed the edges of the raft, counterbalancing it as a wave of water washed over her. Not knowing whether Jack had been shot, she scrambled to her knees and hand-paddled to the log.

"Jack!" She screamed his name, frantically searching as the largest capsules she'd ever seen bobbed to the surface. She snatched a couple and shoved them in her pocket to show Jack later.

"Help me collect them!" Brett thrashed about, shrieking obscenities, snatching at the capsules, losing a few each time he reached for more.

A quick glance at the far bank almost paralyzed Kitarna. The caiman was up on its stumpy legs and snaking toward the water.

"No!" Sweat broke out all over her body. She gasped in air, her heart hammering so hard stars danced before her eyes. If she didn't put her head between her knees she'd pass out, but Jack needed her. She paddled faster, calling him, searching for a glimpse of him on the dark surface. If he'd been shot, the blood would bring piranhas. Maybe they were stripping his flesh at this very moment. "Oh God, please help me find him."

The caiman had reached the water. With a morbid fascination she watched, transfixed as it sank beneath the surface, leaving only its eyes visible and locked on Brett who thrashed about, screaming at her to help.

Turning away, she spotted an arm beneath the surface and shrieked.

"Please don't be dead." Leaning over her knees, she reached out and pulled Jack up, every muscle in her body straining as she hauled him onto the raft. It sank lower, almost tipped, then settled, but left nowhere to sit, except astride his hips.

Pinching his nose, she placed her mouth over his and blew several breaths into his lungs. Hoping for the best, she lay over him and paddled for the nearest bank like the very devil chased her.

A piercing scream sent shudders through her. Bile rose in her throat, but she forced it down and kept paddling.

"Kit, over here."

Relief surged at Ahmed's call. She prayed they weren't too late. As she reached the shallower water, Ahmed and Gabe waded out and dragged Jack off. She gripped his feet and helped carry him up the bank.

"Don't you dare die." Placing her hands on his chest, she began CPR.

"Stop, Kit." Ahmed clutched her hands, pulling her back. "He has a heartbeat. We need to roll him onto his side and check his breathing."

"Thank God." She helped push as the two men

pulled. Blood trickled from Jack's head. "He's been shot."

"No," murmured Ahmed, squeezing her shoulder gently. "When Brett fell in the water, he smacked Jack in the head with the oar. We saw everything from the bank."

Kitarna placed her hand above Jack's mouth, almost collapsing with relief at the warm puffs fanning her palm. "He's breathing." She ran her eyes and hands over him frowning. "With all this blood, why didn't the piranhas attack?"

Gabe shrugged. "He is lucky. Another few minutes and it would have been very different."

"We should get him back to camp," said Ahmed. "He needs stitches and there is a risk of infection and fever."

"Of course." She stripped off her shirt, thankful for her bikini and tank top. After wrapping the shirt around Jack's head, she began cataloguing the best tonic within the Amazon arsenal of medicines. She needed something to ward off fever and treat infection. Several things jumped to mind that were readily available.

Ahmed handed Gabe the machete. "Kit can watch Jack while we turn the raft into a a stretcher."

"Thank you." Kitarna kept her eyes off the river. Thinking about Brett torn to shreds made her queasy. Instead, she kept a vigil by Jack's side, holding his hand to her heart and praying he had a hard head.

Ahmed dragged the flimsy raft ashore, while Gabe cut flexible vines. Using the skills Jack had taught them, they crisscrossed clingy-vines between and wove in palm fronds.

As they lifted Jack onto the stretcher, she asked the question that had been niggling. "How did Jack know to come after me?"

"I told him," said Ahmed. "I was with Piers when we heard the shot. We were making our way back when we saw you on the raft with Brett. Piers went to alert Jack and I followed you." He picked the stretcher up at Jack's head, leaving her and Gabe to take the other end.

"Other than Doris, no one was in camp," said Gabe. "So Piers headed for the waterfall. He ran into Jack and me on our way back, then some of the others came out of hiding and told us about Roscoe."

"Is he alive?" Kitarna looked to Gabe, dreading the answer but needing to know.

He shrugged. "I don't know. Jack said he found drag marks on the bank, but no sign of Roscoe. He asked the others to search for Solana and Lexi. We set off after you."

"The native could have taken Roscoe. I saw him from the raft." She gripped the stretcher with both hands afraid she might drop it.

"Look!" whispered Gabe. "It's the native."

They all stopped to stare at the lone man watching them as he paddled his canoe down the middle of the river. Baskets of fruit sat on a bamboo shelf fitted most of the way along the canoe, leaving enough space for the native who wore Roscoe's pack.

Kitarna gasped. "That's the native I saw near the estuary. What's he doing with Roscoe's pack?"

"Natives are very proud people," whispered Gabe. "He would not steal the pack from a dying man. Look how low the canoe sits. I think Roscoe is under the fruit and the native is taking him to the nearest mission."

The native raised one hand before continuing to paddle down the river.

"I hope you're right." Kitarna blinked away tears. "No one would think to stop and search a native on his way to market."

They continued, panting. Jack was no lightweight. His stillness worried Kitarna. The group's endurance and survival depended very much on Jack's ability to defend them.

~ 21 ~

Darkness had fallen by the time they reached camp, and although Jack had regained consciousness and insisted on walking, he looked to be in pain. To Kitarna's frustration, no one had gone in search of Lexi and Solana. They were alone in the jungle and to make matters worse, no one could confirm if the native had taken Roscoe.

Leaving Ahmed and Piers to stitch Jack's head, Kitarna checked on Doris, bathing her flushed face and holding her hand until her own back ached. When Juliette came to relieve her, Kitarna crept over to Jack who had fallen asleep. She picked up her bloodied shirt and pulled on her headlamp to search the ground. Thousands of flies covered a large patch where Roscoe had been shot. Drag marks led to the estuary. Had he been dragged this far and loaded onto a canoe, or had something much stronger taken him under the giant water lilies?

Standing by the edge, exhausted and laden with guilt, she sank to her knees to wash the blood from her shirt. People were dead, dying, seriously injured and lost through no fault of their own. With no military helicopters or rescue planes crisscrossing the sky, she had to face facts. The plane had been brought down on purpose, but had it been so *El Jaguar* could retrieve Lexi or kidnap Bernie, and if so, why? Could it be the ransom money or some other reason?

Raised voices drew her attention to the group huddled round a small fire. They were arguing whether to stay or to set sail immediately. Most agreed with Robert, that if they paddled all night, tomorrow they'd be far enough down river that a rescue plane might spot them. Only Ahmed mentioned looking for Lexi and Solana. Juliette and Piers confirmed Doris wouldn't last the night. No one conferred with Jack, as the sedative Piers had given him held him in a deep sleep. To Kitarna's astonishment an argument broke out whether to leave the dying woman.

She pulled up her tank top and wiped her eyes and nose. The time had come to add her voice. She would not desert any member of this group and neither would Jack. If Doris died, she would be buried with dignity, not left to the scavengers.

"I say we leave," called Robert.

"Wait." Kitarna jogged over and faced the six people who looked to her expectantly. "Whatever you decide, Jack is staying here. Doris will have a proper burial. When Jack wakes, I know he will back me up in looking for Lexi and Solana."

Victoria scowled. "Jack is in no condition to go trekking. Stay if you must, but he should come with us."

Like a bubbling volcano waiting to blow its top, Kitarna stood her ground and glowered at the self-centered bitch. "Jack can't defend you against mercenaries, or a caiman if it rams the raft. He's not up to swimming or running, and he'd never leave anyone to die or perish in the jungle. Jack stays here with me."

"We can't stay here," snapped Robert. "Our priority and yours should be getting out of this godforsaken jungle and sending help back for the others. Doris won't know, and she'll be protected in the zipped tent until the authorities find her."

"He's right." Juliette squeezed Kitarna's hand. "Jack could develop a fever, and Doris is beyond our help. We don't know where to look for Solana and Lexi, so it's best the rest of us leave tonight."

"I'm staying here with Jack." Kitarna held her hand up as Gabe went to speak. "I know how to treat fever. If Jack woke up and discovered you'd taken him and left the others, he'd likely drown the lot of you. So go, but you're not taking him."

She stalked across to a tree, picked up the rifle and machete then sat beside Jack. "I will shoot anyone who tries."

"You are a brave woman, Kitarna Ashford." Ahmed stood and dusted off his trousers. "I will stay, but once Jack wakes, I am leaving. With luck Solana and Lexi will come back in the morning."

"Thank you." Kitarna sniffed and blinked away her tears of gratefulness. "I appreciate your kindness."

Piers ran his hands through his hair, shifting from foot to foot. "We will leave you the first aid satchel and two hammocks. And send help as soon as we can."

"Thank you, Piers." She held onto the rifle as the others packed a frond basket with fruit and took all the water bottles. As they were about to leave, Gabe ambled over.

"Please reconsider, *señorita*. It is very dangerous here for you. We should stay together as a group. The mercenaries would never believe we have made it this far, so the river will be safe."

"Thank you for your concern, Gabe, but I'm staying here with Jack."

Ahmed helped pushed the raft into the estuary. He stood beside Kitarna as the other five paddled away. She hoped with all her heart they made it, and that no harm befell Ahmed and Jack by staying.

Once the others were well away, Kitarna checked on Jack and Doris, sponging both their faces. Then she donned her rucksack and headlamp, picked up a large stick and put Jack's knife in a basket.

"Ahmed, when Jack wakes give him water. I'm going to draw some sap from a *sangre de drago* tree. The red sap is known as dragon's blood because of its color and ability to heal wounds. There is a tree near the waterfall. I also need some *icoja* bark. The alcoholic maceration is good for treating fever and cuts. Can you watch over Doris too?"

"You shouldn't leave camp alone."

"I'll be fine." Switching on the headlamp, she ran for the narrow animal trail.

Not far from the waterfall, two *sangre de drago* trees stood side-by-side almost smothered in strangler vines. She worked fast, cutting into young limbs to fill several specimen jars.

Thunder boomed in the distance. With all the

usual chirping, rustling and trilling, she hadn't paid attention to the faint rumbling. She would need somewhere dry and sheltered to light a fire. She hoped she'd made the right decision to keep Jack and Doris with her.

Picking her way warily, Kitarna thumped the ground with her stick and wove around low-hanging branches to avoid any chance encounter with snakes. Seeing the other tree she needed, she stripped off several pieces of *icoja* bark and headed back to camp.

"Ahmed, it's going to rain. We should move Jack and Doris behind the waterfall."

He looked up from where he sat beside Jack, his eyes shrouded in despair. "This jungle is a death trap."

She ran to Jack's side, praying she wouldn't find his eyes lifeless. His eyelids were closed, but his color looked good. "Ahmed, what is it?"

"Doris passed away." He gripped one fist in the other. "She was a nice lady, and so looking forward to exploring this country with her friend."

Kitarna's legs wobbled as she sank to the ground, her gaze locked on Jack's rugged face. A wayward lock falling across his forehead, his bristly, ginger whiskers sprouting all over his jaw, his thick eyebrows and the straight edge of his regal nose, those full sensual lips.

"I liked Doris too." She took several deep breaths. "How about we wrap her in my hammock and bury her near the bromeliads by the waterfall?"

"She'd like that."

Kitarna glanced up as a jagged streak of lightning snaked across the black sky, illuminating the canopy.

Predators came out to hunt at night and if Jack got wet, he might catch a chill. "Will you help me move Jack behind the waterfall? Once he's settled we can take care of Doris."

"Of course."

Taking the lighter end, Kitarna held the stretcher behind her and, with the beam from her headlamp, picked the easiest path through the forest. It was slow going, exhausting and a killer on her exhausted body, but eventually they made it up the rocks and behind the waterfall. Once she had Jack settled on his side in the sleeping bag, she smeared dragon sap over his stitches, then set about lighting a fire.

Ahmed picked up the empty stretcher. "If you could wrap Doris, I will make a shovel and dig her grave." He trudged out of the cavern.

Kitarna set up her miniature gas burner and brewed the *icoja* bark in her camp pot. Setting it aside to cool, she leaned over Jack and touched her lips to his. "Rest, my courageous lion. I need you by my side."

He didn't stir.

Sighing, she went to help Ahmed stretcher Doris to her temporary resting place surrounded by the bromeliads she'd loved so much.

The storm broke as Kitarna climbed back up the rocks, so weary she could barely keep her eyes open. Her parents and colleagues would have a fit if they saw her jagged fingernails clogged with dirt, and her sweat-matted hair clinging to her scalp, or knew she'd dug a grave. Such things were beyond their comprehension. With a last-ditch effort, she ignored her aching back and staggered around the gush of water, her headlamp illuminating the cavern.

"Here, have some fruit." Ahmed eased past, and placed a woven lopsided, basket of bananas and figs in her filthy hands. "Sit down before you fall down."

"Thank you, Ahmed. You should get some sleep, I'll look after Jack tonight."

He nodded then arranged Roscoe's sleeping bag along the back wall. After eating some fruit, he crawled into it, falling asleep instantly.

Edging closer to the unbroken jet of invigorating water, Kitarna scrubbed her hands and face, cleaned her filthy nails as best she could then dunked her head under the spray. The shock was enough to recoup much needed energy.

Every muscle ached, her eyes were gritty, and she'd lost her hair tie. Her back screamed from supporting Jack's neck as she squeezed droplets of the fever-reducing potion onto his tongue. Her heart wept that he might succumb to fever because of a drug lord's greed to ransom Bernie. Taking her bolero, she held it under the spray then squeezed out the cool water and wiped her face.

Her mother would be appalled to know the expensive wrap had been used as a bark sieve for an Australian sniper, who had made love to her daughter on a cave floor deep in the Amazon jungle. *At least my hands and face are clean.* She bit her lip, holding in a hysterical laugh. This wasn't the time to freak out.

Reaching for Solana's black satchel, she dug

through the contents hoping to find a candy bar or chocolate, anything with a little sugar in it. No luck. Instead she found a make-up purse, toiletries, headache tablets and a pack of moist wipes. They were handy, as her own had been used by the ladies as toilet tissues.

A foolscap sheet with names on it caught her eye. The passenger manifest.

Adjusting her headlamp, she ran her gaze down the list, stopping at two names that had been highlighted. Bernadette and Kitarna Ashford. The sheet dropped from her stiff fingers. Solana works for *El* Jaguar.

Knowing the plane had been brought down because of her and Bernie would have to be dealt with later. Solana had Lexi and she would bring the mercenaries back here. Andrés Pérez couldn't be *El* Jaguar, or he would have boasted of it, but he would want revenge on Jack.

She prayed for Jack to recover quickly and that Lexi and Bernie were safe, and nothing happened to Ahmed because he'd stayed here. She had so much more she needed to pray for, but her brain would not cooperate.

Thunder boomed and crackled above. The downpour and cascading water obscured the usual rainforest racket. Surrendering to the pull of fatigue, she climbed into Jack's sleeping bag and, spooning her body to his, pulling his arm across her waist. She'd have a catnap then check on Jack again.

# 22

This had to be the motherfucker of all hangovers. Whooshing and piercing whistles competed as sharp splinters dug into his scalp. Wherever he'd passed out, it was as black as the devil's soul and like lying on bloody rock.

He registered the warm, familiar body curled against his chest and memory flooded back. His crushing fear he wouldn't find Kitarna, the elation and alarm at seeing her on a flimsy raft—with no protection against the watching caiman.

He'd burned to pop Brett, but a splash would provoke the caiman, yet waiting could result in them making for the opposite bank. Jack had known the river widened round the next bend in a big sweeping curve, so he'd had to come up with a plan fast, and it had almost worked. Kitarna had seen him and distracted Brett, momentarily.

Touching the back of his skull, he winced. *Brett's aim had been way off, but Jack hadn't counted on a wayward paddle.* He did a gentle exploration, detecting six stitches. Better than having a bullet in his brain. He remembered walking but was still fuzzy as to who fished him out of the river. Kitarna lay safe in his arms, but where were they?

Turning his head carefully, he realised the whooshing was water. They were in the cavern behind the waterfall, but why? And what of the disgusting taste in his mouth? Sledgehammers pounded inside his skull and he groaned.

"Jack!" Her abrupt movement jerked him.

"Fuck." Closing his eyes, he breathed through the pain.

"Darling, I'm so happy you're awake. How do you feel?"

"Like someone hit me with an axe."

"We have to watch for infection and fever." She shuffled away from him.

Light blazed.

He jerked away, further intensifying the hammers crashing about in his skull.

"Sorry." She pointed her headlamp away. "How do you feel?"

"Like shit. Why are we in here? Where is everyone?"

"Ahmed is asleep behind you. He is the only one who stayed to help me. Solana took Lexi and ran off, and the others have taken the raft and gone for help."

"They left without us?"

"They wanted to take you and leave Doris, so I threatened to shoot them. And they weren't prepared to search for Solana and Lexi. I hope I did the right thing."

"Yeah, you did. Am I right in thinking Doris died?"

"Yes. I helped Ahmed bury her."

He nodded then winced. "At first light, we'll look for Roscoe, and the others."

"It's possible the native removed him in a canoe."

"That makes sense. Roscoe had been dragged to the edge, but not by a caiman. I saw a deep groove in the bank and suspected a small boat or canoe."

"When Brett forced me to go with him, I saw the native watching. And we saw him again, paddling down river, just before you regained consciousness. Gabe thinks the native might be taking Roscoe to a mission."

Jack pushed himself to a sitting position, grimacing at the mounting pain. "How bad was Roscoe's wound?"

"I'm not sure. He had blood all over his chest, but he spoke to me."

"What did he say?"

"He wanted me to...*help* you get Lexi back to her mother."

"Help me, or tell me?" Jack raised an eyebrow. "You are not going anywhere near those mercenaries, darlin'."

"You are awake!" Ahmed crawled over on his hands and knees. "I am very happy to see you recovered, Jack."

"Thanks, Ahmed. I should have thanked you and Gabe for pulling me out of the river. Sorry, I wasn't with it earlier."

"Kitarna rescued you from under the water and got you on the raft, as the caiman attacked Brett."

Jack looked at Kitarna, kneeling beside him, her hand in his. "Thank you, kitten. I was supposed to rescue you."

"Thank you for coming after me. I've discovered something you and Ahmed should know." She handed him a sheet of paper. "I found this in Solana's bag."

He picked up the headlamp and glanced at the list of names, noting two had been highlighted. "Solana must be allied with whoever brought the plane down." He passed the list and lamp to Ahmed. "*El* Jaguar is probably stalking Kitarna's sister with the intention of demanding a ransom. Solana's job could have been to identify their target so the mercenaries could kill the rest of the passengers, leaving no witnesses."

"Why your sister?" Ahmed frowned at Kitarna. "Who are you?"

"My father is a United States governor, and my mother is now married to an English attaché in Paris. Our American grandparents are wealthy philanthropists and the English ones are aristocrats. *El* Jaguar could likely ask for millions. I'm so sorry."

Kitarna got further out of his reach every day. Jack folded the list then sealed it in one of her zip lock bags.

"Here, put these in too." She handed him three grape-sized tablets. "They are what Marley and Brett died for."

Ahmed turned to Jack. "Do you suppose Solana intends to return the child to *El* Jaguar and lead him here to collect Kit and execute the rest of us?"

"That's my guess, unless we can find Solana and Lexi first. We do however, have to leave this camp at first light."

"I do not think you are up to trekking." Ahmed scowled. "As a doctor, my advice would be to rest for several days."

"You're right, I'm not up to trekking. I need to hijack a boat. Once we're on board I'll radio for help. The sooner I find Lexi, the sooner we get out of here."

Ahmed shook his head. "I stayed because it knew it wrong to leave Kit on her own with you and Doris so ill. I had hoped Solana and Lexi would come back, but knowing Solana plans to betray us, it would be madness to go back up river."

"Neither of you are coming with me," said Jack.

"No!" Kitarna glared at him. "Everything has happened because *El* Jaguar wants Bernie and probably me too. I will not let you go alone."

"Not negotiable, kitten. Mercenaries have no honor. Even if your parents paid the ransom, there is little likelihood they would release you. If I don't catch up with Lexi, I'll have to gain access to the village, or *El* Jaguar's compound."

"This is madness, Jack."

"Getting in will be difficult. Getting out with a child will be a nightmare. Bottom line—I won't risk your safety." He looked to Ahmed. "I suggest you build a raft. Then you and Kitarna travel downriver before dawn breaks. Find a safe place to hide and only travel by night. Stay close to shore in case you have to avoid mercenaries."

Kitarna lifted her chin defiantly. "If *El* Jaguar wants me, that means *I* am your best chance to find Lexi. I can give myself up and you can follow me."

"Not happening." He winced as the vice around his skull tightened. "I can't help cut the balsa, my head would explode."

Kitarna rummaged through Solana's bag. "These tablets contain codeine. A couple will ease your pain."

She squeezed two into his hand. "Swallow them with this."

One whiff had him drawing back. "What is it?"

"I stewed *icoja* bark. It will ward off fever, and it's good for healing."

"You're the boss." He popped the pills and swallowed the liquid. It tasted as bad as it smelt. "Once the pain's gone, I'll see you off." Carefully, he eased down, grateful when Ahmed left with the lamp, leaving him in darkness.

"Stubborn lion." Kitarna wiggled into his arms.

How much longer he could claim that privilege he couldn't guess, but he'd cherish every second while it lasted.

The next time he woke a small amount of natural light showed he was alone. A worry since he normally woke at the slightest sound or movement. His head injury must indeed be substantial. The sledgehammers had eased to a tolerable throbbing, so he downed another couple of tablets with a new batch of warm bark liquid.

A torn off piece of paper had been propped against Kitarna's rucksack. He smiled as he read the message.

*Good morning, sleepyhead, I've gone to pick fruit. Don't forget to smear dragon sap on your stitches. Trust me, it has amazing healing powers.*

"I trust you, kitten." He picked up the specimen jar and peered at the bright red matter inside. "Dragon sap?" He applied the stuff then wrapped his head in a bandage left beside the jar. Flies would be his worst enemy if he left the wound uncovered.

Climbing out of the sleeping bag, he washed his

face. Time to get back to the land of the living. This was day five in the jungle, and if they weren't rescued today, he could kiss the shack goodbye. Strangely that didn't bother him. There were other shacks and other beaches, but only one Kitarna Ashford. She'd become his priority, along with returning Lexi to her mother and finding Roscoe, dead or alive.

He rolled up the sleeping bag and pushed it into her rucksack along with the billycan, a portable gas stove and her rolled-up tent. His own pack and jacket were lying at the bottom of the Putumayo River, which pissed him off big time.

After coating the *urucu* dye over his face, neck and arms, Jack crammed the jars in the rucksack, slung it over his shoulder then picked up the rifle. Ahmed and Kitarna should have left before dawn, the note suggested otherwise.

Ducking past the flow of water, he studied the surrounding forest. Leaves sparkled with droplets, and the rocks and ground were wet. Parrots were back in their tree, surrounded by vivid bromeliads. Close to the spectacular array he noticed a raised mound of freshly turned dirt and a roughly twined-cross covered in orchids. His throat tightened as remorse settled heavily on his shoulders. Another death he should have prevented.

Aside from the chirping, whistles and screeching within the canopy, he could hear a voice humming behind the tree.

"Bipperty-doo-dah, bipperty-ay, God help us on this beautiful day. We're here in the jungle in the middle of May. Bipperty-doo-dah, bipperty-ay."

The lyrics were interesting, and she sounded as

cheery as the feathered legion above, but singing, even softly wasn't a good idea. He wondered if she'd eaten fermented fruit. Circling the bromeliads, he found her picking figs. "Hey, bipperty, you can sing when we're safe, but not here."

"Good morning, my handsome lion. Would you like breakfast?"

"Thanks." He took a handful of figs. "Where's Ahmed?"

"He finished his raft and set sail. As soon as he reaches the mission, he will alert the authorities and send help. So, it's just the two of us."

"Damn it, Kitarna. I wanted you to go with him." He raked his hands over his face. "I can't leave you here alone."

"No, you can't." She stretched up and kissed him. "We're a team."

The low purr of an engine caught his attention. "Kitten, a boat's coming along the estuary. We need to find cover."

"Shouldn't we hide behind the waterfall?"

"No, in case it's mercenaries. If they've picked up the others, they might know about the cavern." He veered to the left, away from the animal trail and closer to the estuary where giant water lilies covered the still water. A grove of golden bamboo blocked their path. Taking the machete from her, Jack sawed through the bottom of the bamboo, creating a narrow path almost all the way through the thicket.

Sweat trickled down his face and back, his skull vibrated as though a dozen castanets clanged inside, but that sixth sense he relied on screamed at him to hurry. He guided Kitarna inside the tight channel and followed, driving the last few rods into the ground, sealing the entrance.

They were cocooned inside the copse with little chance of being discovered. Lifting the rifle, he used the slightest amount of pressure to lever the stems apart, giving him a glimpse of their old camp and the estuary.

An army-green, flat bottom boat with machine guns mounted on the bow and stern putted into view. "It's not a rescue boat."

A quick head count showed four men in army fatigues and Solana, who held her hand over Lexi's mouth. *Does she think we wouldn't hear an engine?*

Even from this distance, the stiffness in Lexi's arms and legs proclaimed her terror. Surrounded by armed men, the innocent, vulnerable kid had to be terrified. Fury and contempt rose in equal measure.

No way, would he allow those bastards to hurt the little girl.

～ 23 ～

Spluttering, the boat drifted into the bank. The mercenary Jack had knocked out the evening their plane crashed, jumped clear. He carried another high quality automatic rifle. Along the lower left side of his face, a jutted line of stitches covered a raised welt. *He'll want my guts for garters.*

"Can you see anything," whispered Kitarna, attempting to peer around him.

He gently pushed her back. "Four mercenaries, including the man who confronted you."

"Andrés Pérez."

"Hmm. Solana and Lexi are there too. I can't risk them getting caught in the cross-fire, which means if they think we are close, they will use Lexi to force us to surrender."

"You can't shoot anyone in front of Lexi." She leaned against his shoulder, stretching up on her toes. "What are they doing?"

"Looking for an advantage. Shush." He studied Pérez as the man did a three-sixty-degree turn, his gaze wandering from the ground to the surrounding foliage.

"They must have left before the storm." Pérez spoke in Spanish, which thanks to Jack's years in the SAS, he was fluent in, along with Arabic and Afghani Persian.

Solana called out, also in Spanish. "Ross Dalton would not leave his granddaughter willingly, so he must be dead. I told you Jack Callaghan would go after Brett and the girl." She jumped out of the boat, dragging Lexi with her and switched to English. "What do you think, Alexandra? Have they all deserted you?"

"No! Kit and Jack would never leave me. They're searching for me right now, you stupid lady." She slumped to the ground, sobbing into her hands.

Kitarna wiggled beside Jack, snapping a piece of bamboo under her foot.

The man behind Lexi twisted, his hand dropping to a gun holstered to his thigh.

Jack raised the rifle, scoped his target's forehead. If the man reached for Lexi, Pérez would eat the next bullet.

Kitarna's breath came in short gasps. He could almost hear the cogs whirring in her brain, seeking an alternate way to save Lexi without exposing their hideout.

"Span out and search the area," yelled Pérez. "The child might be right."

Two mercenaries trudged along the animal trail, passing within four feet of the bamboo grove.

Jack tracked their footsteps, releasing his breath when they kept moving.

Pérez paced back and forth, the rifle hanging across his chest. "I am disappointed in you, *señorita*. You have failed *El* Jaguar."

"No, I have not, Andrés." Leaving Lexi, she marched over to Pérez, her hands on her hips. "I fulfilled my instructions by confirming Bernadette Ashford was on the plane. It is I who discovered her younger sister accompanied the archeologist. You and your men messed up."

Without a tripod, Jack's arms were beginning to ache, but he maintained his stance. A large proportion of canopy blocked the morning light, casting a protective shadow over the grove of bamboo, an upshot he welcomed. The man beside Lexi kept his hand by his thigh, his gaze remained riveted on their clump of bamboo. If he could see the rifle, why hadn't he alerted Pérez?

Jack's interest grew as he noted the man's cleanly shaved face and pressed clothing. He didn't reach for the gun, and although his gaze shifted to Pérez and Solana, his lips were moving as if whispering to Lexi. Could this be the undercover operative?

Solana gave a shaky laugh. "I have not failed *El* Jagua*r*. He will reward me for discovering his granddaughter was also on the plane. Not lost by natives in the jungle, but snatched by an Australian called Jack Callaghan."

*Fuck.* Jack scoped Pérez.

"Are you positive Callaghan is the man who also attacked me?"

"I think so. He killed two of your mercenaries for attempting to rape the blonde woman. From what her boyfriend told me, Jack is very handy with a knife. I saw him shoot five bullets into a caiman. He wrestled and stabbed another.

"Describe him." Pérez had his hands clenched as he stared at Solana.

"He's ruggedly handsome, six-foot-four, and only interested in one woman, even though I made it blatantly clear he could have me." She huffed.

Jack bent close to Kitarna's ear. "She can't hold a candle to you, kitten."

"Does she have green eyes and red hair?" Pérez began pacing again.

"Yes, and she's no fool. Kitarna Ashford knows what is and isn't safe to eat."

Jack checked on the man with Lexi. He had crouched down to wash his hands in the estuary. For some reason, Lexi had taken off her shoes.

One mercenary came pounding back. "Lieutenant, I found a cave behind a waterfall with scorch marks on the rocks, and a fresh grave."

"That will be Doris," called Solana. "She was bitten by a pit viper."

"Or it could be Ross Dalton." Pérez prowled to the dead campfire. "So, they slept in the cave last night and left this morning. Radio the other boats and tell them to search further down river. Make sure they understand Kitarna Ashford and Jack Callaghan are to be captured alive. Let's see how long the Australian lasts after being dropped into a pit of stinging ants. The redhead is mine."

"That's out of the question." Solana stalked after Pérez, who had stopped to sift through the wet ashes with his boot. "*El* Jaguar will insist you bring him both sisters. Once he doesn't need them, you can ask for Kitarna. And *El* Jaguar will want to personally punish the man who stole his granddaughter. If you refuse, I will inform him of your defiance."

*Silly woman.* Jack lowered his rifle.

"No, you won't, *señorita.*"

In one fluid motion, Pérez drew his handgun and fired, hitting Solana above the left eye, and sending her flying backward, her body landing by the estuary.

Jack covered Kitarna's mouth, cutting off her scream. He held her tight, rubbing her spine in soothing strokes. He should have killed Pérez when he'd had the chance.

"Where is the child?" Pérez marched across to the estuary, shouldering the other man aside. "Where did she go?"

*Shit.* Jack released Kitarna and lifted the rifle to scan the bank. Lexi had vanished.

"I don't know, Andrés." The man looked baffled. "She was sitting on the ground beside me as quiet as a mouse." The man spoke calmly; his voice devoid of humility. Whoever he was, he didn't answer to Pérez.

"Perhaps after seeing her grandfather shot and hearing the others have deserted her, the child drowned herself."

Pérez snarled. "*El* Jaguar will want my head for this."

"He doesn't know you had the child, so her disappearance will not be attributed to you."

"True, and my men are loyal." Pérez gazed about, then snapped his fingers. "Come, she is of no importance. We will continue down river. Stay alert. I want Kitarna Ashford and Jack Callaghan. We must remove all witnesses." He strode to the boat.

"Yes, Andrés." The other man glanced toward their hiding place before boarding the boat.

Kitarna whimpered. "Jack, we need to find Lexi."

"Wait. That guy could be the operative who told Roscoe where to find Lexi."

"Really?"

"Yeah, and he just helped Lexi escape."

"But where can she go without shoes?"

"I think he suspects we're here and has told her to hide, or it's a very clever trap." Jack resumed his watch.

Two mercenaries picked up Solana's body. With barely a splash they let her sink into the murky depths then jumped on board the boat. Its motor roared to life.

The operative cast a furtive glance over his shoulder, not at the bamboo grove, but up the small inlet. He gripped a side rail as the boat zoomed away.

Lexi's sneakers had been left on the bank.

"Let's go, but if you hear anything, run along the animal track. I will catch up." Jack removed the loose sticks and eased out.

Kitarna barged round him, sprinting to the estuary. "Lexi, where are you?"

"Here." Lexi's muffled voice seemed to come from the water.

Jack slid to a stop beside Kitarna, his gaze searching the thickly packed, giant lilies covering the surface. They stretched as far as he could see. To the right the lilies had been torn apart by the mercenaries' metal boat, creating a narrow channel leading to the river. Opposite, the bank rose steeply, impossible for a small child to climb up to the overhanging bracken ferns. "Lexi?"

"Jack!" A water lily flipped over, revealing the little girl, spread-eagled on another underneath. "You didn't leave me."

Jack met Kitarna's wide gaze and laughed. "No wonder Pérez and his men couldn't find her, she's a lily fairy."

Lexi giggled. "I'm not a lily fairy. The man told me to hide here. He said you were close, but I had to stay quiet until the boat went away."

"He told you to hide?" Kitarna chewed her lip, glancing down the estuary. "It could be a trap."

"No, it's not." Lexi scrambled up and ran across the lilies, grinning from ear to ear. "He's the man who came to the village and told me I would be rescued soon."

"Do you know his name?" Jack lifted her onto the bank.

"No, but he said if I ever saw him, I had to pretend I didn't know him, so that's what I did. Where's horrible Solana?"

"Gone. I'm so glad to see you, sweetie." Kitarna hugged Lexi. "We didn't know what happened to you."

"Solana said Brett wanted to shoot me, but I told her Jack wouldn't let him and we had to save you. She kept pulling me along, so I bit her hand and ran."

Jack squatted in front of her. "Lexi, how did you end up with those men?"

"I climbed a really high tree and you'll never guess what I saw?" She didn't wait for an answer. "The river curving like a giant snake, and lots of trees, but there were no houses anywhere, not even for as far as I could see. And I shared a branch with my favorite animal. A *kinkajou*, this big." She held her hands a foot apart. "It let me give it bits of fruit."

He was about to hurry her along when Kitarna spoke. "That's wonderful. Put your shoes on as you talk. What happened next?"

Lexi pulled on her sneakers. "I saw a black monkey with fuzzy ears in another tree, but the biggest eagle I ever saw swooped down from the sky and took it. Its wings were bigger than this." She held her arms out wide. "Its talons were longer than my hands. I cried for the monkey."

"I've seen a few harpy eagles flying around. What happened then?" Jack's patience had waned. They needed to get away from here.

"It got dark, but no matter how much Solana yelled I wouldn't come down, not even when the thunder woke me. You should have seen the flashes."

Jack rubbed his eyes. They were well hidden here in the estuary, but they couldn't hang around too long. "Tell us about the men on the boat, Lexi."

"I woke up when a boat came along. Solana started screaming again. The nice man climbed up. He promised to send me home, but it had to be our secret, because Andrés is second in command to *El* Jaguar."

Kitarna raised an eyebrow at Jack. "Looks like you were right. He must be the undercover operative."

"I think so, but he won't blow his cover to help us. Lexi, we need to find Roscoe and get you both on a plane to Florida."

"And what do you plan to do with me, Jack?" Kitarna had her arms crossed under her breasts and chin tilted stubbornly. It was a wonder she wasn't tapping her boot.

"I plan to get you home safely too, kitten."

"I'm not ready to go home. We have a rendezvous, remember."

"Very well. Let's make for the river. Dive for cover if you hear anything. The mercenaries are searching for us, and they're not likely to give up."

# ∽ 24 ∼

Carrying a sturdy stick and the first aid satchel, Kitarna trooped behind Lexi and Jack. It bothered her that he insisted on wearing her rucksack and leading the way, as every chop of the machete had to be akin to shooting nails into his hard, stubborn head. By his silence and drawn face, he suffered big time.

Back at the camp, she'd kept Lexi near the estuary, and listening for any approaching boats, while Jack retrieved Solana and wrapped her in a space blanket. He buried her alongside Doris. Digging the grave would have exacerbated his headache, and after walking three hours in suffocating humidity, he had to be fatigued and hungry. She definitely had no energy left, and by Lexi's hunched shoulders and dragging steps, she felt the same.

They came to a tall clump of large banana like leaves and brilliant red bracts.

"These are the *Zingiberales*, or ginger, we used on the fish a few days ago." Kitarna picked a few, jumping when a red-eyed tree frog hopped out of one.

"My legs are tired, and I'm hungry," whined Lexi. "Can we make camp?"

"No." Jack tripped, shouldering a tree. "We have to keep going."

"Jack?" Kitarna sidestepped Lexi and gripped his arm. "Stop, you're pushing your body and us too hard."

He clutched his thigh, swaying. "We can't stop."

"Yes, we can. Are you cramping?"

"Yeah."

"I'm an idiot. The high humidity reduces our ability to sweat. Cramps are a side effect. We should have been taking salt tablets. I've got some in my emergency kit." She turned him around so she could dig in the small pocket of her rucksack. In her haste she dropped the kit, spilling the contents over the ground.

Lexi scrambled to help pick everything up. "Why do you have dental floss in your emergency kit."

"Aside from cleaning my teeth, it can be useful for tying things, or even as a fishing line, which will come in handy today. My sister helped me put this together, in case I got lost while she worked on a dig."

"What's a dig?"

"An ancient site. My sister is an archeologist." Kitarna gave Lexi a salt tablet, swallowed one herself and passed Jack two. They downed them with water from her hydration pack. "That should ward off the cramps for a while."

Jack staggered. "God almighty, my head hurts."

"You've had a head injury and your pupils are dilated. We're making camp here, and you're going to rest for a couple of hours." She looked around, irritated to find no convenient logs or fallen trees to sit him on.

"Gotta keep going, don't wanna be put in a pit of giant ants." He leaned against a tree and slid to the ground. "They've got razor sharp jaws, and the poisonous sting is worse than a bee. Ten bites will kill a man." His chin slumped to his chest.

*Oh no! He's delirious! His temperature must have spiked.* She crouched beside Jack, easing the rucksack off his shoulders then pulled the packet of headache pills from her pocket. "Here, take more of these." She broke the seals and placed two on his tongue, pressing the drinking tube between his lips. "Suck."

He did, closing his eyes.

She kissed his whiskery cheek. "Rest and let me take care of you."

"Sounds good."

Tears ran down Lexi's cheeks as she squatted on the other side of Jack. "Is he going to be okay?"

"Of course. He's as strong as a bull." Kitarna prayed she was right. "Help me clear the ground so we can pitch the tent. Jack will be safe inside while we catch some fish."

"Roscoe's going to be all right too, isn't he?"

"I hope so, sweetie."

Lexi picked up the machete beside Jack. "What will we use for hooks and bait?"

"Safety pins, and we can dig for worms." Placing the rucksack beside Jack, Kitarna pulled out the tent. Using the machete, she dragged the leaf mulch away in case they were setting up on ants or termite nests. She rolled out the tent and Lexi helped her erect it then they spread out the sleeping bag.

Jack was harder to shift, mumbling about bazaars and carnage as he crawled into the tent. Once they had him settled, Kitarna unwrapped the bandage and smeared more dragon sap over the stitches before rewrapping his head.

Screwing up her face, Lexi leaned over Jack. "What are those things on Jack's neck?"

Kitarna took a closer look. "Ticks! They could be all over us." Kitarna whipped off her bucket cap and ran her fingers over her neck and through her hair. She found one of the nasty little bloodsuckers behind her right ear. Opening her shirt, she checked her chest and armpits, finding another one. "We can cover them in sap and they will drop off. Let me check you, sweetie."

"Ugh." Lexi dragged off her cap and let Kitarna run her fingers over the short fuzz.

"None on your head. Take your shirt off and roll up your jeans."

Lexi had a tick on her shoulder and a leech on her ankle, which got a dose of salt. They used the dragon sap to get rid of the ticks. Jack had three on his head and two on his neck. He didn't stir as Kitarna removed them.

Sitting back on her heels, Lexi sighed. "No wonder he didn't feel well."

"Sleep will help. Let's get organized and catch some fish." Kitarna stowed her first-aid supplies in her rucksack then the left the tent.

Lexi stayed close, digging for worms with the machete while Kitarna set up her portable stove and stewed more *icoja* bark. The tent was well hidden from the river, but when they took their dental-floss line to the bank, Kitarna found a well-worn trail with human footprints.

"Come look," whispered Lexi, crouching and pointing down the bank.

Heart thumping, Kitarna squatted beside Lexi, breathing a sigh of relief when she sighted eight fat little animals drinking at the river edge. "They're capybara, a distant relative of the guinea pig. They're herbivores, so they won't hurt us. Oh, look."

White egrets and purple herons stalked through the shallow water on long stick-like legs, pecking up small fish. The array of color was magnificent. She edged off her rucksack and pulled out the camera.

Lexi gasped and pointed. "Giant otters."

They both sank lower, eyes wide with wonder as the family of seven frolicked among the herons. Two of the largest ran along the muddy edge, sniffing the ground and yapping like dogs. Another sat up on its haunches and ate a fish clutched between its front-webbed feet. Four others dived and cavorted, their heads popping up to check on each other.

Kitarna kept shooting photos until she spotted a caiman, weaving its way across the river. "Oh no."

The otters immediately took to the water, surrounding the five-foot predator, snapping at its tail and jumping on its back, pushing it under. The herons and capybara observed the disturbance with mild interest.

Fear for the otters had Kitarna biting her fingernails, but she needn't have worried, the otters chased the caiman away, ending the riverside entertainment.

Shaking her head, she nudged Lexi. "Here in the

Amazon, what astounds us is run-of-the-mill for the inhabitants. Let's catch a fish before any boats come along."

Twenty nervous minutes passed before they hooked a fish longer than Kitarna's arm. Copying Jack's methods, she scaled and gutted the fish and wrapped it in banana leaves. They built a small pit of river stones near the tent. It was a big risk lighting a fire, but Jack needed sustenance. She hoped the trail didn't get a lot of use, and Jack recovered quickly.

To her relief, he slept three hours then drank the billy of *icoja* liquid and ate a huge helping of ginger-seasoned fish.

"I feel much better. My stitches are pulling a little, but the headache is gone."

"Good." Kitarna pointed a finger at him. "You were covered in ticks. We're taking it slow from now on. The minute you notice pain, we stop and rest. Okay?"

"Yes, darlin'. I wouldn't dare argue with such a fine fisherman."

Lexi giggled. "Kit used the dental floss, a safety pin, and squiggly fat worms."

"She is a woman of many talents, Lexi."

They were telling him about the capybara and otters when he cocked his head. "Shush, I hear voices."

Their lighthearted moment vanished as all three looked through the forest toward the river. A group of naked natives wearing crowns of brilliant parrot, macaw and toucan feathers, walked in single file, heading up river.

"Get down," whispered Jack. "The ferns will hide us."

"What about the tent?" Kitarna fell to her stomach and wrapped her arm around Lexi, who scrambled between them.

"It blends with the vegetation. With luck, they won't look this way."

The closer the natives got, Kitarna realized their bodies were painted in red, purple, and black squiggles and lines. They wore twisted string round their hips, with a three-inch fringe covering the women's pubic area. Three men with missing teeth and weathered faces carried long bows and tapirs over their shoulders. Two teenage boys held spears and dead monkeys.

A couple of women carried babies in slings across their chests. All the females wore necklaces of seeds and slivers of wood through their pierced noses and lips. Feathers adorned their pierced ears. Four giggling girls, Kitarna guessed to be between eight and fifteen brought up the rear. The natives disappeared round the bend, their chattering fading until only rustling in the undergrowth and bird whistles filled the air.

Lexi whispered. "The girls think wearing feathers in their ears and pine needles in their lips and nose make them pretty. If a boy likes her and she agrees to be his future wife she hangs her hammock beside his."

Jack raised an eyebrow at Kitarna. "You're already sharing my hammock, so don't stick anything through your pretty nose and lips."

She couldn't hold in her grin. "As long as you don't wear a fringed apron." She covered Lexi's ears. "It wouldn't cover your...assets."

He replaced her hands as she pulled them away. "If you wore a 3-inch fringe, I'd have to chase you through the jungle."

"That's an idea. Would you swing on a vine like Tarzan?"

"I would if it meant getting you into my feathered bed, darlin'." Jack stood, holding out his hand for Kitarna to take. "I don't think they would have attacked us, but best to be cautious. Let's pack up. It looks like we're in for another thunderstorm. We'll take advantage of the native track, rather than slashing our way through jungle."

The storm hit two hours later, making it hard to hear approaching river craft. Several times a helicopter flew over the canopy, and twice they dived for cover when mercenary boats rounded a river bend. The up side was Kitarna managed to fill her hydration pack with fresh water, and she found guarana creeper. Its red seeds could be pounded into power to make a nutritious energy drink, so she filled a zip lock bag.

Eventually the rain stopped and as evening drew near they moved off the trail to make camp. Kitarna made up the energy drink and they drank it with the leftover fish. She'd also found some peach palm fruit lying at the base of a forty-foot tree. They were delicious, but climbing for more wasn't an option, given the razor-sharp spines that ringed the tree.

Since seeing the capybara and otters, Lexi had become a bundle of energy, running about photographing geckos, and humming birds with Kitarna's camera. She found a giant armadillo, and seven-inch beetle, and a monster caterpillar with fluffy, wispy, lime colored hair. It could have been Jurassic Park.

Discovering a log covered in blue morpho butterflies topped off Lexi's day. Kitarna managed to photograph the delighted little girl standing close to the oasis of shimmering, metallic shades of blue wings, before they became defensive, raising the mottled brown underside, to reveal a pattern that looked like black and yellow eyes.

Dusk was settling when everything suddenly went eerily silent. The nightly chorus they'd grown familiar with stopped, then a high-piercing yowl made them jump. A deep, rumbling growl, answered it.

"Damn, I wish had my night vision goggles." Jack picked up the rifle, braced his feet wide and raised his rifle toward the disturbance. "Get inside the tent."

The caterwauling escalated to a deafening pitch. Fear gripped Kitarna as she urged Lexi inside. "I recognize the jaguar, Jack, but what's that other animal?"

"A possum or some sort of wild cat. It doesn't stand a chance against the jaguar. Close the zip, and don't open it until I tell you."

~ 25 ~

Kitarna helped Lexi into the sleeping bag. "It'll be okay, sweetie. Jack will protect us." She picked up the machete and crawled to the flap.

He hadn't moved. "Shut the zip, Kitarna. I'll be…"

A sickening squeal cut Jack off. A golden jaguar with black markings leaped through the bracken, a small cat of similar coloring, hanging limply from its jaws. The jaguar stopped and stared at them.

Jack fired, blasting bark from a tree beside the massive cat. It flinched and bounded away in the opposite direction. "Phew. I only have one bullet left, and I didn't want to kill the animal."

"Will it come back?" Kitarna scrambled to her feet.

"No, he's got what he came for. I don't understand why the smaller cat didn't takeoff or climb a tree. It could have gone much higher than the heavier jaguar."

"Is it safe to come out?" whispered Lexi.

"Yes, sweetie." Kitarna opened the flap. "Do you need to pee before bed?"

"Yes."

Jack frowned. "Give me the machete. I want to check something."

Lexi ran behind the tent, leaving Kitarna trying to watch the two of them at once. "What if the jaguar comes back, or it circles our camp?"

"I don't think it will." Jack poked about the ferns and palms then pushed further into a dense thicket, disappearing behind a tangle of vines.

A bird squawked, making Kitarna jump. Crickets and frogs started their trilling and croaking. The canopy above rustled and the night birds began chirping. It seemed the animals knew it was safe to come out again.

Lexi crept back, sliding her hand into Kitarna's. "What's he looking for?"

"I'm not sure."

Jack backed out of the vines and turned. He had the rifle strap slung over one shoulder and cradled a tiny ball of gold and black fluff. "This is the reason the small cat didn't run. She had a little one to protect."

"Can I hold it?" Lexi ran to Jack. "Did the jaguar get the mother?"

"I'm afraid so." He passed Lexi the tiny kitten. "She won't survive on her own."

"Can I see?" Kitarna stroked the big-eyed kitten. "A guide once explained the differences between ocelots, margays and oncillas, but they're all similar. I'm guessing this cutie is about five or six weeks old, and as there is only one kitten, and her mother wasn't very big, she is probably an oncilla."

"I want to take her home?" Lexi raised pleading eyes. "She will die here without me to look after her. Please, Kit."

"Lexi, this kitten is wild born. It would be wrong to domesticate her. I know she can't stay here, but she should be raised by a wildcat organization then released back into her natural environment."

"I guess so." Lexi stroked the kitten. "I'll look after her until we're rescued."

"That's a good girl." Kitarna knelt beside Lexi. "I know being kidnapped and hunted is scary, but you've experienced and done things in the Amazon rainforest that few people will ever do. Hopefully one day you'll become a spokeswoman for conserving the world's rainforests, and protecting the animals that live in them. How about I take a photo of you with the kitten, so you can show your friends when you go home?"

"Can you send me photos of the frogs and monkeys and otters?"

"Of course. I'll send you photos of *all* the plants and animals I've taken."

"Will you come visit me?"

"I'd love to."

Photographing Lexi and Jack with the kitten, and having Jack take pictures of her with Lexi, made Kitarna realize the bond between them would last a lifetime if allowed.

She handed the camera to Lexi. "I need a memento too."

While Lexi put the kitten inside the tent, Kitarna wrapped her arms round Jack's waist, and pressed against his chest. "You are an amazing man, and whether you believe it or not, you have captured my heart. I want a picture of the two of us, here in the rainforest to treasure for the rest of my life."

"So do I, darlin'." His arms tightened about her then he lowered his head, touched his lips to one corner of her mouth, and brushed kisses across her lips until she opened for him. He deepened the kiss, leisurely tangling with her tongue as heat built between them.

"I've got enough photos of you kissing, now you have to look at the camera."

They jerked apart, laughed and came together again, turning to Lexi. She took the photo then crawled inside the tent. A twig snapped.

Jack whirled round and reached for the rifle. "We've got company."

"Where?"

"River bank. Get Lexi and find somewhere to hide." He crept forward.

She lifted the flap and signaled Lexi forward, whispering, "Someone or something is on the river bank, so we're going to hide in the vines."

Lexi rolled her eyes. "Here we go again." She put the kitten inside her cap and clutched it to her chest.

Snatching her rucksack, Kitarna gripped Lexi's free hand and they ran behind a tree as wide as a car. The cloud cover had cleared, but the canopy screened most of the moonlight, only allowing thin slivers to light the forest floor. They crouched between two massive roots and waited. It was impossible to know where Jack or the intruder had gone.

Movement drew Kitarna's attention to a shaft of light above their heads. Curled about the thick branch, a pale-green emerald boa lifted its head to stare at her from big yellow eyes. Pulling Lexi close, she kept her gaze glued to the large snake. It really had turned into a day of spot the rare and exotic animal.

Five minutes passed before they heard Jack calling, "Ladies, you can come out now. Our visitor is Ahmed."

Kitarna peeped round the tree and saw Jack had her headlamp in his hand. He stood by the tent talking to Ahmed.

"Come on, Lexi, let's see what Ahmed has to say." Holding hands they tramped heavily over the soft earth, hoping to scare off any creepy crawlies.

"Ahmed, what are you doing here?"

"Hello, Kitarna. After I left you, I paddled for an hour until I found a safe place to hide. The mercenaries have been going up and down the river all day. They also have a small helicopter which flies low over the water. Once it became dark, I set off again. I was passing this place when I heard the gunshot and saw a jaguar streak along the bank. I wondered if you and Jack were here."

"Yes, and we have Lexi."

"Jack told me. I am glad to see you safe, Lexi."

"Thank you, Ahmed. Would you like to see my kitten?" She held the tiny creature up for him to stroke. "This is Amazonas."

"A fine name for a young jaguar."

"She's not a jaguar. We think she's an oncilla." Taking her pet with her, Lexi crawled inside the tent.

Ahmed fidgeted. "I found the other raft on a bank. It had broken in half and there were five sets of prints in the mud. Our friends have continued on foot."

Jack sighed. "I will go after them. Can you take Lexi and Kitarna with you and keep paddling by night? It can't be that far to a major settlement or mission."

"My raft is too small for three. I will take Lexi, but Kitarna must stay with you."

"All right. We will keep going on foot. If we catch the others, we'll build another raft. You take the rifle, it has one bullet left."

"I will do my best to keep Lexi safe." Ahmed bowed his head.

Kitarna worried her lip. She didn't want to part with Lexi, but if Jack's stitches became infected, she'd have her hands full and, all things considered, the river held fewer dangers than the jungle. "I will send the first aid kit with you, and give you antiseptic for scratches and more *urucu* paste to keep insects off. You can also take my hydration pack. Jack and I can find water when we need it."

"You are a courageous woman, and you have my respect and gratitude."

"Thank you, Ahmed. You should go now." She ducked inside the tent, where Lexi sat cross-legged with the kitten. "Sweetie, we want you to go with Ahmed. If you get far enough down river tonight, you might make it to a mission."

"I'd rather stay with you and Jack."

"I know, but the mercenaries are after us and they think you drowned, so it's really important they don't discover you're alive. I promised Roscoe we'd get you back to your mother."

Lexi shook her head. "What about Roscoe? I'm not leaving without him."

"We're hoping the native took him to a mission. You might even catch up with them tomorrow."

"Can I take Amazonas?"

"Of course you can."

"Okay." She crawled over and hugged Kitarna. "I'll wait for you at the mission."

Kitarna hugged her tight. "You're the bravest little girl in the world."

Once Ahmed had everything he needed, they crept to the riverbank, using only the light of the moon to guide them. Jack helped Ahmed uncover the raft and lift it into the water. He handed him the rifle and shook his hand.

"Don't take any chances. Stay close to the bank and take cover if you hear an engine. Resume your journey when it's safe."

"That is my plan. I hope to see you both soon."

"Look, I've found a tortoise." Lexi held the kitten in one arm and a tiny tortoise in the palm of her other hand. "Can I keep him?"

"No, sweetheart." Kitarna leaned over to examine it. The brown shell had yellow circles over it and the tortoise's legs were covered in red spots. "I've seen these before. It's a red-footed tortoise. He's very cute, but you have to let him go."

Lexi gently eased him back into the water and cuddled her wide-eyed little kitten. "Don't you go thinking that's your dinner, Amazonas, because it is not."

Jack lifted Lexi onto the narrow raft behind Ahmed. "I've rigged up an oar to act as a rudder."

Lexi tucked the kitten between her crossed legs and took hold of the bamboo stick. She experimented, pushing them up and down. The raft moved. "We'll go really fast now. Thanks, Jack." She gave them a bright smile. "See you tomorrow."

Ahmed waved then dug his double-ended paddle into the water. The raft moved further out into the river and soon disappeared from view.

Praying they'd stay safe, Kitarna turned into Jack's arms. "I don't understand why *El* Jaguar wants me and Bernie, but I feel so guilty."

"This is not your fault, darlin'. Somehow, he found out your sister was coming to the Amazon and saw an opportunity to extort a ransom. There could be more to it, but as you decided to come at the last minute, it can't have anything to do with you."

"I hope Bernie made it out."

"So do I, darlin'. Let's hit the sack. We've a big hike ahead of us tomorrow."

"How's your head?"

"A bit sore, but I don't have a headache. In fact, I'm feeling extremely good." He grinned. "I know we don't have a proper bed, but we do have a roof over our heads and my sleeping bag is reasonably comfy."

"Jack Callaghan, are you suggesting we have sex?"

"With you, it will always be making out." He scooped her into his arms. "We're in the jungle, baby, so let's go explore our wild side."

❦ 26 ❧

Treading warily, Jack carried Kitarna up the bank. He followed the trail until they came to a barely discernible break in the thick foliage. "Sadly, you're going to have to push through this yourself, darlin'."

"It does look that way. At least no one can see us from the river or from this path."

"No." He glanced about, but other than the usual chirping and rustling, nothing stirred. He lowered her to the ground and flicked the flashlight on. "Stay close."

At their campsite, he stopped again and listened. They were hemmed in on all sides by colossal trees, ferns and strangler vines. Not even an adventurous caiman could fight its way through. They were safe for tonight, yet his sixth sense thrummed. Come daylight, Pérez would mount an aggressive search to prevent them escaping. At least Ahmed and Lexi had a better than average chance.

A soft hand slid into his. "Darling, you've done everything possible to keep us safe. Let's go to bed. I want one more night in your arms."

"Only one?"

"There may not be much alone time once we reach the mission." She squeezed his hand. "You could always run away with me?" Her eyes implored him.

It was an invitation he burned to accept, but reality could be a bitch sometimes, and bottom line— she'd regret the invitation once she knew the truth.

"I'm done running, darlin'. It's time I faced facts. I am who I am, and what's done is done. First thing in the morning, I'll tell you what haunts me, and you can decide whether you want a relationship with me."

She pursed her lips and considered him for a couple of seconds. "Tell me now."

*Damn. I should have kept my mouth shut. If I unload on her now, she won't look me in the eye. Hell, she won't want to be anywhere near me.* "I'd rather tell you tomorrow."

"No. We need to settle this tonight."

"As you wish." He followed her inside the tent then zipped the flap shut and hung the flashlight from a hook in the dome. Sitting on his backside, he drew up his knees and leaned on them. "What I'm about to tell you is confidential, so you can't breathe a word of it to anyone."

"Except you." She sat cross-legged, clasping her hands in her lap, waiting.

"I need your promise, that no matter what you think of me, you will let me keep you safe tomorrow?"

"Very well."

He drew a deep breath.

"I served in the regular army for five years then spent six years in a special unit within the Special Air

Service Regiment. A year ago, we were sent to a small town in Afghanistan. Intelligence pointed to a terrorist cell operating thereabouts. The locals were wary of us, but I made friends with a little kid, Baharah. She was a fountain of information."

"She could speak English?"

"No, we spoke to her in Afghani Persian. For weeks we patrolled the region, watching for unusual activity. Whenever I ran into Baharah, I gave her sweets and loose change to share with her siblings."

He cleared his throat. "We got word members of the terrorist cell were coming to the weekly bazaar for supplies, so I took up a position overlooking the central square."

Closing his eyes, he inhaled, reliving the babble of voices, heat and spices from the lively markets. All too real. Opening his eyes, he stared at his scratched hands. "At first light, I set up my tripod and waited, studying every person who entered the bazaar. I saw Baharah with her older brother, but I couldn't leave my post. They were walking slowly toward the center where all the stalls and a group of US soldiers stood. The brother would have been about thirteen, a skinny kid, but that day he seemed overly bulky, so I scoped him and saw perspiration running down his face. His eyes kept darting from side to side. He held onto Baharah's arm too tightly. I realized it was a set up and they planned to blow up the US soldiers and all the innocent civilians nearby."

"The boy was a suicide bomber?" Kitarna clutched Jack's hands. "What did you do?"

Staring into her concerned eyes, he balked, but it only prolonged the inevitable. "I radioed it in and got the order to take the kid out. I had no choice but to shoot him, or let hundreds of innocent people die. So, I took the shot, killing him instantly."

Kitarna gasped, her fingers tightening. "No wonder you have nightmares."

He shook his head, unable to maintain eye contact. "Baharah turned and stared in my direction as if she knew I was the shooter and couldn't believe I'd do such a thing. She raised her hand and I saw the thick vest under her clothes, but my brain didn't compute fast enough."

"Oh my God! She wore a bomb too."

"Yeah. I pulled the trigger, but a second too late, and I've had to live with that guilt, and memories of the carnage ever since. Other than you and the psychiatrist, I haven't spoken about it to anyone. I sank into a well of depression and anger. Drink and pills numbed me, but I wasn't a nice guy to be around."

He sighed, looking up. "So now you know...and I completely comprehend what's going through your mind. I live with it every day."

"You have no idea what is going through my mind." She scowled at him. "I can only imagine how harrowing your nightmares must be. Unfortunately, there will always be extremists capable of brainwashing susceptible children into doing their dirty work."

She wasn't showing the repulsion he'd expected. Confusion reigned as she came up on her knees and placed her hands either side of his face.

"Your friends and family have a right to know what you've told me. It would help them understand what you're going through. Promise me, when all this is over, you will go back to Australia and talk to them."

"I don't know. It may be too late to salvage those relationships." He looked into her beautiful eyes. "Don't you despise me?"

"Of course not. You're the bravest, most caring man I know, but we do have a problem."

*Here it comes, the gentle let down. She's too soft-hearted to hurt me outright. I can play along.* "And what would that be, darlin'?"

"I'd like to get to know you better, but you're headed for your Caribbean beach shack." She chewed her lower lip and gave him an apprehensive look. "I specialize in rainforest botany, and it's more than a job for me. I won't give it up."

"I wouldn't ask you to give up your passion. Hell, without your knowledge we'd have starved and never made it this far."

Her eyes dropped. "So, if you're in the Caribbean and I'm in a rainforest somewhere, we won't see a lot of each other. I'm not the trophy girlfriend type."

"I'm not into trophy girlfriends. It would mean we'd both do a bit of traveling, but I'm keen if you are?"

She blinked several times before her face broke into the most wondrous glowing smile. "Yes, yes." She surged forward, wrapping her arms around his neck as he fell backward. "You make me crazy, Jack Callaghan."

"Not half as crazy as you make me, darlin'." He held her slender hips, searching for any sign of pretense in her clear open gaze. Elation filled him from head to toe. She still desired him, wanted a relationship with him, knowing what he'd done. This beautiful, sexy woman offered him a chance of happiness, if he dared take it, and if he could keep her safe for one more day.

"You are gorgeous and amazing. I'm bloody grateful for whatever force brought us together."

"Stop gasbagging and kiss me."

"Yes, ma'am." Holding her tight, he rolled to the side and kissed every inch of her face, neck and ears. Her soft little moans spurred him to take possession of her lips and mouth in a drugging kiss that left them panting.

"Take this off." She dragged his T-shirt up his chest. "I need skin to skin."

Sitting, he wrenched it over his head then, with fumbling fingers, unlaced his boots and heeled them off. His pants and briefs quickly followed. He helped drag her cargo pants off before pulling her back into his arms. "This is not going to be slow."

"Wait." She threw off her tank top and pulled the strings of her bikini undone then wiggled out of the panties and come up on her knees facing him. "Take me, my brave lion. I'm yours."

Crazy with lust, he skimmed his hands down her smooth as silk arms, his gaze locked on her plump breasts, his erection straining between them. "Turn around, kitten."

She did, leaning against his chest and tilting her head, allowing him access to her neck as her fingers grasped his thighs. "What next?"

"This." He stroked her hips, skating his fingertips across her stomach, smiling when a quiver rippled under her skin. He captured her mouth as he closed his hands over her breasts, absorbing her hitched gasp.

She rubbed purposely against his erection, uttering delighted cries when he thumbed and lightly pinched her nipples. A moan escaped her lips when he kneaded and weighed her bounty. "You like this, kitten?"

"Oh yes."

Spreading one hand over her stomach, he pushed a knee between her thighs, opening her to his questing fingers. "So wet, darlin'." He circled her nub then pushed two fingers inside, stretching her, plunging in and out.

"Harder." She arched, thrusting against his fingers, her fingernails digging into his thighs. "Do it harder, Jack."

"Stay on your knees and put your hands on the sleeping bag, darlin'. Yes, like that." He spread her knees wide then grasping her hips, nudged inside her tight sheath.

"Oh my God, that's so good." She pushed, taking his cock to the hilt.

They both moaned.

Savoring the moment as long as he could, Jack withdrew and pushed in, slowly at first, then thrusting faster and faster, his balls smacking against her slick bottom.

Matching his fervor, she cried out, "Yes, Jack, yes." She shuddered; tightening round his engorged cock, uttering a strangled cry, taking him with her.

Giddy with exhilaration, he pumped his seed into her. It left him lightheaded and adrift. Still deep inside her and fully sated, Jack wrapped her in his arms and fell sideways. The realization they might one day do this to create a child—children—a family together, filled him with jubilation.

He traced his fingers up and down her spine, indulging his fantasy further. Children needed extended family. Maybe it wasn't too late to mend bridges with his parents and brothers. His closest mates in the SAS had resigned to work for their Colonel's security firm. Jack had been offered a job, which remained an option, but there might be a better alternative, if Kitarna chose to take him on.

Kissing her shoulder, he withdrew from her warm clutch, spooning against her curves. "I've bruised your hips."

"You were wonderful, and I'm tougher than I look." She squirmed closer, entwining her fingers over his right hand and bringing it to rest on her stomach. "I can live with those kind of bruises, as long as you can live with my fingernails." She abandoned his hand to brush his thigh, sending tickling goose bumps skittering along his skin. "I've scratched you."

"I don't care."

"Imagine what I'll do to your back when you're on top of me."

"Behave." He reached up and flicked off the flashlight then pulled the sleeping bag across her. "We will indulge in that position when we have a real bed."

"Why not here, when I re-energize?"

"The ground is hard, darlin'."

"I'm not made of porcelain, and we do have a sleeping bag."

"Hmm, that we do." He cuddled her, relaxing as her breathing settled into gentle puffs. *How did I get so lucky?* Against all odds, fate had brought them together. The next twenty-four hours would seal their destiny. He'd make sure of that.

～ 27 ～

Waking from a sensual dream to the reality of being caressed intimately was a pleasure Kitarna could happily endure every morning. She tried not to react as Jack drew lazy circles over her belly, tiptoeing his fingertips up her ribcage, closing his warm hand over her breast.

It was harder to ignore the leg pushing between her thighs, boldly brushing against her highly sensitive genitalia. Total failure ensued when he nibbled on her neck, his warm breath tickling a giggle from her.

"At last, Sleeping Beauty awakes, and so must grant me a reward, if she is to find eternal happiness." His deep drawl vibrated against her skin.

She stretched, pushing her breast further into his hand, rubbing against his hard thigh. The solid length pressing against the base of her spine flexed. "What did you have in mind?"

"I should like to explore the possibilities." He shifted her thigh forward and withdrew his knee, replacing it with his fingers, to rub, circle and thrust, working his magic until she squirmed, wet and desperate.

"Jack, I want you inside me."

"I know you do." He rolled her beneath him, spreading her thighs, pressing into her, inch-by-inch. Lavishing her collarbone with open-mouthed kisses. "I intended to take you from behind, but as you're not made of porcelain…"

The thickness of his substantial length filled her, nudging her cervix and sending hypersensitive, salsa dancing atoms rioting throughout her body. He withdrew and thrust again and again, harder and faster, until her body fizzed like a newly opened bottle of champagne. Any moment she'd explode in bubbles of ecstasy.

"Is this what you want, kitten?"

"Oh, yes." Locking her ankles at the base of his spine, she clung to his wide shoulders, meeting each thrust with panting gasps and wild cries. Deep in her core a mounting pressure rose, sending waves of electrifying currents shooting through her quivering limbs. "Jack!"

He cut off her scream with his mouth, thrust once more and shuddered, a low growl radiating from deep in his throat, before he collapsed on top of her.

She held him bemused. *Did a meteorite hit earth as I climaxed?*

With his solid weight pressing her into the sleeping bag, but loathe to lose the connection, she caressed his smooth back in sweeping swirls and kissed his stubbled cheek. "Jack Callaghan, you're a mind-blowing lover. Thank you for not kicking me out of your seat. That tree would have crushed me, and I'd have died never knowing you, or experiencing so much pleasure."

He raised himself on an elbow and gave her a crooked smile. "You're an inspiring woman, darlin'. Meeting you has turned my life around. You've given me back my self-worth and inspired me to join the human race again."

"Damn, I liked you wild." Smiling, she traced the scratches on his shoulders. "Dare I hope you retain some of your wild ways, my beautiful lion?"

"Count on it, darlin'." He lowered his head and kissed her, long and leisurely, the fervor escalating until they were devouring each other with hands, lips and tongues.

Heart pounding, and panting, Kitarna rode wave after wave of euphoria as Jack smothered every inch of her in open mouthed kisses, backing off each time she neared completion. She pushed him onto his back and returned the torture, moving steadily down his torso, swirling her tongue around his nipples. Licking a path to his magnificent erection. She clasped his testicles, stroked and licked his length, then took him into her mouth, laving and sucking until he bucked, almost choking her.

Suddenly he flipped her onto her back again, spread-eagled and being kissed voraciously. Beyond desperate, she moaned, wrapped her arms around his neck, her legs around his waist and pressed against the broad head of his erection.

Braced on one elbow, his other hand gripping her hip, Jack nudged her entrance, and with one powerful thrust, filled her, igniting an adrenaline-fueled frenzy of lovemaking. She met each driving thrust with gasping shrieks, lifting her hips to meet him, urging him on and on. Her orgasm hit fast, her sheath clenching around his width, shudders racking her body as she bit his shoulder, muffling her scream.

He held in his roar, thrust again then heaved a deeply sated sigh before rolling to the side, holding her tightly to his chest.

Still joined intimately and breathing hard, they clung to each other.

Eventually Jack eased away and kissed her forehead. "We should pack up and attempt to catch up with the others."

"I just need a few minutes to wash and dress."

"No worries." He pulled on his clothes then picked up her sharp rocks, which must have fallen out of her cargo pants. "I can make fishing spears by strapping these to bamboo sticks. We can use them as walking sticks or weapons if necessary."

"Before you do that, I'll put some dragon sap on your head and rewrap it. We need to cover our bodies in more *urucu* seed paint. After seeing what the bot flies did to Brett, we don't want them laying their larva on our skin." Sitting up, she reached for her rucksack and pulled out the vials she needed and the almost empty packet of moist wipes. No way would she wash in the river.

Attending to Jack was no simple matter. Smacking his hands away didn't deter him from stroking any part of her body he wished. In the end, she pulled on her shirt and ordered him to turn around, so she could finish wrapping his head, otherwise they'd never catch up with the others.

He left her to finish dressing and repack the rucksack. Her fingers lingered over the thin spikes of her *kansashi* hairpin. When embedded in a lady's hair, only the oriental dragon showed, giving no indication of the deadly hidden fork. On impulse, she braided her hair and concealed the pin inside.

Emerging from the tent, she discovered weak sunrays breaking through patches of the canopy. On a thick branch above her, four emperor tamarin monkeys held court, watching her with age-old wisdom in their dark eyes. Two stroked their long white mustaches, reminding her of a pair of ancient Chinese emperors, debating her right to be here.

Jack sent her a sexy smile as he bound the rocks to bamboo sticks with palm twine. After blowing him a kiss, she set about packing up the tent and sleeping bag. With luck, they would reach the mission today and sleep in a real bed, but with mercenaries hunting them, they had no guarantees. She picked fruit, handing Jack some as they started along the river path. "I present you with delicious tidings."

He raised an eyebrow. "Are these the brown things you gave us that first night?"

"Yes, they're the ones with the fruity chocolate flavor. And these are *camu camu*. They're sour, but high in vitamin C." She passed him a handful of the small red fruit.

As she followed Jack along the well-worn track, Kitarna kept glancing behind, listening for voices and engines. The usual chatter, screeches and chirping abounded in the canopy, along with curious spider monkeys swinging through the branches, following until distracted by ripe mangoes.

River life remained much the same. Long-legged birds stalked through the shallows, filching small fish. Under the eye of a large caiman, a mother tapir and her colorfully striped baby drank from the river.

No natives crossed their path, but three boats of mercenaries motored past, binoculars to their eyes, scanning both banks. Thankfully, the dense foliage provided an abundance of cover to hide behind.

They trekked for several hours, stopping at clumps of bamboo for water and once so Kitarna could photograph a toucan's magnificent bright-orange beak, a beacon against the multiple shades of green foliage. He ruffled his shiny black feathers at the interruption to his grooming regime.

"Thank you, Mr. Toucan." Kitarna slid the camera into her pocket and grinned at Jack. "I love capturing animals in their natural environment."

A gunshot blasted, sending the birdlife into panic.

"Christ." Jack dragged her through a tangled mass of strangler vines. He urged her behind a high tree root. "Stay here, I'll be back in a minute."

Sitting in the gloom between moss-covered roots, she counted off five minutes before he returned, almost jumping out of her skin when he landed beside her with a soft thud.

"Pérez and two of his men are up ahead. They've captured Piers, Juliette, Victoria and Robert. I can't see Gabe, and there's no sign of Ahmed and Lexi."

"We have to rescue them?"

He hugged her. "My little Amazon. Of course you want to help the people who abandoned you?"

"They did what they thought best. What's your plan?"

"I can't do much against three armed men. Don't stand on anything brittle."

"Okay." She followed on his heels, putting her feet where he stepped, crouching when he waved her down.

Jack stopped at the widest tree she'd ever seen, its aboveground roots twice her height. "From here we maintain silence. As long as we keep the trees between us and them, we are invisible."

"I'm right behind you." She looked about in wide-eyed wonder. They were in a forest of ancient trees, possibly over a thousand years old. It blew her mind.

She followed Jack until he stopped and leaned his spear against another giant root. He dropped to his belly and crawled forward, motioning for her to join him. It was awkward slithering commando style along moldy leaf matter with a spear, but she wasn't giving up her weapon. She reached his side to discover him peering through a bushy shrub she didn't recognize. Quick as a flash, she filled her pockets with small spiny fruit. It was hard to repress her excitement, but her research would have to wait. She wriggled closer.

Jack pressed a finger against his lips. He pointed ahead to where two mercenaries circled the four crestfallen passengers.

Victoria, Robert, Piers and Juliette stood shoulder to shoulder, their hands tied behind their backs, terror-filled eyes following Andrés Pérez as he strode back and forth, muttering in Spanish. He stopped and lashed out at Piers, knocking him to the ground. "I will not tolerate lies. Tell me where Kitarna Ashford and the Australian have gone?"

"I'm not lying." Piers awkwardly clambered to his knees. "We had a snakebite victim and Jack was unconscious from a head injury. Kitarna insisted on staying with them. We tried to convince her to come with us, but she refused."

"The Australian was unconscious?"

Piers gave a step-by-step account of Brett shooting Roscoe and taking Kitarna and how Jack got injured rescuing her. His voice cracked. "Brett was taken by a caiman."

"A just end." Andrés Pérez spat on the ground. "That weasel and his skinny girlfriend reneged on a deal with one of my agents. They stole from me. If they weren't already dead, I'd feed them to the piranhas."

Kitarna glanced at Jack. He signaled for her to stay put and that he would circle round. Nodding, she returned her attention to the horror unfolding.

Juliette sank to her knees beside Piers. "My husband and I are doctors. We've been volunteering at the mission, and can't possibly be of any value to you."

"You are correct, *señora*. Three of you are of no value whatsoever, but my men shall enjoy your blonde friend."

*Oh no.* Kitarna bit her knuckle.

"Wait!" Robert called. "I'm a director of a substantial building and real estate company owned by my father-in-law. He will pay anything to get me back to my wife and children."

Pérez pressed his rifle into Robert's cheek. "But once you are free, you will tell the world what I did to your friends."

"No, I won't. They are nothing to me."

"You selfish bastard." Victoria kneed Robert in the groin, knocking him to his knees gasping. "Without me to do your power-point presentations and research, you're a useless prick. As for promising to leave your whining, dull wife, I should have known it was all lies. You cowardly, worthless slug."

Pérez struck out, slapping Victoria's face so hard she fell backwards.

Kitarna clenched her fists, appalled but unable to look away as Pérez dragged Victoria up by her hair and snarled, "Do not speak unless I give you permission."

"Pérez!" Jack bellowed from behind a thicket of bracken fern. "I'm Jack Callaghan. Hurt my friends and I'll ensure *El* Jaguar knows you're responsible for the death of his granddaughter."

Pérez twisted round, raising his rifle. He wore a bandage along his jaw.

To Kitarna's horror, Jack waved then took off. For a big man, he moved like lightning, dodging between trees, heading away from the river. He dived as a barrage of automatic gunfire erupted.

She crouched low, praying Jack got away safely. The alternative was unthinkable.

Pérez yelled at his men to go after Jack. To her amazement Pérez followed, leaving his four captives in a stupefied huddle.

Jumping to her feet, Kitarna picked up the machete and rushed forward. "Quick, turn around. I'll cut you free, but it's every man for himself." She sawed through Juliette and Piers' bindings then gave them a shove. "Go!"

They did, holding hands as they ran toward the river path.

Victoria scrambled to her feet. "It's you he wants, Kitarna. You need to go."

"Once you're free." She grimaced at the red welt across Victoria's cheek. It was nothing compared to what the mercenaries would do to her in their camp. "Hold still." She cut the rope. "Follow the river and hide if you hear boats. The mission isn't far."

"What about you?"

"I'll hide and wait for Jack. Go."

"Thank you." Victoria tore off after the doctors.

Robert held out his hands. "Hurry up, they could come back any minute."

"I'm going as fast as I can." She sawed through the rope. "You are a self-centered slug. One day, karma will catch up with you."

"I'm a survivor, babe, and I'm not the one who sabotaged the raft or betrayed everyone." He snatched the machete and ran.

"That's mine!" Incensed and with her heartbeat pounding in her ears, she had no choice but to creep back through the ancient forest to her hiding place and hope Jack made it back to her.

Reaching for Jack's spear, she leaned against the giant root and exhaled. *Safe.* A twig snapped. Clasping the spear, she swung round, sagging with relief when she recognized the man standing in front of her. "Gabe?"

"I am very glad to find you, Kitarna. Where's Jack?"

"Leading mercenaries on a wild goose chase." She slumped against the root. "That creep Pérez caught the others. Where were you?"

"Guarding the patrol boat for *Capitán* Pérez and waiting for you, Kitarna." He smiled. "I see you are confused, yes?"

A chill ran through her. "*You* sabotaged the raft and betrayed us to a mercenary?"

"*Capitán* Pérez is my uncle, *señorita,* and a great man." Gabe moved so fast, she didn't have time to block his fist.

His punch winded her. Tears blurred her vision as she crumpled to the ground, curling into ball, clutching her tender stomach, gasping for air.

~ 28 ~

Leaning against a thick trunk, Jack slowed his breathing. After their initial heavy-handed barrage of firepower, the mercenaries were conserving their bullets and hunting him.

Ripping off the white bandage, he shoved it in his pocket. A head target was the last thing he wanted to give those mongrels. He'd prefer to take each one out separately, except they stuck too close together.

A quick glance at his compass indicated he needed to go southeast to get back to the river. By now his brave little kitten would have ignored his request to stay put and set the others free. In which case, they'd be running for their lives and she'd be hiding somewhere close. Alone and unprotected. Not for a second did he believe she'd leave without him.

His thoughts returned to the broken raft. It had been plaguing him since Ahmed mentioned the wreckage. Plaited vine wouldn't shear through that quickly, but why sabotage the best chance of escape?

Of the five people on board, four had been captured, so what happened to Gabe?

The hairs on the back of his neck bristled. Solana, Gabe and Doris had stumbled across the group at that small creek, leaving a trail any moron could follow. Solana had been working for *El* Jaguar. Did they have another spy in the group?

*Shit.* Gabe had known a lot about the drug lord's operation, yet he genuinely seemed to hate *El* Jaguar. But so did Andrés Pérez. Jack didn't like what that equation added up to. He needed to get back to Kitarna.

Edging around the tree, he spotted the three mercenaries. Pérez was ahead of the others, but not by much, and moving cautiously. One man lagged, his red face and bulging belly indicative of his fitness. It was the man Jack had locked in his trunk at the airport. Now he used his rifle to lean on while he muffled a coughing fit. A loud fart sent two humming birds into panicked flight.

"*Tranquilo, estupido bastardo,*" yelled Pérez without looking back.

Moving with the stealth he'd perfected in the SAS, Jack eased onto his stomach and slithered over the rotting mulch to the next tree, bringing him to the rear of the fat mercenary. One soundless step at a time, he closed the gap, keeping his eyes fixed on all three mercenaries.

It was now or never. Sweeping the rifle aside, Jack clamped a hand over the man's mouth and dragged him behind a tree, dropping him with a hammer punch to the kidney. The man's eyes rolled back in his head and he went limp. Wary, Jack lowered him to the ground and checked for a pulse. Whether from obesity or shock, the man's heart had stopped. No great loss.

Pérez and his companion were still moving forward, so Jack snatched up the dead man's rifle, steadied his breathing and took aim. Pérez must have sensed something. He dived to the ground. The other man whirled, opening fire on several trees. Jack shot him with one well-placed bullet to the chest then took off running.

He reached the clearing where the others had been and found it empty. Kitarna wasn't behind the bushy shrub either. Staying off the narrow animal trail, he crept through thick foliage, heading to the river, where he found a patrol boat and two more mercenaries on guard.

Fury burned deep in his gut at the sight of Gabe standing behind Kitarna, a gun pressed to her head. Her hands were tied in front, but by her paleness and the way her body slumped, she had to be nursing an injury. Sinking to the ground, Jack crawled closer, taking advantage of the overhanging ferns. Damn, he couldn't get a clear shot at the bastard.

As if she sensed him, Kitarna lifted her head. "Gabe, you don't need Jack. He's sure to have killed those mercenaries and gone for help. I'm the one *El Jaguar* wants."

"No, we wait for my uncle."

*Uncle?* Jack frowned.

Kitarna's anxious gaze settled on a thicket close to where Jack had taken shelter. "Andrés Pérez doesn't care that you're his nephew. He murdered Solana to keep her quiet. He will shoot you too."

"No, I am his only nephew. Soon my uncle will take over *El* Jaguar's empire and put an end to the drugs. My family will not live in fear anymore."

"You're a fool, Gabe. Andrés Pérez is as bad as *El* Jaguar, maybe worse, and anyone who doesn't do what he wants will disappear. You, your friends, your family."

"A warning you should heed, *señorita*." Pérez stepped from behind a tree, pushed Gabe aside and locked his arm around Kitarna's throat, pressing his handgun against her ribs.

*Shit.* Jack kept the rifle up, waiting for an open shot. If he could take out Pérez, the others might flee, and Pérez knew it.

Gabe looked about nervously. "She said Jack would go for help."

"She will say anything to protect the Australian." Pérez rubbed the gun across her breasts. "Jack Callaghan won't leave her. He's somewhere close."

*Yes, I am, you bastard, and I'm coming for you.* Jack barely breathed, his finger hovered over the trigger, waiting.

"No, Jack is long gone." Kitarna pushed the gun away with her bound hands. "Don't touch me."

Pérez gripped her throat, calling out, "Give yourself up, *Señor* Callaghan, or I will choke the life out of your pretty lover."

*Fuck.* Jack held his position as Kitarna struggled, her gurgle ripping his heart open. *Come on, Pérez, give me one clean shot.*

Kitarna passed out, but Pérez didn't release his hold.

"Christ, let her go." Jack clambered to his feet,

forging his way through the ferns. His gaze locked on Kitarna. "You're no leader, hiding behind a woman. Show some guts and fight me one on one."

Pérez's lip curled. "You think I can't beat you?"

"I know it."

"Get the rifle." Pérez waited until Gabe had taken Jack's rifle. He nodded at the other two mercenaries who had jumped onto the bank. "Secure him."

They seized Jack's arms. Only then did Pérez let Kitarna fall to the ground and approach. He halted far enough to avoid Jack's fists and steel-capped boots.

Desperate to get to Kitarna, Jack surged forward dragging the men with him. He used them to hold his weight as he kicked out, slamming both boots into Pérez's chest. The impact knocked the bastard off his feet.

Jack clamped onto one of the men's arms and twisted. Bone cracked under his vise-like grip. He ignored the strangled scream and drove his knee into the other guard's jaw. It crunched like shattered glass. Running on adrenaline and instinct, Jack launched a roundhouse kick, striking Gabe in the hip and sending him toppling onto Pérez, who held his chest, wheezing. Another couple of kicks relieved both men of their weapons.

Snatching up the rifles, Jack hurled them into the river and shoved Pérez's handgun into his waistband. He ran to Kitarna. Fingerprint smudges on her throat stood out against her pale skin. He found a pulse, and when he laid his cheek against her lips, felt a faint puff.

"Thank God." He exhaled. The knot of terror unraveled into waves of relief, bringing moisture to his eyes. A week ago, he would have scoffed that this gutsy little lady could become the center of his world. Take possession of his heart. A week ago, he'd been emotionally dead.

He wanted to kill Pérez and Gabe with his bare hands, but his priority was getting Kitarna onto that patrol boat and down the river to safety. Keeping an eye on the battered men, he bent down to pick her up.

A mercenary burst from the jungle, discharging a volley of bullets. Dirt and debris exploded as the bullets tore along the ground toward Jack.

"Fuck." Whipping out the handgun, Jack flung himself over Kitarna, took aim, and fired, hitting the maniac in the throat. He squeezed the trigger again as Pérez clambered to his feet. Nothing happened, he'd run out of bullets.

Pérez sneered. "Now I beat you to a pulp."

Jack smiled. "You're welcome to try." Planting his feet wide, Jack waited with the patience born from years of stakeouts. Pérez would have to come to him, as he wasn't letting the bastard anywhere near Kitarna.

Pérez parried to the left. Jack blocked his path and waited.

"*Estúpido*," called Gabe before limping to a tree.

*Not as stupid as you.* Jack waited, half amused as the traitor turned to a tree and snapped off a couple of short, stocky limbs. He tossed one to Pérez.

They limped toward him, their faces smug. He'd faced down three guerillas armed with knives and barely taken a scratch. The trick was to go in hard and fast, using opponents as shields. His old friend, James Talarico had taught him that.

Jack dived to the ground, swept Gabe's feet from under him then snatched the limb and bounced to his feet. The cocky bastard's winded gasp barely left his lips before Jack slammed his fist into the younger man's nose, spreading it across his face. Gabe howled as blood spurted down his shirt.

Jack leaped back, avoiding Pérez's wild swing by inches, the momentum kept the mercenary turning, leaving an opening for Jack to come in hard with his chunk of wood. He hit Pérez across his back, sending him sprawling into rotting leaf litter.

Jack raised his weapon, ready to silence Pérez for good, when the cocking of a rifle caught his attention. He dived again, rolling toward a tree, expecting a barrage of bullets to follow him. They didn't. He raised his head cautiously and silently cursed.

A sleek speedboat he hadn't heard had nosed into the bank, and standing over Kitarna was the man who'd encouraged Lexi to hide. He held a rifle pointed at Jack. *Fucking hell.*

Jack had no choice but to stand and place his hands behind his head. He watched the smooth-looking man warily. *If he's a covert, he won't want to blow his cover, but will he give me a chance?*

Glancing behind, Jack observed Gabe helping Pérez stand. The promised retribution in the mercenary's eyes came as no surprise, but at least the odds were a little more in his favor. Gritting his teeth, Jack strode purposely forward.

The operative held up a hand. "That's far enough, *señor.* If you value the *señorita,* you will put your hands on your head."

Halting, Jack considered the man's barely discernible American accent. With his coloring, he easily passed for a South American. Finding no sign of malice in the watchful dark eyes, Jack decided to go with his gut. They were far enough from Pérez and Gabe not to be heard. "I realize you're undercover, but I need you to get Kitarna to safety."

The man raised an eyebrow. "You are mistaken, *señor*, however, I do not condone the kidnapping of women, so I will do my best to help her."

"No." Kitarna croaked, holding out a shaking hand, her beautiful eyes shimmering with tears. "Jack, save yourself."

"I can't, kitten. Not without you."

She sobbed brokenly. "Pérez will kill you. Please go."

He shook his head as all his dreams trickled away with her tears.

The man glanced quickly behind Jack. "Andrés will insist on torturing you himself, so all I can do is give you a little extra time. What you do after that is up to you. How well can you fake unconsciousness?"

Jack grimaced and lowered his hands. This might hurt, but any lifeline was better than none, and his gut insisted this guy was their only chance. "Let's find out."

"I don't understand." Kitarna looked up at Jack.

Jack's head exploded like a grenade had gone off inside. He heard a far-off scream before blackness engulfed him.

～ 29 ～

"You didn't have to hit him." Kitarna cradled Jack's head on her lap, his blood soaking into her pants. "Untie my hands this instant. I need to stop the bleeding." She looked up at the tall man standing over her. She would have considered him an extremely handsome if he hadn't hit Jack.

For several heartbeats, his brown eyes seemed to waver between concern and remorse, before a cool loftiness descended. "Do not make the same mistake as your boyfriend, *señorita*. I don't take orders."

The callousness in his voice rattled her. He had lied to Jack? Her last hope disintegrated.

The man turned his back on her and strode to where Andrés Pérez had stopped, clasping his chest and breathing shallowly. His eyes glowered with rage, his damaged face twisted into an ugly snarl.

Anger mounted as she listened to them converse in rapid Spanish. The man apologized for knocking Jack out, professing angrily that he couldn't stand by and do nothing after witnessing such insolence. He assured Pérez that the Australian would recover, and it would be a pleasure to witness his punishment.

Her heart sank.

Pérez seemed mollified, but his gaze stayed on Kitarna. The cruelness in his black eyes petrified her. He switched to English, no doubt for her benefit. "I would appreciate you loaning me your boat. I want to transport these two to the village quickly."

The man looked amused. "I suppose I am to convey your injured men in the patrol boat?"

"*Sí.*"

"Very well, but I insist on bandaging the Australian's head. I do not want his blood staining my upholstery."

"Certainly, but do not injure him further. I want the man coherent when I slice the muscle from his back. He must die an agonizing death, bleeding out slowly to the sound of his whore's screams. It will be interesting to see who loses consciousness first." He laughed then clutched his chest. "*Mierda*, I will make him pay."

Bile rose in Kitarna's throat. She could barely breathe as she held Jack closer. Visions of what Pérez intended filled her head.

She stroked Jack's forehead, her tears splattering his face. How would they ever escape this nightmare?

The man squatted in front of her. "*Señorita*, I will need your help."

"Go to hell." Fury and hate seared every syllable. She would not help this liar. She lifted her chin and opened her mouth, determined to expose him.

"I will do my best to help both of you." The gentleness in his eyes confused her.

Glancing away, she watched as Gabe assisted Andrés Pérez into the speedboat. They were both moving gingerly, Gabe holding a blood-soaked rag to his nose. The other two injured mercenaries supported each other as they shuffled toward the river, leaving their dead comrade where he'd fallen.

None of these pigs would be a match for Jack when he regained consciousness. She shuddered. It could take hours, maybe days, and by then it would be too late.

Gabe met her gaze and mouthed, '*I'm so sorry*'. He looked utterly shell-shocked. Had he truly believed his uncle wasn't a vicious beast? Pérez was a mercenary, a drug runner, a killer.

The man tapped her knee. She glanced down to see him wedging a smooth, sharp rock between her tied hands.

"If you work it on the rope, you will fray the threads." He ripped Jack's T-shirt down the middle then with a flick knife, slashed the short sleeves, displaying Jack's magnificent chest and shoulders.

The man folded the T-shirt into a pad and handed it to her. "Hold this against the wound."

He bound Jack's hands in front of him, which surprised her. Maybe she wouldn't expose him just yet. "We need something to bandage Jack's head." She started unbuttoning her shirt.

"No, leave it on." The operative strode to his boat, rummaged under a seat then jogged back.

"What are you doing, *señor*?" Pérez leaned to the side, his gaze suspicious.

"Give me a moment, Andrés. I am making sure this man survives long enough for you to take your vengeance. I am almost done."

Kitarna held the pad while he wrapped the bandage around Jack's head, securing it with a flimsy, pronged clasp. She eyed the closed flick knife lying beside her knee. Damn, she should have grabbed it when he went to the boat.

The man stood dusted down his spotless, pressed trousers. "I will take his shoulders, if you can lift his feet."

"And how do you suggest I do that, *señor*? My hands are tied."

He considered her for a moment. "Don't forget your rucksack." He squatted behind Jack, lifted him into a floppy sitting position then after sliding his arms around Jack's chest, heaved him up.

Kitarna pulled her rucksack closer, reached for the flick knife and pushed it between her sock and boot. She squashed her panic as the man hauled Jack into the speedboat and lowered him to the carpeted floor. He opened a side panel and pulled out a revolver, which he passed to Pérez. "The woman shouldn't give you any trouble, but one never knows."

Pérez shuffled to the front passenger seat then aimed the gun at her. It was threat enough to have her lifting her leaden feet. Bernie would never concede defeat and she wouldn't either.

Hostility and aggression coiled in Kitarna's stomach, smothering her panic. She had a rock and a knife. They were better than nothing.

The other two mercenaries were on the patrol boat, their downcast eyes and slouched shoulders making her wonder if they feared punishment.

Clenching her jaw, she scrambled into the speedboat and sank to her knees. Jack's face was smeared with dirt. His breathing appeared normal, but he lay terribly still. She lifted his head and nudged her rucksack underneath it with her knee.

The operative snatched her hands. "Let me check this rope is tight enough." He stood leaning over her, his back to Pérez and Gabe. "Stay calm, *señorita*," he murmured. "They are taking you to a wharf guarded by two mercenaries. A jeep will transfer you to the village."

He tugged at her bonds. "Very secure. Now for the Australian." He knelt beside Jack, lowering his voice again. "If your friend comes around in time, he should overpower Pérez before you reach the wharf. The first two bullets in the gun I gave him are blanks. Take my boat and do not stop until you reach a sizeable town. If you don't escape, I will see what I can do later. Good luck, *señorita*."

"Why are you helping us, if you're not undercover?"

"I have my own score to settle with Andrés."

"You warned my father about *El* Jaguar and told Roscoe where to find Lexi, didn't you?"

"You are mistaken, *señorita*." He stood and turned to Andrés. "Neither will escape, *Capitán*." He leaped onto the bank without a backward glance.

Tentacles of fear spread as she caught Pérez watching her with narrowed eyes. Defiantly, she raised her chin. If they failed to escape, she'd have to find the courage to end Jack's life mercifully. After that, it would be easy to plunge a knife into her heart. She touched her bound hands to her braid and felt the *kansashi* hairpin. Did she have the nerve to use it? *Oh yes.*

Gabe looked pasty, as if he might puke, but with a nod from Pérez, he started the motor and putted out into the river.

She lifted her chin. "I have a right to know why *El* Jaguar brought down the plane. Is it because he intends to ransom me and my sister?"

Pérez sneered. "*El* Jaguar didn't know *you* were on the plane. Your sister is his target. Now she will be his downfall."

Kitarna clenched her fingers over the sharp rock, fighting nausea. "Where is my sister?"

"I do not know. Perhaps when I dispose of *El* Jaguar we will find out."

*Oh, please let Bernie be safe.*

Gabe pushed the throttle forward and the powerful boat surged ahead. Within seconds they were hurtling upriver, passing plenty of mean-looking caiman. She'd throw herself to them without a second thought if Jack stopped breathing. At least the high-powered engine inhibited her having to converse with Pérez.

Several droplets splashed her face and looking up she observed a leaden sky of thick, bluish cloud. A crack of thunder vibrated through her and the heavens opened.

Jack stirred. The heavy rain aided her in wiping the grime from his face. He moaned again. Thankfully the engine-hub sat in the middle of the boat, shielding him.

She dropped the rock and leaned over. "Hush, darling. I will protect you."

His eyelids fluttered. "You're very brave for such a little thing." His murmur held faint amusement.

Relief filled her with bravado. "I won't let that pig touch your beautiful muscles."

"Thata girl." His thick eyelashes settled.

*Blast.* She couldn't let him drift into unconsciousness again. She needed to shock him into full awareness. He wouldn't shock easily, so it would need to be a bombshell. Something a man like Jack couldn't ignore.

Pressing close to his ear, she whispered, "We may have created a baby."

His eyes snapped open. "You said it was safe."

She bit down on her lip. A smile would make Pérez suspicious. Raising her bound hands, she pulled out her hair tie and finger-combed her hair, sliding the pin between her hands. She leaned close again. "It *was* safe the first time, but I wasn't thinking last night, or this morning." She grimaced. "What's done is done, so for the baby's sake we need to come up with a strategy to escape."

"When were you planning to tell me?"

She bit down on her bottom lip. "That depended on you."

"Me?" His eyes widened. "I deserve to know if I'm going to be a father."

"Yes, but you prefer dogs. Children need to know they're cherished and loved."

"*Our* children will be. As for their mother..."

It took supreme willpower to keep her expression blank. "Their mother?"

He huffed. "Don't act the innocent with me. First you commandeer my seat on the plane then lure me into a web of carnal delight. As if that's not bad enough, you slide under my guard and lay siege to my heart."

"Your heart?" Along with the rain, tears streamed down Kitarna's face.

"Damn right. You can't wave a rosy future at me then walk away. Whether we've created a baby or not, I plan to be there for you, and any children we have."

"Always?" She so wanted to believe him.

He turned his head and winced. "For the last twelve months, I've barely existed day to day. My heart's function was to pump blood through my body. Now it's brimming with anticipation. You've turned my life around and given me a future I look forward to."

She wanted to smother him in kisses, have him hold her so tight she couldn't breathe. Instead she cleared her throat. "In that case we better make sure we have a future. I've got a knife in my boot and a deadly hair pin."

His lips twitched. "Of course you do."

Squeezing down beside him, she whispered. "Pérez is taking us to a village where he intends slicing you to bits, which isn't going to happen. I think that man who hit you is definitely an undercover operative, even though he denies it."

"So do I."

She wriggled closer. "If you play unconscious, there is a chance we can escape."

He frowned. "Tell me everything that happened after I blacked out, and I mean everything. I need to know what I'm up against."

"What *we* are up against. You need to trust me, Jack."

~ 30 ~

A wall of steady rain surrounded them, adding to Jack's dilemma. He doubted Pérez would toss Kitarna to his men, at least not until he'd tired of her, and as broken ribs had a way of spoiling any kind of bed sport, that wouldn't be any time soon. He hoped.

His vision kept blurring, fatigue and nausea lingered. He winced as the boat hit a cross-current, sending razor-sharp splinters shooting into his brain. He was in no state to fight anyone, let alone a pack of mercenaries or villagers with poisonous darts. No matter which way he looked at it, Kitarna's plan seemed their best hope.

Faking unconsciousness wouldn't be a problem, and he now had the operative's knife. The fly in the ointment lay squished alongside him, drenched and shivering, using her body to buffer him from the worst of the jolts and bumps. At any moment, his brave little angel would go head-to-head with these vicious bastards. He happened to be the trained soldier, but would that stop her? Unlikely.

She'd wanted his trust. Of course he trusted her. It was the mercenaries he didn't trust. The thought of those mongrels getting their hands on her infuriated him. He'd give anything—everything—to have his five ex-SAS mates and Colonel Jarred Steele backing him up. The mercenaries wouldn't stand a chance against a unit of elite special force soldiers and one ferocious kitten protecting her mate.

The engine revs dropped, and the boat taxied slowly through the water to bump up against a pylon. They'd arrived. Through his eyelashes, he counted three armed men standing on a wharf and a fuel bowser he'd like to blow up. No sign of the operative, but Kitarna said they were following in the patrol boat. Time might not be to their advantage.

Nudging her with his elbow, to let her know he was ready, Jack played the unconscious captive, as Pérez issued a volley of orders in Spanish.

"Be good." Kitarna left his side and began stomping like a spoilt, little rich girl, screeching that when her daddy found out she'd been kidnapped, he'd send the entire United States Army to rescue her.

A sobering thought. Her father was the governor of Florida after all. Maybe he'd already demanded a contingent of soldiers be sent to search for his daughters.

The boat rocked as a man gripped him under both arms. Another lifted his feet. They hauled him onto the wharf roughly, where someone strapped his ankles together.

Kitarna continued to rant, informing anyone who would listen that her stepfather was an extremely important diplomat within the British Government, and a close friend of the Royal family, so he would send the entire British Army to find her. She yelped then screeched. "You don't have to hold my arm so tightly, *Señor* Pérez. I can walk to the jeep by myself."

"Get in the back seat and be quiet or I will shoot your boyfriend now."

"Where are we going? Jack needs urgent medical attention."

"The natives will take care of him, Kit." Jack recognized Gabe's apologetic mumble. "Please get in the jeep. I will drive you there."

"No," snapped Pérez. "You will refuel the speedboat and hide it in the estuary."

"Won't your friend want it back, uncle?"

"Not today. He can fly the *señorita* to a secret location. Once I've dealt with the Australian and *El* Jaguar, I will be in charge of the cartel."

After another volley of Spanish, hands gripped Jack under his arms and feet. He was lifted and carried along the wharf. They dumped him on the rear seat of a jeep. Kitarna scooted across and huddled beside him.

Risking a peek, Jack discovered an armed mercenary climbing into the driver's seat. By the rocking motion, he deduced another had climbed into the back tray.

Pérez awkwardly maneuvered into the front passenger seat then twisted, pointing his gun at Kitarna.

She'd told Jack that the operative insisted the first two bullets were blanks. They'd better be. With his hands tied in front, Jack plotted. He'd need to wait until they were out of sight of the wharf to deal with the mercenary behind. Pérez would die next followed by the driver.

The jeep jerked forward, thumping Jack's head against the headrest. Pain exploded behind his eyes. He groaned, collapsing against Kitarna.

She screeched at the driver to be careful. Her fingers touched Jack's face, wiping the rain away. "Darling, are you all right?"

He didn't answer. If this was to work, he needed to stick to the plan, even though her agitated movements and quickened breathing revealed her worry.

She knelt beside him, lifting each eyelid, checking his eyes. It gave him a brief glimpse of Pérez. The bastard's gaze had locked on Kitarna's backside. Her breath hissed. She knew he was conscious.

Using her as a screen, Jack charted their surroundings while he worked his hands free of the rope. The knots hadn't been tight. Thick jungle screened the rough, winding track. He was about to make his move when the two-way radio buzzed loudly. The gun wavered as Pérez leaned forward and flicked a switch.

"*Hola,* Jaguar, *soy* Andrés."

A torrent of Spanish curses filled the jeep. *El* Jaguar wasn't in a good mood. Jack tensed as the drug lord swore vengeance on the Ashford sisters. It momentarily distracted Pérez, who insisted he hadn't known both sisters were on the plane. *El* Jaguar appeared to believe him.

Tossing off the rope, Jack pushed Kitarna onto the floor, twisted then ripped the rifle from the mercenary behind him. One brutal jab with the butt and the man tumbled onto the rutted track. His face would need reconstructive surgery.

Jack swung the rifle hard, catching Pérez in the shoulder.

Pérez bellowed and fired his rifle, taking out the windscreen.

The jeep skidded sideways.

Jack braced his body as the jeep slammed into a wall of thick vegetation, throwing Pérez onto the road.

Kitarna scrambled onto the seat behind the driver and wrapped rope around his neck, pulling back with all her strength.

Jack wrenched out the operative's knife and slashed the binding round his ankles. A burning zing shot across his hip. The gunshot sent a troop of howler monkeys on the rampage, their noise drowning out Pérez's shouting.

Jack lunged at Pérez, clouting the gun from his hands. The bastard punched Jack in the kidney, winding him. On reflex, Jack slashed out, slicing Pérez's cheek. The man roared and came at Jack like a demented elephant.

They crashed to the wet mud and rolled, each trying to get the upper hand. Jack finally got a clump of Pérez's hair and slammed his head into the ground.

"Help me, Jack," screamed Kitarna.

Leaving Pérez dazed, Jack snatched up the rifle and leaped to his feet, but the sight before him brought him up short. Kitarna had her feet braced against the front seat. The driver howled, his hairy fingers clawing at a coil of rope anchored round his throat. She held him anchored with one hand, while using her other to jab his shoulder with two thin stickpins. Blood soaked the driver's shirt.

With a shake of his head, Jack slogged the man and threw him out of the jeep. "You drive, darlin', I'll ride shotgun."

Tossing the rope aside, she wiped the pin on her trousers then jumped over the seat. "Are you okay?"

"My head is fit to explode. Let's get out of here."

She handled the jeep like a pro, ignoring the pelting rain as they slid round tight corners at a speed Jack thought freaking reckless.

"You never cease to amaze me, kitten."

"Gabe's taken the speedboat to an estuary, so what are we going to do when we get to the wharf?"

"Find somewhere to hide and wait for our operative with that patrol boat."

"That could take ages."

"Let's hope not. When we get to the wharf, I want you to drive straight at the remaining guard. We can't allow him to call in reinforcements."

"All right. Let's sink the jeep so Pérez can't use the radio."

"Brilliant idea." He pursed his lips. "We didn't make a baby, did we, kitten?"

"No, but it's all I could think of to get your undivided attention. You should have seen your face."

"I can imagine. You certainly got my attention."

She grinned as they skidded around another bend. "I do like babies though, and I meant everything I said."

"So did I." Jack couldn't help but grin. "You'll make an incredible mother."

They rounded another bend and there stood the wharf in front of them. The remaining mercenary came running then stopped, his eyes widening.

A new tension gripped Jack, as Kitarna pressed her foot to the accelerator and the jeep surged forward. She grinned at him. "I'll slow down at the last minute. Get ready to jump."

*Fuck, she's serious.*

The mercenary raised his rifle.

Jack unloaded the belt of ammo, sending the man diving off the wharf.

"Jump," screamed Kitarna.

"Christ." Jack tossed the rifle and flung himself sideways, jolting his head as he landed on the rough boards. He registered the almighty splash, but couldn't see a thing through his blurred vision.

"Jack, there's a patrol boat coming down the river with more mercenaries."

"Fuck." Perspiration trickled into his eyes as he crawled to his knees. Things were hazy, but after blinking frantically, he could make out Kitarna picking up her rucksack and the rifle.

The wharf lurched, throwing him off balance. Looking up he saw the blurred shape of a man at the wheel of the speedboat.

"Get in," called Gabe. "You don't have much time."

Jack rolled to the edge of the wharf and sat, his legs dangling over the side.

"We can't trust him," yelled Kitarna. "He sabotaged the raft and betrayed all of us." Rifle at the ready, she came to stand beside Jack. "I should shoot him now."

"I'm sorry for everything that's happened," called Gabe. "My uncle intends to overthrow *El* Jaguar and take over the drug cartel, but I had no idea he could be so cruel or vindictive. You must hurry. I will pretend you knocked me out."

"You won't have to pretend." Jack pushed off the wharf, landed on his feet and smashed his fist into Gabe's soft stomach, doubling him over. He would have slogged him again only shouts rang out, followed by machine gun fire.

Reaching for Kitarna, Jack hauled her into the boat then snatched the rifle. With his vision slightly off and the boat rocking, his aim was anything but steady as he tried to focus on two men running down the track toward him.

He let off two shots. One man flew backward, he didn't get up again.

Choking, Gabe clambered onto the wharf, gasping for air as he fell to his knees. "Who are you?"

"A man who doesn't take shit from anyone. You are only alive because your testimony will help put Pérez behind bars."

"If he thinks I might testify, I won't make it to trial. Go. My uncle is coming, and the patrol boat will be here in minutes." Gabe curled into a ball, clutching his stomach.

"I'll drive." Kitarna pushed Jack onto a rear lounge-seat and jumped into the driver's seat. "Hold on."

The speedboat's nose lifted out of the water as she pushed the throttle all the way forward, throwing Jack against the padded backrest. His kitten had come to the rescue again. What a woman.

Gripping the chrome sidebar, he squinted at the chaotic scene behind. The patrol boat rocketed toward the wharf, where Pérez waved wildly. Gabe hung onto a post, vomiting into the river.

The patrol boat slowed for Pérez to jump aboard then shot out of the water, its powerful engine on par with the speedboat. The bastard wouldn't give up.

Jack cursed, ducking as a volley of bullets blasted from a machine gun mounted on the front of the patrol boat.

Balancing the rifle on the backrest, Jack scoped the driver and returned fire. He shattered the windscreen, but the boat kept coming.

"Stay low, kitten. I'll try to slow them down." Wrenching the seat cushion free, he hurled it at the fast approaching boat. They were close enough for Jack to make out Pérez in the passenger seat. "Shit, does that guy never quit?"

The driver swerved, but in doing so lost a man overboard. The boat didn't slow.

Jack's vision improved, but he could do without the heavy rain. He lifted the rifle, scoped the man behind the machine gun and emptied the rifle, ridding them of their biggest threat.

Only two remained; the driver and Pérez, who crouched low.

Jack threw every seat cushion and the backrest at them, forcing the driver to take constant evasive action. He hurled fuel cans, tools and finally the engine cover. It hit the water and bounced, smashing across the front of the patrol boat, decapitating the driver.

The patrol boat did a three-sixty-degree turn, flipped and ploughed into the riverbank, splintering on impact.

"Wow." Jack exhaled and sank back on his heels. He dropped his chin to his chest in an attempt to ease his headache and quell the nausea.

Fiery heat seared his hip from where Pérez's bullet had scorched his skin. "Fuck."

## ~ 31 ~

Turning from the wreckage, Kitarna searched the bank and river but couldn't see any sign of Pérez. Better all-round if he'd died in the crash, but it left a sick feeling in her stomach.

Taking a deep breath, she checked the river ahead then glanced back at Jack. He had his naked back toward her, sitting on the floor, slouched forward, his broad shoulders lifting and falling as he drew in breath. A shiver ran down her spine.

"Jack?"

"I'm…okay. Keep…going."

He didn't sound okay. He sounded odd. Stretching up and leaning sideways, she tried to see what he was doing. Her gaze dropped to his right hand, pressed against his hip, where she noticed bright-red blood.

"Jack, you're hurt." She cut the engine and ran to him.

"Just a scratch. It's my head that hurts."

"There's blood everywhere." She lifted his hand

and flinched at the deep gouge running across his hip. "A scratch? When did this happen?"

"In the jeep." He rolled onto his knees. "We can't stop, kitten. Gotta keep going."

"In a minute." She stripped off her shirt and tied it round him, cinching it tight. "Lie on the floor and rest your head on my rucksack." She helped him then ran back to the driver's seat and started the engine.

Grasping the wheel, Kitarna ignored her cramping fingers and absorbed every jolt as the speedboat lifted and smacked down on the fast-flowing river. The rain had moved east, leaving a light breeze and overcast sky. Every few minutes she glanced back at Jack. His eyes were closed, and he hadn't moved. She prayed his head injury wasn't serious. To lose him now would destroy her.

Heading into a wide bend, she glanced back again. His chest rose and fell evenly. That had to be a good sign.

A booming horn blasted.

"Argh."

She yanked the wheel to the left, her heart jumping into her throat as the speedboat ploughed across the top of the water almost on its side, straight toward the steel hull of a very large boat.

The horn blasted again, vibrating through her body. She yanked the wheel right and pushed the throttle fully forward, missing the larger hull by several feet.

Perspiration covered her face and ran between her breasts as she fought for control, terrified she'd added to Jack's injuries. The speedboat continued its sideways slide, rounding the other boat's stern. She pulled back on the throttle and shut off the engine. The boat listed violently for a minute then settled, facing back up the river. She sank onto the seat, her jelly legs unable to support her any longer. Dragging in oxygen, she looked over her shoulder terrified she'd find Jack gone.

He lay curled in a ball, holding his head.

"Jack!" She stumbled like a drunk and fell to her knees, wrapping her arms around him. "Please say something."

"Who the hell taught you to drive?"

"My sister." Giddy with relief, a giggle escaped.

He pushed himself into a sitting position. "In that case, the bloody woman could probably defeat a whole army on her own."

A large shadow fell over them.

Terrified *El* Jaguar had caught them, Kitarna's gaze slid up the steel hull to the deck where a group of smiling, uniformed men stood. The Navy had come to their rescue.

"Kit, Jack. I am pleased to see you." Ahmed leaned over the railing, smiling and waving like crazy.

"Ahmed?"

"Lexi and I made it to a small settlement this morning and they radioed the authorities to pick us up. The rescuers have been searching in the wrong location."

Bemused, Kitarna could only watch as a rope ladder dropped over the side and two uniformed men scampered down. One tied a rope to the front of the speedboat, the other crouched in front of her.

"*Hola, señorita.* Are you hurt?"

"I'm fine, but Jack's been shot, and he has an open

wound on his head. Please help…him." She choked on a sob and trembled as tears streamed down her face. "Don't let him die."

"I'm not dying, kitten. I just need something for this fuc…bloody headache."

"*Señorita*, please climb the ladder." A crewman waved her up. "We will help your friend."

"I'm fine," muttered Jack. He came to his feet, swayed slightly then gripped the side of the boat. "You go up first, kitten. I'm right behind you." His jaw looked rigid in pain.

"Men and their damn pride." Handing one of the crew her rucksack, Kitarna reached for the ladder. She clambered up, climbed over the rail and looked down. Jack climbed slowly, but steadily.

"Kit!"

She turned and gasped as Ahmed caught her in a hug and swung her round. A wide grin split his face. "I am so happy to see you. Piers, Juliette, Victoria and Robert were brought in at midday and they told us how you and Jack helped them escape. I have been so worried for you both."

"Put me down, Ahmed. I'm dirty and wet."

He lowered her. "You are a heroine, Kit, and Jack is a hero. I owe you both my life. You have made me a better person, and I will be much more tolerant in the future."

"Good for you."

Jack climbed over the rail and shook Ahmed's hand. "Good to see you, mate."

Ahmed clapped Jack's shoulder. "You too, my friend. Lexi will be delighted. She is waiting at Santo Antonñio do Içá with your brothers."

"My brothers?" Jack blinked several times.

"Yes. Once the news got out that Roscoe had been found then I turned up with Lexi, relatives and film crews began descending."

Kitarna gripped Jack's hand. "Ahmed, is Roscoe all right?"

"He was unconscious and in a serious condition when a native brought him to a small settlement. The people there organised an emergency flight to Manaus Hospital, but no one realized he'd been a passenger on the plane until later. I believe his daughter and wife are with him."

Kitarna accepted her rucksack from a sailor. She followed Ahmed as he led them through an open door and down steep, narrow steps. "This is a naval patrol boat. Captain Varela will speak to you shortly, but first, he has made his cabin available for you to shower and change. A doctor is waiting to examine you both."

"I am looking forward to a hot shower and shampoo and soap." Kitarna sighed. "And clean clothes."

Ahmed stopped at a doorway. "Here we are." He stood aside so they could enter a small cabin with a single bed and desk. "Towels and clothes are on the bed for you and everything else you need is in the bathroom. The dining area is along the hall. I will meet you there with the captain for coffee and food."

"Thank you, Ahmed." Kitarna closed the door, feeling a little overwhelmed. Meeting Jack's gaze, she saw the haze of pain in his eyes. "Right, shower time." She pushed the door open to reveal a tiny bathroom. "Too small to shower together. Come on, I'll help you get your pants off.

"I'll have to take a rain check, darlin'. My hip is on fire and my head is throbbing. I'm in no condition to have your hands anywhere near me. You take the first shower and I'll let you take my pants off when we have a real bed at our disposal."

"Nothing like a little anticipation." She stripped off and blew him a kiss before sashaying into the bathroom.

The shower did wonders for Kitarna. She shampooed and conditioned her hair, luxuriating in the warm water. While Jack showered, she braided her hair then pulled on trousers and soft-blue cashmere sweater, which was a little big, but it felt heavenly to wear clean clothes and smell of soap. After washing out her bikini and dress she hung them up to dry and carefully transferred the spikey fruit to her rucksack.

A freshly shaven Jack was a sight to behold. Kitarna couldn't but stare as he taped a thick wad over the raw graze then dressed. The shirt strained across his chest and the pants were several inches too short, making her smile.

Once the doctor had examined them both and given Jack painkillers, they made their way to the small dining area.

As they consumed coffee and hot paella, they wrote statements of their ordeal and handed the captain the drugs Kitarna rescued from the river.

"Captain Varela. Has there been news of my sister?"

He shook his head. "Since we turned our attention to this area, army helicopters have found the plane wreckage and picked up a Brazilian family. They were suffering exhaustion, dehydration and severe bot fly infection. Ross Dalton is in Manaus Hospital, and the six other survivors from your group have been examined and interviewed."

The captain stood. "Soldiers have been dispersed to search the region for the mercenaries and any other survivors. Please excuse me. I will radio my report through then we shall deliver you to the town of Santo Antonñio do Içá. Andrés Pérez is probably dead, but if he survived it is unlikely we will find him, or the hidden headquarters of *El* Jaguar."

As Captain Varela walked away, Ahmed placed a packet of biscuits in front of them. "I have an amusing story to tell you."

"Oh." Kitarna sipped her coffee, reveling in its aromatic flavor. She sat hip to hip with Jack, who steadily munched through the biscuits.

Ahmed laughed. "I was standing on the wharf beside Robert's wife and father-in-law when a fishing boat arrived with Robert, Piers, Juliette and Victoria. Robert pushed Victoria aside to leap onto the wharf and embrace his wife, as if she were the love of his life. Victoria marched up to Robert and announced their affair had ended, and from now on he could do his own power-point presentations and research. Victoria told the wife Robert lied and constantly whined about his dismal marriage. The wife went as pale as a ghost."

"Good on Victoria." Jack laughed.

Ahmed nodded. "She was magnificent. She took

the wife's hand and told her Robert only cared about money and climbing to the top of his father-in-law's empire."

Kitarna clapped her hand over her mouth. "Oh, my God. Is that karma or what?"

"There's more," said Ahmed. "Robert's father-in-law sacked him. And, the wife announced her lawyers would arrange a divorce. Robert ran after them, but they left in a private helicopter."

"The miserable bastard deserved to be shamed," murmured Jack.

Kitarna looked at Ahmed. "You said Jack's brothers are here?"

"Yes, they hired their own plane and pilot to help with the search effort. The resemblance between you and your brothers is very strong." Ahmed grinned at Jack. "Your brothers are also very determined men."

Jack's hand tightened around hers. "Yes, they are. Thanks for getting Lexi to safety, Ahmed. I'd like to take Kitarna up on deck now and we'd appreciate a few minutes of privacy."

"Of course. I will bring you fresh coffee."

Knowing Jack's brothers were here filled Kitarna with a joyous relief. He came from a close-knit family, who if he let them, would welcome him back with open arms. Whereas all she had was Bernie. No way would their parents leave the safety of their palatial homes to expose themselves to the wilderness of the Amazon.

Relieved to see the rain had stopped, Kitarna followed Jack to the bow.

The boat's engine pulsed under her feet as they churned through deep water. A crisp breeze toyed with an escaped curl. It had to be late afternoon, yet they were surrounded by a never-ending variety of riverbank animals and birdcalls. She looked up at the thick cloud-covered sky. "I wonder what happened to the undercover operative?"

Leaning on the rail, Jack stared out across the river. "If by some chance Pérez survived, the operative will continue with his mission. Otherwise it's back to square one. He'll go after *El* Jaguar some other way."

No words could express Kitarna's jubilation at escaping the mercenaries, but alongside her euphoria a veil of grief hung heavy. Her heart mourned those who were dead. Worry gnawed at her for those still missing, perhaps forever.

*Where are you, Bernie?*

While there was a chance her sister lived, all Kitarna could do was trust in Bernie's stubborn will and intelligence. If anyone could survive, it would be her gutsy sister.

Tears welled as she cuddled closer, resting her hand against Jack's solid chest, thankful for his warmth and strength.

He kissed her forehead. "We'll continue the search for your sister, and no matter what happens, I'll be there for you."

"Promise?"

"Yes, as long as you'll have me." He lifted her chin and touched his lips to her eyelids. "You are my heart, darlin'."

She stared at him, unable to believe the truth in his eyes. "What if I want forever?"

"I would be the happiest man on earth. I'm yours to command."

"I command you kiss me."

"It will be my pleasure." He kissed her deeply and leisurely, uncaring that they were in full few of anyone on deck.

The horn blasted, making her jump. Kitarna looked over Jack's shoulder. Up in the bridge Captain Varela saluted her.

She grinned at Jack. "If I hadn't misunderstood your proposition on the plane, we might never have grown this close."

"I'm ashamed I ever issued such an invitation, but thank God you accepted."

"I love you, Jack."

His lips curved into a wicked smile. "Marry me?"

For a second she couldn't believe he was serious, but his beautiful lion eyes burned with desire, tenderness and love. His hands shook as he cupped her face. "Say yes and let me love you, and take care of you."

"I'm not keen on commuting across the world for a week or two here and there. I'd want to be with you every day."

"So, we find a way to make it happen."

Her heart welled and overflowed with love for this big, gentle, wonderful, sexy man. Time stood still as their days together flashed through her mind. They complemented each other, their connection and desire undeniable. He embodied everything she'd ever wanted in a partner, lover and life-long friend.

Smiling, she stretched up to kiss his smooth cheek. "Yes. I will marry you, my darling."

He pulled her into a bear hug. "Thank God."

~ 32 ~

As evening fell, they cruised toward a well-lit wharf, swarming with people and film crews. Santo Antonñio do Içá appeared to be a sizeable town.

Jack's gaze fastened on two men pushing their way through the crowd. Tom and Rick were sixteen months younger, and until the fall-out had been his best friends. They were decent men, hard workers and both married with a kid each. Their lives were full, and they thrived on it.

The envy that had ridden Jack for the last few years fell away like a heavy winter coat, leaving him buoyant. Seeing relief and joy in their exhausted faces had him blinking hard. It humbled him that they'd come to Brazil to join the search.

For so many years the Callaghan boys had stood side-by-side, an impregnable wall bullies soon learned to avoid. That had changed a year ago when Jack snapped and turned on his brothers in an alcohol-fuelled tirade. It had ended in an all-in brawl, leaving all three battered, bruised and estranged.

The ferocious clash had shaken the whole family and broken his mother's heart. Severing ties and walking away had been Jack's only option at the time. But now Tom and Rick wore identical grins as they waited, feet spread wide and hands on hips.

"Twins." Kitarna beamed at him. "They certainly look happy to see you."

"They do, don't they?" He pulled her closer under his arm as the naval boat slowed. "Stay close. I don't want to lose you in the crowd."

"I'm not going anywhere, Jack Callaghan. You promised me a lifetime of loving, so you're stuck with me now."

He smiled into her sparkling eyes. "Come to Australia with me? If my family has forgiven me, we could make a life there and you'd have the Daintree to explore."

"What about your beach shack?"

"That's not what I want anymore. If you're agreeable, I'd like to join my brothers and father in the family business. I spent my leave from the army croc-spotting and leading treks through the rainforest. You could do research and give talks. You might even discover a new plant or two."

"Oh!" She clutched the handle of her rucksack. "I think I *have* discovered a new species." She mangled her bottom lip with her teeth. "I might need to come back here or explore other rainforests and dig sites with my sister. How do you feel about that?"

He chuckled. "I'll never put restrictions on your research, but I'll accompany you or employ a bevy of armed guards to protect you."

She hugged him tight. "One ex-sniper will do

nicely." She leaned against him. "Darling, I can't leave Brazil until I find Bernie. Alive or…"

"We will both stay for however long it takes."

A rapid whoop, whoop, whoop had them both looking up river to where a helicopter swooped in low over the water.

Kitarna clutched his hand. "Do you think it's carrying more survivors?"

"Could be."

"Bernie's alive. I feel it in my heart. And, if she's had half the adventure and excitement we have, she'll have an incredible story to tell."

The naval boat eased alongside the wharf and sailors ran to tether the lines.

"*Señorita!*" Captain Valera handed Kitarna a paper bag. "The items you left in my cabin."

"Thank you, Captain."

He hesitated. "One of my crew found this in the speedboat." He held out the six-inched-two-pronged dagger, Kitarna had used to stab the jeep's driver. A green dragon curled around the tiny disc at the top.

"It's mine." She took the implement and slid it into her braid. "Thank you, Captain. It's a traditional *kansashi* hairpin. In feudal Japan, women of Samurai families used them as hair accessories. As a defence, it's a deadly weapon."

"Ah, this is the thing you stabbed the driver with, *señorita*?"

"Yes."

The captain looked to Jack. "Take care of this brave lady, *señor*."

"I will, Captain. Thanks for the rescue." They shook hands.

As the captain walked away, Jack stepped onto the wharf, grinning at his brothers, "Am I glad to see you two."

Tom wiped at his eyes. "We figured you were big and tough enough to survive, but the oldies and our wives were anxious, and we had nothing better to do."

Jack laughed. "Unless business has dropped dramatically, I find that hard to believe." He helped Kitarna onto the wharf. Uncaring of the crowd, he hugged his brothers in a ferocious three-way embrace. "I've missed you guys, more than you'll ever know." Eventually he let them go and cleared his throat. "I'm sorry for what I've put you through over the last twelve months."

"Forget it," said Rick. "We would have been more understanding if we'd known exactly what you were up against. Hell, it would send any sane man round the twist."

Jack looked at them blankly.

Tom shrugged. "Your ex-Colonel came to see us. He explained everything."

Kitarna pushed between them and leaned against Jack's chest, smiling at his brothers. "My goodness, you are a handsome lot."

The fact she wasn't intimidated, surrounded by three hulking men, had Jack grinning.

Tom raised an eyebrow. "This is Rick and I'm Tom. And you are?"

"Kitarna. It's nice to meet you."

Jack turned her in his arms. "This kansashi Amazon is my fiancée." He kissed her soundly to the cheers of everyone on the wharf. He didn't give a damn if the camera crews and journalists were closing in. He loved Kitarna and the whole world might as well know it.

When he finally consented to set her down, they were both breathing hard.

She placed her hands on his chest, her lips twitching. "Are you sure you want to take on a kansashi Amazon, Jack?"

"Bloody oath I do." He hugged her tight. "I love every inch of you."

"And I love you, my handsome, courageous lion." She blinked rapidly before turning to his brothers. "Has anyone had an update on Ross Dalton?"

"He's in a stable condition," said Rick.

"Thank goodness. Do you know where his granddaughter is?"

Tom chuckled. "At the hotel. She's got a wild kitten that no one can pry away. And she's inviting everyone, including the film crews, to her birthday party in Manaus."

The smile faded from Kitarna's face. "Has there been any word on my sister, Bernadette Ashford?"

Tom's eyes widened. "Yes, actually. Got word from the search and rescue guys a few minutes before you turned up. They've received a mayday call from a remote village."

Kitarna's fingers tightened in Jack's hand.

Rick injected, "Geez, Tom, don't keep the lady hanging." He grinned at Kitarna. "Your sister is alive."

She collapsed against Jack's chest. "Bernie's alive."

He wrapped his arms around her as the last weight lifted from his shoulders. "Tomorrow the two of you will be reunited, kitten, but tonight you're mine."

She raised her hand to his cheek, her eyes sparkling with tears and happiness. "I've so very much to tell Bernie."

He quirked an eyebrow. "I hope some things remain our secret."

She winked. "Not a chance."

"Let's get out of here," said Rick. "We've secured a couple of rooms at a local hotel tonight, so how about we adjourn to the bar and celebrate. You can tell us about your adventure over dinner and a few cold beers."

Jack laughed. "I'd love to boys, but first we need to fight our way through this crowd. I assume the search and rescue people need to speak to us too. And, Kitarna will want to ring her parents, if they're not already here somewhere."

Her small hand slipped into his. "They won't be." She turned to his brothers. "As your future sister-in-law, I'm commandeering one of those rooms. I have need of a real bed tonight."

Tom's lips twitched. "No worries. Welcome to the family, Kitarna. You're going to fit right in with our mother and wives."

"Thank you." She cuddled against Jack as his brothers cleared a path through the curious onlookers. "Is your head still aching?"

"The headache has gone." Smiling wickedly, he lowered his mouth to her ear. "It's another part of my body that's throbbing and needs relief."

"Anticipation, remember." Stretching up, she kissed his cheek, her eyes brimming with mischief. "I need a new pair of sandals to wear with my dress." She waved the paper bag at him.

He groaned at the memory of her in that miniscule dress. "That's playing dirty."

"Yes, it is." She chuckled. "And, after dinner I'm going to drag you to that hotel room and have my wicked way with you."

She smiled so confidently that he almost felt guilty teasing her. "Darlin', you can have your wicked way with me, once I've kissed every delectable inch of you."

"Jack!" Her beautiful eyes flared.

Catching her hand, he chuckled. "Anticipation, kitten... Anticipation."


## The End

# Acknowledgements

While researching this series, largely set in Brazil's Amazon Rainforest, I discovered an extraordinary world of poisonous, exotic and medicinal plant life. This magnificent sanctuary, often described as the lungs of the earth, is home to rare, deadly, bizarre, and beautiful creatures. I admire the people who fight to protect and conserve its biodiversity for the enjoyment and wellbeing of future generations.

My sincere thanks to cohort, friend and critique partner S E Gilchrist for inviting me to be part of this thrilling series. Aside from her enthusiasm and cheer, she continually motivates me to reach for the stars.

The lovely Juanita Kees for her exceptional editing skills and delightful sense of humor.

Fiona Jayde Media, for her patience and another stunning cover. Amy Atwell of Author E.M.S for her formatting expertise. My other wonderful critique partner and friend, Susanne Bellamy, and special thanks to Samara Abrego, for assisting me with the Spanish translations.

# ABOUT THE DEADLY FORCES SERIES

My fellow Hunter Romance Writer, S E Gilchrist often comes up with intriguing ventures. When she suggested bringing down a plane and then writing separate stories involving two groups of survivors, I was delighted to come on board.

What could possibly work better than a bunch of strangers with secrets finding themselves trapped together in an inhospitable environment? We could add deadly animals and plants. Suddenly we were off and running, barely able to draw breath.

We had so much fun brainstorming locations and characters for each story—emails flew back and forth. We made up a character database and timeline of events and weather conditions. Plots, scenarios and hours and hours of research filled our heads. I created a journal with pictures and information.

SE and I were in total accord during the whole process. Our stories were to be action packed, romantic adventures with a good dose of suspense and intrigue.

The first two books can be read as stand-alone, but if reading in sequence, **Beat of the Jungle** comes first, followed by **Scent of the Jaguar.**

We hope you enjoy our *Deadly Forces* series.

~

**Books in the Deadly Forces series:**

*Beat of the Jungle* – Erin Moira O'Hara
*Scent of the Jaguar* – S. E. Gilchrist

Discover Bernadette Ashford's adventures in the Deadly Forces series, *Scent of the Jaguar*, by S E Gilchrist.

*Excerpt from*

# SCENT OF THE JAGUAR

## A DEADLY FORCES NOVEL

## S. E. GILCHRIST

~ 1 ~

The storm had hit hard and fast, not long after take-off from São Paulo de Olivença, a municipality in the western section of the Amazon Basin. Several passengers had drifted off to sleep, lulled by the drone of the engines and the stuffy air.

An afternoon nap was the last thing on Bernie's agenda. Not with so many anxious thoughts squirreling through her mind. Inside the cramped restroom, she pressed her pounding forehead against the cold glass, recalling her father's phone call. The storm interference had transformed his voice into a bubble of white noise, his frantic words difficult to make out.

She'd only deciphered, 'get to the US Consulate... Jaguar hunting you...' before the call had been cut off and he was gone.

The Jaguar had to be a person. Her father had too much respect for her profession to believe a wild animal would make an archaeologist give up the prospect of a new dig. Especially one as exciting and wreathed in mystery as this. But what *had* he been talking about?

She hadn't waited to find out. Whatever was going on had been enough to germinate fear in her father and, as an ex-marine, he wasn't a man easily intimidated.

She'd been galvanized into action, leaving messages for the professor and the guides she'd intended to meet up with tomorrow. If she'd been alone, she would have risked continuing her journey to the dig—jaguar or no jaguar—but not when she had her younger sister, Kit, with her.

Within three hours, they were in the air, flying back to Manaus. Now worry plagued her that she'd made the wrong decision by insisting they change their plans. Maybe heading to a remote area of the jungle would have been a safer bet than isolating themselves on an airplane.

The Jaguar could be here, with them. He could be anyone. Waiting to spring his trap, to take her down. Or worse...Kit.

# ABOUT THE AUTHOR

**Erin Moira O'Hara** grew up in the Blue Mountains of Australia, with a garden backing onto native bushland, hidden caves and fabulous lookouts. Weekends were spent exploring, climbing trees and creating secret bases. Her love of reading began with visits to the local library, where she became absorbed in a world of intrigue, fantasy and action-packed adventures. The moment Erin read her first romance; she recognised the importance of finding the right man to share her life. She now lives with him close to the largest saltwater lake in Australia. Their home overlooks bushland and is surrounded by an abundance of bird life and an ever-growing garden.

Erin's writing encompasses everything she loves—intrigue, suspense, passion and romance.

If you would like to know more, please visit:
http://www.erinmoiraohara.com